# Praise for *The Perfect Family*

"The talented Robyn Harding peels back the sleek facade of suburbia to show its disturbing reality. . . . Incredibly cinematic and jaw-droppingly devious, this book will have you turning the pages as fast as you can."
—Hank Phillippi Ryan, *USA Today* bestselling author of *The First to Lie*

"Harding creates powerful character studies, reflects on societal expectations from a variety of viewpoints, and ramps up unmanageable chaos in a tale that is unforgettable on many levels. . . . A great choice for fans of Celeste Ng, Gillian Flynn, and Liane Moriarty."
—*Booklist* (starred review)

"A highly entertaining domestic thriller from Harding . . . Harding is sure to win new fans with this one."
—*Publishers Weekly* (starred review)

"Unsettling and darkly sublime . . . A mesmerizing, compulsively readable thriller, this one smolders from the first page to the last."
—Christina McDonald, *USA Today* bestselling author of *The Night Olivia Fell*

"Robyn Harding wields deep community ties like a garrote and redefines terror in suburbia. Breathless pacing and an inescapable sense of menace make Harding's latest an absolute must-read . . . This one's a stunner."
—P. J. Vernon, author of *Bath Haus* and *When You Find Me*

"A propulsive, constantly surprising read that both entertains and chills . . . From the opening page to the shocking last line, I was hooked."
—Laurie Elizabeth Flynn, author of *The Girls Are All So Nice Here*

# Praise for *The Swap*
## INSTANT #1 NATIONAL BESTSELLER

"There are books born for summer reading and *The Swap* is one of them. Steamy sex, obsession, partner swapping—this one has it all."

—*The Globe and Mail*

"[A] deliciously scarifying story . . . No reader is likely to guess at the tantalizing path that winds its way to murder."

—*Toronto Star*

"A wickedly delicious, addictive, utterly compelling read about obsession, toxic relationships, and dangerous secrets. . . . An absolute must-read."

—Samantha M. Bailey, #1 bestselling author of *Woman on the Edge*

"Page-turning and completely riveting. . . . Harding deftly explores toxic friendship, desire, and obsession. . . . This is a clear-your-night-and-read-in-one-sitting book!"

—Kathleen Barber, author of *Follow Me*

"Harding is an expert at slowly building creeping dread. . . . Undoubtedly her best book yet."

—Kate Moretti, *New York Times* bestselling author of *The Vanishing Year* and *In Her Bones*

"Dangerously addictive."

—*Kirkus Reviews*

"[A] convincing tale of obsession and celebrity worship . . . Fans of psychological thrillers will be satisfied."

—*Publishers Weekly*

# Praise for *The Party*

"Tense and riveting . . . I was hooked from the opening scene and could not look away until I reached the very last page."

—Megan Miranda, bestselling author of *The Girl from Widow Hills*

"Cleverly constructed and brilliantly paced. . . . Impossible to put down."
—Bill Clegg, *New York Times* bestselling author of *Did You Ever Have a Family*

"Fast-paced and tension-filled, *The Party* explodes the myth of the perfect family and is one invitation you can't turn down."
—Rebecca Drake, author of *Only Ever You*

"Engrossing and unflinching in its portrayal of the dark side of human nature, *The Party* takes the concept of 'mean girls' to a whole new level."
—A. J. Banner, bestselling author of *The Good Neighbor* and *The Twilight Wife*

"A domestic drama that spins off the rails with hellish consequences."
—Erica Ferencik, author of *The River at Night*

"With teenagers worthy of *Mean Girls*, and a healthy dose of suspense, *The Party* reads like a cross between Megan Abbott and Jodi Picoult by way of James Patterson."
—*Booklist*

## Praise for *Her Pretty Face*

"A fast-paced, thrilling, gut-wrenching novel with sharp teeth and daring observations about the inner lives of women. . . . Positively exhilarating."
—Taylor Jenkins Reid, *New York Times* bestselling author of *Daisy Jones & The Six*

"A haunting tale of friendship and loyalty, secrets and betrayal—a book that will grab your insides and give them a twist."
—Janelle Brown, bestselling author of *Pretty Things*

"This one might be the thriller of the summer."
—*Toronto Star*

ALSO AVAILABLE FROM
ROBYN HARDING
AND GALLERY BOOKS

*The Swap*
*The Arrangement*
*Her Pretty Face*
*The Party*

# THE
# PERFECT
# FAMILY

# ROBYN
# HARDING

POCKET BOOKS

NEW YORK   LONDON   TORONTO   SYDNEY   NEW DELHI

Pocket Books
An Imprint of Simon & Schuster, Inc.
1230 Avenue of the Americas
New York, NY 10020

This book is a work of fiction. Any references to historical events, real people, or real places are used fictitiously. Other names, characters, places, and events are products of the author's imagination, and any resemblance to actual events or places or persons, living or dead, is entirely coincidental.

First Pocket Books paperback edition October 2023

POCKET and colophon are registered trademarks of Simon & Schuster, Inc.

For information about special discounts for bulk purchases, please contact Simon & Schuster Special Sales at 1-866-506-1949 or business@simonandschuster.com.

The Simon & Schuster Speakers Bureau can bring authors to your live event. For more information or to book an event, contact the Simon & Schuster Speakers Bureau at 1-866-248-3049 or visit our website at www.simonspeakers.com.

Interior design by Davina Mock-Maniscalco

Manufactured in the United States of America

10  9  8  7  6  5  4  3  2  1

Library of Congress Cataloging-in-Publication Data is available.

ISBN 978-1-6680-2163-7
ISBN 978-1-9821-6940-4 (ebook)

*For John*
*(Thank God our family isn't perfect.)*

# *Prologue*

I STOOD ALONE in the street, watching the silent house turn down for the night. One by one, the lights blinked out, like stars dying in an inky sky. The upscale suburb was eerily quiet, no sound but my own breath. My own heartbeat. Still, I waited. And then I waited some more. The occupants had to be asleep. All of them. If someone heard me, if someone woke up, everything would be ruined. If I got caught, there would be serious consequences. Violence. Or even jail. But I wasn't going to get caught.

It was a beautiful house; anyone would say that. It was Craftsman style; they were everywhere in Portland. Older, two-story homes with covered front porches, chunky wood columns, big picture windows. This one had been renovated and updated. It wasn't huge or extravagant, but it was definitely expensive, and well maintained. The yard was manicured to perfection and you could probably eat off the paved driveway. Inside would be the same . . . an open floor plan with high-end furniture, valuable paintings, and designer knickknacks. All the shit that made a house appear elegant and refined.

But the people who lived there only looked perfect. They had done horrible things. They kept horrible secrets. People like that made me sick. Fakes. Phonies. Pretending they were better than everyone else, when they were rotten inside. Now, they were stressed, panicked, falling apart. The thought made me smile.

Pulling my hood over my head and drawing the strings tight, I moved down the driveway. My sneakers were nearly silent on the pavement, but the red plastic jug banged against my leg, so I held it aloft. The scent of gasoline was already strong in my nostrils. Good thing I'd thought to wear gloves. The smell would linger on my hands and give me away.

I stepped onto the grass, cool and damp, and cut across the lawn to the side of the house. The camera over the door blinked at me, but I'd be nothing more than a dark blur on the screen.

The family thought the surveillance would be a deterrent, but it wasn't. There was no way to identify me, no way to know who I was. Just another faceless figure lurking in the night.

At the side of the house, I squatted down, bouncing on my haunches. Adrenaline was coursing through me, my body vibrating with the need to enact my plan, but I forced myself to wait. And then I waited some more. To be safe. And to build up my courage. Because what I was about to do was serious. It could be fatal. But I couldn't back out now.

I don't know how long I crouched in the dark, but my knees were getting stiff and my right leg was starting to fall asleep. It was time. Bursting out of the shadows, I scurried to the decorative hedge that ran along the front of the house. Removing the lid from the gas can, I dumped the accelerant onto the shrubs, dousing the shiny green leaves with the toxic substance. A plant like this wouldn't burn easily, but the gas would erupt. It would burst into flames, fire skittering across the foliage. There was a chance the porch railing could catch fire, that it could climb the wooden posts and ignite the second story. If the smoke alarms didn't work . . .

Well, the world would be a better place without people like the Adlers.

I lit the match. And let it drop.

# SIX WEEKS
# EARLIER

# *Vivian Adler*

## (Viv)

I SAT CROSS-LEGGED in a pool of spring sunshine, my palms pressed together at heart-center. The morning light offered little warmth, but it bathed the bedroom in a flattering glow, and the color palette I'd chosen—muted blues and creams—created a seaside aura despite our suburban locale. My eyes were heavy, but not quite closed, as I breathed through my nose and took a conscious moment of gratitude. It was a *thing* I had been trying: starting each morning with a grateful heart. According to a podcast I'd recently listened to, being thankful was the key to health, happiness, and abundance.

Thomas was downstairs in the kitchen making coffee with his usual amount of banging and clatter. I tried to conjure some gratitude for my husband of twenty-two years, but that full feeling in my chest, that warmth and lightness, refused to materialize. I loved him, I did. He was an excellent provider, a great dad, and every morning, he got up and made coffee. But it's hard to be thankful for a man when he's cheating on you.

I had no proof, just a sick feeling in my gut. Thomas had been distant, distracted, and irritable of late. His job as a real estate agent was always frenetic, he'd always kept odd hours. An affair would have been easy for him. But I'd trusted him . . . until now. We'd had rough patches before; what marriage hasn't? But even in our darkest moments, we'd always been a team, a unit. These days, we felt like two solo performers who'd left the band to go out on our own. He was George Michael. I was Andrew what's-his-name.

It could have been a midlife crisis; Thomas had turned forty-eight in February. Or perhaps something had happened at work. But another woman seemed the most logical explanation. My partner was attractive in a beefy, middle-aged sort of way. He had charm and style, a twinkle in his hazel eyes. I'd seen women flirt with him. Thomas had always acted oblivious, but maybe he wasn't? I exercised, ate salads, dyed away my grays. But we all know affairs are not about the spouse.

Sniffing his jackets for perfume and checking his collars for lipstick had provided no evidence. If I wanted proof, I'd have to search through his phone and his laptop. But he kept his devices close, protected by ever-changing passwords and facial ID. This was a relief, in a way. I wasn't ready to deal with the truth. I wasn't ready to blow apart my family. My entire life.

Abandoning my attempt to be grateful for my husband, I focused on my son, Eli, sleeping two doors down. He was home for the summer, had just finished his second year at the prestigious Worbey College. The sporty little boy with the green eyes and crooked smile was a man now, taller than his father, and the starting goalie for his college soccer team. But he was still my baby and I was grateful to have him home for four months. Or *longer*. . . . Eli had recently announced that he was dropping out of school. Thomas was devasted. He had gone to a state college, couldn't afford to attend an esteemed school like Worbey. We'd made significant financial sacrifices for Eli's education, and now he was quitting. Thomas had blown up, had accused Eli of being ungrateful, of throwing his future—and our money—away. But our son held firm. He refused to explain his decision, simply saying, "I'm not going back."

I had insisted that we refine our approach: no more yelling, badgering, or interrogation. We would simply pretend that everything was normal, let Eli have time to process his issues. He had the whole summer to deal with whatever had upset him. And then, when he had, he'd realize that returning to school was his best option. The flicker of warmth elicited by thoughts of my adorable toddler was extinguished by our recent struggles.

There was no point in trying to summon gratitude for my seventeen-year-old daughter. Tarryn was going through the most unlovable of stages. She was sullen and condescending, seemed to consider her father and me (but mostly me) to be irrelevant, ignorant, tone-deaf boomers. (My explanation that we were, in fact, Generation X was met with an eye roll.) Tarryn still got good grades, she seemed to have friends, but my bubbly little girl had transformed into a surly, angry grouch.

But despite our struggles, we were the same family we'd always been. We were all healthy. We had a lovely home. And for that, I was—

"FUCK!"

It was Thomas. My heart jumped into my throat, constricting with dread. It's not as if my husband never swore, but he never swore at the top of his lungs at seven thirty in the morning. Something was very wrong. I scrambled up off the floor and ran down the stairs in my pajamas. The front door was wide open, and the living area appeared to be deserted. Peeking my head outside, I searched for my chagrined spouse. I folded my arms across my braless chest and stepped onto the porch.

"Thomas?" I called. But he was nowhere to be seen.

He rounded the corner then with the garden hose in his hand. His handsome face was darkened by a scowl.

"What's going on?" I asked.

He looked up, scowl still in place. "Some goddamn kids threw eggs at the house last night. And at my car."

That's when I noticed the shattered white shells littering the driveway, the viscous goop already congealed on our plate glass window. Thomas's BMW had been assaulted, too, shards of shell glued to the black paint.

"Why?" I asked.

"I have no idea," he grumbled, screwing the hose onto the tap at the corner of the house. "Ask Tarryn. She might know what this is about." He turned the water on and blasted the side of his car.

I retreated into the house, shutting the door behind me. Tarryn would be up soon. Perhaps our teenage daughter could shed some light on the assault. But Tarryn was seventeen, a junior in high school. Wasn't throwing eggs a bit juvenile for her peer group? And she'd never had enemies before. She saved all her snarky comments for her family, seemed perfectly pleasant with her friends.

As I climbed back up the stairs, I felt fluttery and agitated. Logically, I knew this was not a big deal. Bored, unsupervised kids roamed the streets in search of mischief on a regular basis. But this had happened at night. While we slept. The master bedroom was at the front of the house, so I would have heard the attack, had I not been in a deep sleep. What kind of parents let their children out after eleven on a school night? And why us? Our neighbors' houses appeared untouched.

Abandoning my attempt at gratitude, I stepped into the walk-in shower. I was meeting a client at nine, and I didn't want to be late. My interior decorating company was small but thriving, no longer a "hobby business"—unlike my client's vegan ice cream shop. Her hedge-fund-manager husband was backing the venture. It didn't matter that she was entering a saturated market, that ice cream was highly seasonal, or that her downtown location was not ideal. This wasn't about turning a profit. It was about creating something that was viable, that was *hers*. I understood that, and I was eager to help.

As I shaved under my arms, I reflected on my own business. It had never been funded by Thomas outright, but I still owed its success to him. I'd been working as a graphic designer (packaging mostly) when he asked me to help him stage his listed homes. I'd always had a flair for décor. And I loved sourcing furniture and unique treasures that would turn an empty or dated house into an inviting home. Word spread about my abilities, and other realtors hired me for staging. When buyers started employing me to decorate their recently purchased abodes, I quit the graphic design firm. My business was doing well, but we still relied on Thomas's income. I made a fraction of what he did.

Stepping out of the shower, I grabbed a towel off the heated rack. As I dried myself, I still felt jittery and my jaw was tense. It was an over-reaction. The appropriate response to one's house being egged was irritation, not this unnerving sense of vulnerability. I was being ridiculous. But I slipped into my robe and hurried to my bedroom.

My recent closet renovation filled me with instant gratitude. We'd knocked out the wall between the master suite and the small nursery next door. I'd had wardrobes installed allowing me to color-code my outfits. Angled racks held my shoes, cubbies displayed my purses, and shelves showed off my sweaters. In the center sat a small island with several drawers for lingerie, nightgowns, and jewelry. The project had gone way over budget—we were still paying it off—but the results were worth it.

Slipping inside, I shut the door on the sound of the hose running in the driveway. Thomas was still washing away the mess; I didn't need to worry about him interrupting me. I opened the third drawer of the center island and removed the mishmash of hosiery I kept in it. Then I lifted out the false bottom and set it aside. The secret compartment wasn't necessary in our safe Portland suburb, but it was the perfect place to keep my treasures: a bottle of deep-plum nail polish;

showing across town. The listing in Grant Park had been sitting for way too long. It needed a price adjustment, but the sellers were difficult. The potential buyers I was meeting were from out of town, starting new jobs; they were desperate to find a home. I couldn't afford to be late.

"Hey, Siri. Text Eli."

She obediently responded: "What do you want to say?"

I wanted to say: *Get your lazy ass out of bed, you entitled millennial. Go get a job flipping burgers, then tell me why you want to throw away your parent-funded, top-tier education.*

But Viv would have killed me if I spoke to our son that way. When I'd lost my shit on him, he'd gone quiet, turned inward. He'd always been a gentle, anxious boy—even now that he was six foot three, athletic, and handsome. Life was hard enough for sensitive souls like Eli, Viv said. College was intense. He was playing high-level soccer. Goalies always felt the most pressure. It was a lot for anyone, but particularly for Eli. Viv said our best strategy was to act like nothing was wrong. Eventually, our son would open up to us about his issues. We'd arrange support—counseling, maybe some medication. An institution like Worbey would be well-equipped to handle Eli's problems. He'd go back in the fall. It would be fine.

And I wouldn't take out my anger at the little shits who'd egged my house on my own son. I might not understand my eldest child, but I loved him. Cleaning the egg off the house was not punitive. It just had to be done.

"Hey, buddy," I said into the silent car. "Some little brats egged the house. Can you clean the front window with soap and a squeegee? There's a ladder in the garage. Thanks, pal."

After reading my genial message back to me, Siri sent the text to my sleeping offspring.

I was approaching the office now, and my pulse began to escalate. Fifteen minutes, in and out, I told myself. No big deal. But sweat was soaking through the armpits of my crisp white shirt, and my hands felt clammy on the wheel. Head office, once a place of support and camaraderie, now felt daunting and hostile. My colleagues, many of whom I had considered my friends, were not. Friends didn't stand by and watch while you fucked up your entire life.

The gate to the underground parking lot opened automatically, and I drove into its gaping maw. My reserved spot was next to the elevator; I was one of the top agents, after all. The prime parking spots were based on last year's sales figures; if things didn't pick up, I'd be parking on the street next year. But I deposited the BMW and then strode to the adjacent elevator. Stabbing the button, I waited. In and out. I could probably do it in ten.

As I rode up, my mind drifted to that golf weekend on the coast. Roger, a forty-six-year-old colleague, was getting married (for the third time), and had felt the need to celebrate the end of his sporadic singledom. It was ridiculous for a bunch of middle-aged guys to party and carouse like we were in our twenties, I could see that now. I thought we'd golf, rent dune buggies, have a few beers. Never, in a million years, could I have predicted what would happen on that trip. I should have stayed home. I should have said I was too busy at work, that my family needed me.

But I'd gone.

The elevator lurched to a stop and the doors opened with a ding. Taking a deep breath through my nostrils, I strode into the office. It was early, quiet, just a few harmless junior staff milling about. Most of the agents trickled in around ten, and then only to pick up paperwork, access online realtor tools, or catch up with colleagues. We were self-employed, and we lived in our cars. Lucky for me. The tension in my shoulders was beginning to ease as I headed toward my assistant's desk. I shared Emma's services with three other brokers, but she managed to stay on top of everything. I'd told her to have my feature sheets and paperwork for the house on Hancock Street waiting in a manila envelope. Emma was usually a very conscientious assistant, but she'd been slipping lately. She was distracted by her upcoming wedding to her college sweetheart, a video game designer. Or was he an animator? Something like that.

"Morning," I said as I approached.

"Oh, hey, Thomas." She clicked the mouse, shutting down her screen. No doubt she'd been looking at bridesmaids' dresses or bouquets. It wasn't the first time. "What are you doing in so early?"

"Picking up the new brochures for Hancock Street. I asked you to prepare them yesterday, remember?"

"Oh, right." She swiveled in her chair and began to dig through a stack of papers.

*Oh, right?* I'd specifically told her to have the updated marketing materials ready, that I was in a hurry this morning. I understood that she'd rather google cakes and flowers and wedding rings than handle my paperwork, but I was going to have to have a word with her about her distraction. Just not right now.

Down the hall, I heard the elevator doors open and I caught a glimpse of Leo Grass. Leo had been Roger's best man at his last two weddings. He'd organized the bachelor weekend at the resort and casino on the Oregon coast, and was responsible for the debauchery that had occurred. I wasn't completely blameless—I was a grown man with free will—but Leo had provided the alcohol and the drugs. He had invited the women. He had created the perfect storm.

"Here they are," Emma said finally.

"Thanks." I grabbed the envelope and hustled toward the elevator. I should have checked through the pages. Last month I'd found her gift registry in with the feature sheets. She and the video game guy wanted a full set of Le Creuset cookware. They certainly had expensive taste. I'd tell the office manager to get her a dutch oven from all of us.

As I was punching the elevator call button, Leo strolled up with a cup of coffee.

"Hey, mate," he said in his British accent, which some considered charming but I'd recently decided I hated. "Haven't see you around much. Still recovering?"

He winked at me then, and I had the distinct urge to punch him in his smug face. The bachelor party was over a month ago. Yeah, I'd been fucked up, a mess, disgusting even. But it didn't take a *month* to recover from one night of depravity.

"Been busy," I said, with a forced smile that felt like a grimace.

"You shifted the house on Hancock?" he asked, and I caught something taunting in his tone.

"I'm headed to a showing right now."

"Why isn't it selling?" He took a sip of his coffee. "Was someone murdered in there?"

*I'd like to murder you in there.* But I forced a chuckle. He was joking, but it was still a dig. To my relief, the elevator doors opened, and I stepped inside. They closed on his haughty British face.

Alone in the small box, I closed my eyes, let the tension, anger, and shame seep out of me. This wasn't Leo Grass's fault. Leo, Roger, and the other guys were just bystanders, just witnesses. This was all on me, and the thought made my throat close with emotion. How could I have done something so heinous? So vile and abhorrent? Never in a million years had I thought I had it in me. I still didn't believe it. But the photographs . . .

The doors opened and I hurried to my car. I was not going to fall apart. I was going to sell this house, make some money, and deal with this fucking mess. Viv knew something was up. Her eyes darted to my phone whenever it made a sound, so I kept it on night mode when I was at home. If she got into my e-mails, if she saw what was on there, it would be the end. And not just of my marriage.

Hopping into the car, I reversed out of the space and drove out of the dank garage. The spring sunshine hit me, and I reached for my Tom Ford sunglasses in the console. It had been raining for the past four days and the balmy weather should have been a welcome reprieve. But it barely registered with me as I gunned the car toward Grant Park, lost in my thoughts.

My wife thought I was having an affair, but I wasn't—never had, never would. I wanted to tell Viv that I still loved her, that she was beautiful, that I was loyal. But how could I?

The truth was so much worse.

# *Eli Adler*

## (Just Eli.)

I WAS AWAKE when my dad's text came in. How could I not be? He'd started swearing at the top of his lungs at seven thirty. I knew the house had been egged. I knew he had to get into the office early and that this was *the last fucking thing he needed*. But I didn't get out of bed and offer to help him. As usual, I stayed in my room until the house was quiet. And, with luck, empty.

The prospect of scrubbing dried egg off the front window didn't make it any easier to get up. I lay there, scrolling through my phone. I had two texts: the one from my dad and another from my mom, wishing me luck on my job hunt today. My parents were getting frustrated with me. I'd been home for almost three weeks and I still hadn't found work. And then, a few nights ago, I'd told them that I was dropping out of college. They'd totally freaked. It had been messy, ugly, but it was what I'd expected from them. How could they brag about a son who had dropped out? What would they tell people who asked about me? Their plan to turn me into the perfect reflection of themselves had gone awry. Now they were employing a new strategy: denial. They were pretending that nothing had happened, that I was going back, that everything was normal. I wasn't sure which was worse.

If they knew how little I had looked for a job, they really would have been pissed. But they had no way of knowing that when I left the house in my khakis and button-down shirt, I usually bought a coffee and sat on a bench by the river. If it was raining, I went to a movie, sometimes sneaking into another one right after. I'd dropped off a few résumés, but I still had some money left over from last summer's fast-food job. And I had all the time in the world to work. Because I wasn't going back to college, no matter how much my parents wanted me to.

Propping myself up on my pillows, I checked the news apps, glanced at social media, and studiously ignored all the notifications on Messenger. Six of my soccer teammates had created a group chat for us to keep in touch over the summer. We'd chosen the Facebook platform ironically;

none of us were active on Facebook because we weren't *fifty*. The content of their messages was predictable: internships, girls, parties. I had nothing to contribute. When I wasn't pretending to look for a job, I was home, in my room, gaming. And the guys didn't know I was dropping out of school. If they found out, there would be questions. Questions that I didn't want to answer.

Finally, I slipped on a T-shirt and stumbled to the bathroom in my flannel pajama pants and bare feet. My muscles felt stiff and sore in the mornings, reminders of the rigorous training I'd put them through at Worbey. I peed, washed my hands, then shuffled out to the kitchen. My sister, Tarryn, was sitting at the breakfast bar eating toast and staring at her phone.

"Morning," I mumbled, heading straight for the coffee machine. She didn't respond, just kept eating her breakfast, staring at Tumblr or some other forum for angsty teens or angry feminists. Unlike most of the girls I knew, Tarryn didn't wear makeup, didn't straighten her hair, didn't dress to show off her figure. She was in sweats and an extra-large concert T-shirt, her hair pulled back in a messy ponytail. As I poured a cup, I glanced at the clock on the coffee machine: 9:37 A.M. "What are you doing here?"

She double-tapped her AirPods to mute them; I hadn't noticed that she was wearing them. "I live here," she snapped. "What are *you* doing here? Shouldn't you have a job by now?"

My parents might be walking on eggshells around me (pun intended) but my sister was not. "I thought you had school," I retorted.

"I have a free period. What are you—the attendance police?"

Jesus. Tarryn and I used to get along okay, but since I'd been home, she'd turned into a total bitch. It was bad enough that she'd taken over my basement bedroom the minute I left, hauling her furniture downstairs and mine up. I thought she should have at least asked, but my parents said she lived here full-time and I was only home for a few months in the summer. But now I was here for good, and I longed for the privacy and separation of the basement lair.

I dumped some cereal into a bowl, adding milk to it and to my coffee. As soon as I sat at the breakfast bar, Tarryn got up. "Dad wants you to clean the egg off the front window."

"Yeah, he texted me." I took a mouthful of cereal. "Any idea who did it?"

My sister dropped her plate and knife into the sink with a clatter. "Why does everyone think this has something to do with me? I'm a junior in high school, for fuck's sake. I'm not in sixth grade." She stomped out of the kitchen, down to my basement bedroom.

I finished my cereal and cleaned up the kitchen. As I was dumping out the dregs of the coffee, I heard the front door slam. Tarryn was going to school, finally. I breathed a sigh of relief. My bitchy sister didn't cause me anxiety, not like my parents did. Tarryn didn't give a shit about why I'd dropped out of Worbey. As long as I stayed out of her way, she didn't give a shit about me at all. But I liked being alone in the house. When no one was around, I could almost pretend I was a kid again, before college, before that horrible fucking night that ruined my life.

Eventually, I dressed in an old pair of jeans and a flannel shirt and got the ladder from the garage. The egg was dried on the glass like glue. I probably should have tackled the mess earlier, but with a little elbow grease, and my fingernails, I was able to scrape the gunk off. I scrubbed the whole window with a soapy sponge, rinsed it with the hose, and squeegeed away the excess water to avoid streaks. If my parents got on my case about job hunting, I'd point out their gleaming front window.

I was climbing down off the ladder when I heard my name.

"Eli! Hey, man!"

It was Sam, one of my best friends from high school. He'd gone to college locally, but we'd kept in touch. As I stepped onto the ground, he pulled up on his bike. Sam was small and wiry, with a mop of curly hair in a distinctly triangular shape. He usually wore shorts (in all sorts of weather) and ironic T-shirts, but today he had on a white button-down and black slacks, with a messenger bag slung across his body. He looked happy to see me.

Shit.

Sam rolled to a stop and straddled the cross-bar. "Hey, buddy. When did you get home?"

I lied. "Just last week."

"Why didn't you text me? Tyrone and Derek are back from U Dub. We should hang out."

"For sure," I said, as earnestly as I could. "But I just got home so my parents want me to stick around here." I rolled my eyes. "Family time."

"Sarah Ephremova's having a party on Saturday. It starts at eleven. Your parents will be asleep by then. They won't care."

I couldn't go to Sarah's party. She was friends with Arianna Tilbury, and I couldn't handle seeing her. Not now, not in my current state. I should have been over her; we'd broken up a year and a half ago. But even the thought of her made my heart twist in my chest and hot anger burn in my throat. Because we would be together right now, if it weren't for my parents.

"Maybe."

"Come on, man." He gave my arm a playful shove. "Or are you too tight with your *elite college soccer team* to hang out with your old friends?"

My jaw clenched with the need to tell Sam that he knew nothing about my fucking soccer team, that he knew nothing about *me* anymore. It was a major overreaction. I couldn't attack my old friend. Because this wasn't about Sam. It wasn't about him at all.

He was watching me, his brow slightly crinkled. I probably looked like I was having a stroke or something.

"I'll try," I croaked.

"Okay." He put his left foot on the pedal. "I've got to get to work. You're looking at Bank of the West's junior teller."

I managed a weak chuckle. "Good for you."

"See you Saturday?" he said as he rolled away from me.

"Sure," I called after him.

But I wouldn't.

# Tarryn Adler

(Call me Tarry at your peril.)

BY THE TIME I got to school, my irritation had almost simmered away. *Almost.* Being woken from a deep sleep by my mom's accusations, followed by my brother's nosy inquisition, was not the best way to start the day. I'd been sound asleep, dreaming about playing mini golf with Timothée Chalamet, when my mom knocked on my door at eight fifteen.

"I have a free period!" I'd yelled, my voice muffled by my pillow. I'd been awake most of the night, finally going to sleep around 3 A.M. I needed at least another hour of shut-eye or I'd feel like shit. But my mom didn't know I'd been up all night. And I couldn't let her find out. She entered my room.

"It's after eight, Tarryn. Why are you still asleep?" She perched on the side of my bed. I could smell her familiar perfume, citrusy and expensive. "No wonder you can't wake up. Your blackout curtains make it pitch-dark in here."

"That's the point," I muttered. I'd complained that a streetlamp shone through my window and kept me awake at night. It wasn't exactly true, but my mom had let me order the curtains online.

"Some kids threw eggs at the house last night. Any idea who might have done it?"

"No. Why would I?"

"It's probably schoolkids. We thought you might know something about it."

I rolled over, looked at her groggily. "I'm *seventeen*, not ten."

"Maybe some younger boys have a crush on you. Or they're upset at you for some reason."

"Oh my god!" I turned away from her and closed my eyes. "Don't put that toxic masculinity shit on me."

"I'm not *blaming* you, Tarryn. I was just asking. . . ." She rubbed my arm under the blanket for a moment. "Everything okay with you?"

"Fine."

"You don't seem very happy lately."

A lump formed in my throat. Which was stupid. And embarrassing. It was self-pity and it was fucking gross. But it was the first time either of my parents had commented on my well-being in like . . .

forever. They'd always been so focused on my brother, the athlete, the A student, the golden boy—and now that he was dropping out of college, they were *obsessed*. But my mom's warm hand on my shoulder made me want to tell her that she was right: I wasn't happy. I hated my face, my body, and everyone at school . . . except Luke and Georgia, my besties since first grade. I didn't even know why I hated everything; I just did.

But my mom leaned down and kissed the side of my head. "I've got to run. I've got a meeting downtown." She paused in the doorway. "Tell your brother to clean the egg off the front window."

When I heard the door close, I felt a tear leak from my eye, dampening my pillow, but I wasn't going to cry like a baby. I didn't need my mom's comfort. She wouldn't understand, anyway. She was beautiful—*old*, but beautiful. And she'd been married to my dad for a hundred years. What did she know about growing up average in the age of Instagram? In a postfeminist world with rampant impostor syndrome and an epidemic of anxiety? She was basically a housewife. She had her decorating business, had turned my childhood bedroom into her office, but Dad made the money, Dad paid the bills. My mom's job was just for show.

Besides, I had a new community now. A place

where I felt special and adored. I didn't need to fit into that skinny blond high school girl mold to be appreciated. There were people out there who made me feel unique and beautiful and empowered, not ashamed of my body or myself. They longed for my company, would pay for it even. I wiped my tears and dragged myself out of bed.

WHEN I GOT to school, the hallways were deserted. I headed to my locker, enjoying the squeak of my sneakers on the linoleum floor in the silence. The bell would ring in moments, releasing my peers from first period. I'd lied to my mom about the free period I'd skipped. The school would send an automated call to our home phone that no one ever answered or checked for messages. If the school did manage to contact my parents, I could always fall back on an indignant: *I was there! The teacher messed up attendance!* It had worked before.

Opening my locker, I stuffed my backpack and light spring jacket inside. I had a precalculus test next and I couldn't afford to miss it if I wanted to pass. Not that it mattered that much. Grades were not as important as they once were. I was making decent money and I knew I could make a lot more. But I'd always been a conscientious student; apparently, it was a hard habit to break.

The thought of telling my mom and dad that I wasn't going to college made me smirk to myself. They'd fucking lose it. They'd wring their hands and cry, blame themselves for failing as parents. My dad had dropped out of community college and my mom had a two-year design diploma. They weren't *ashamed* of their education, they said, but they wanted better for their children. Now that Eli wasn't going back to Worbey, they were oh-for-two. Total parental fail.

The bell rang and students flooded into the hall. I ignored them and they me. I wasn't relevant here, didn't even want to be. Everyone thought I was a bitch and steered clear. I'd grown to enjoy my hostile outsider status. Fuck the conformists. I didn't have to dress like them, look like them, try to fit in. I didn't have to smile and make eye contact. It was a relief.

"Why weren't you in English?" It was my best friend Luke. He was tall and slim with black hair, long on top, the sides shaved down to the skin.

"I couldn't deal," I said, grabbing my math book out of my locker. "What did I miss?"

"Mr. McLaughlin looked hot in his corduroys."

"Ewww." Unlike Luke, I was not attracted to our thirtyish English teacher.

"We have to write another paper. I'll send you the assignment." Luke cocked an eyebrow. "Late night again?"

Luke thought I had insomnia. I could have told him the truth about what kept me up at night. He had come out to me in ninth grade, before his parents or anyone else. He was progressive, sex positive, open-minded; he wouldn't have judged me. But my nocturnal life was separate from the rest of my life. It was for me alone. And if my parents ever caught wind of it, they would murder me. For real.

"Went down a YouTube rabbit hole," I fibbed, thinking about last night's conversations, adoration, and tips. I'd made almost two hundred bucks.

"Are you sure you're not a porn addict?" he teased.

"You got me," I said. "My favorite site is Horny Bike Couriers."

"Mine too!"

We both laughed, and suddenly, a precalculus test seemed so fucking pointless. "Want to skip and go for brunch? My treat."

"I guess I can miss precalc, just this once."

I tossed my math book back into my locker, grabbed my jacket, and closed the door.

# *Viv*

I SAT AT the breakfast bar, sipping a cup of rooibos tea and toying with the sleek black tube. Removing the cap, I swiveled the base to reveal the deep-red matte lipstick. It was far too intense for my skin tone, but it had looked great on my client. Alicia had applied it just before we left her unfinished ice cream shop. I hadn't intended to take it—or anything else, for that matter. I never did. But Alicia had triggered my deepest insecurities, my darkest self-doubt. And I had just snapped.

The meeting had started out well. Alicia Fernhurst and I knew each other peripherally through our sons. Eli had played junior soccer with her eldest, Magnus. (She had another son a year older than Tarryn.) For years, I'd stood on the sidelines with Alicia and another mom, Dolly Barber, while our boys ran up and down the field. Eli had been a forward then; he became a goalie when he sprouted up, towering over his teammates. My son had been the best player, followed closely by Magnus. Dolly's son, Nate, had never quite measured up.

We'd made pleasant small talk as we toured the small space. It was painted a tropical blue and had a roughed-in counter with a built-in refrigerated ice cream cabinet. That's where we sat, on utilitarian stools, as I pulled out my laptop to show her the mood boards I'd created for her. I had also sourced and costed all the décor items I was recommending.

"Cute," she said dismissively, "but I had something different in mind. More of a Miami vibe. Like pastels and ferns and flamingos."

I maintained my professionalism. I didn't point out that Miami chic was entirely different from the beach shack theme she'd told me she wanted. And I could roll with this change in direction. It was not unusual for clients to shift their vision.

"I can put together some new boards for you. I'll need a couple of days for the costings."

"Shall we meet again next week?" Alicia

checked the calendar on her phone. "How's Tuesday for you?"

We set another meeting; then Alicia dug in her Ferragamo bag for a lipstick and compact mirror. "How's Eli doing?" she asked as she precisely painted her lips deep red. "Did he have a good year at Worbey?"

My pleasant smile didn't falter. "He had a great year. And Magnus?" I couldn't recall where Alicia's son had gone to school—somewhere out east.

"He *loves* Columbia," she said. "I thought it would be hard having him across the country, but it's not when he's so passionate, and fulfilled, and challenged."

"Is he playing soccer there?" I knew he wasn't, but I allowed myself this little dig. Magnus was not the athlete Eli was.

"He gave up soccer in senior year to focus on his grades and college applications. Ivy League schools are *so* competitive."

Worbey was an excellent school with an excellent reputation, but it was not Ivy League. We didn't have the resources to paddle in that pool. Magnus would have had tutors and ACT boot camps, service trips to developing countries and a pricey college consultant. Without a legacy or significant "hook," the Ivies were unattainable to most people.

Alicia pressed her lips together as she snapped the lid back on the lipstick tube. "Theo has just accepted MIT. He could have chosen Stanford or Brown, but MIT has the best engineering program in the world."

I swallowed the sour taste in my throat. "That's great."

"And your daughter? What's she going to do?"

"Tarryn's a junior, but she's already thinking about Cornell."

God, why had I said that? Tarryn had mentioned Cornell a couple of times in eighth grade, back when she'd wanted to be a veterinarian. My daughter had once been a cheerful, bubbly animal-lover. It was hard to imagine the surly troll who lived in my basement vaccinating puppies.

"Good for her," Alicia said, dropping the lipstick into her bag. "We had a retired college professor help with the boys' applicant essays. She's not cheap but she's worth it. I'll give you her number."

"Please."

She smiled and stood. "I'll go set the alarm and we can leave."

When she was in the back room with the alarm, I had made my move.

Now I swiped the lipstick onto the inside of my wrist. It was silky smooth, but the color made my already pale skin resemble a corpse's. I smudged it with my thumb, turning it into a rosy smear, and pictured Alicia rummaging in her bag while her genius sons did math problems for fun. She'd think she'd misplaced the lipstick or dropped it somewhere. She'd never suspect me of taking it.

Would she?

The front door slammed, announcing that Eli was back from pounding the pavement, or Tarryn had returned from school. I quickly dropped the lipstick into the pocket of my long cardigan and stood. As I walked to the front entrance, my cheeks burned with shame. If my children—or *anyone*—found out about my habit, I would die. Literally die. It was harmless. I never took anything sentimental or valuable. . . . Still, I knew it was horrible, I knew it was wrong. I just wasn't sure I could stop.

It was Tarryn, bent over untying her Doc Martens. "Hi, honey," I said, my voice belying my nerves. I wasn't *scared* of my own daughter, but she was so unpredictable these days.

"Hey."

"How was your day?"

"Fine."

"Are you hungry?"

"No." She righted herself, and I saw her wan complexion, the shadows under her eyes. Without forethought, I reached out and touched her cheek.

"Are you okay? You look tired."

"Gee, thanks," she snapped with heavy sarcasm. "You look nice, too." She pushed past me and headed to the basement.

Christ. It was like trying to hand-feed a grizzly bear.

I went back to the kitchen and tipped the rest of my tea down the sink. Reaching into the fridge, I grabbed a bottle of chardonnay.

# *Thomas*

I WAS HOME by six twenty. Viv was already suspicious, so I didn't want to give her any more cause for concern. I had clients who wanted to see a condo in the Pearl District, but I'd arranged for one of my associates to take them. They were looky-loos, so I knew they weren't going to buy the place. And it was more important that my wife stop worrying, stop wondering. Feeling noble, I'd texted to tell her that I'd be home in time for dinner, that I'd be staying in for the night. I wasn't expecting a *medal*, but her thumbs-up response seemed a little dismissive.

When I entered the house, I heard the sizzling of a wok, smelled ginger and garlic and onions. Viv was making a tofu stir-fry. Again. Tarryn was a vegetarian and Viv tried to accommodate her dietary restrictions a few times a week. "It's healthy and good for the planet," my wife said. But the real reason she cooked veggie was to placate our malcontent youngest. Sometimes Viv made a chickpea curry, but the stir-fry was her go-to vegetarian recipe. Tarryn was probably pissed off at Viv for something. Tofu as peace offering.

"Hi, hon," I said, entering the kitchen.

"Hi." Her smile was weak.

"Smells great." I kissed her cheek.

She allowed it. And then, "Can you call the kids? Get them to set the table?"

Obediently, I poked my head down the basement stairs. "Tarryn! Dinner!" There was no response. If her door was closed, she might not be able to hear me. "Tarryn!" I called again, louder this time.

"Oh my god, stop yelling! I heard you the first time!"

I headed upstairs to change out of my suit and rouse my son. He was playing computer games, the violent sound effects slipping under the door and skittering down the hall. How long had he been holed up in his room staring at a screen? Had he dropped off any résumés today? Had he followed up at places he'd already visited? Viv's admonition to be gentle with him ran through my mind, and I wondered if it was backfiring. Was it giving him carte blanche to become a lazy video-game addict? But I couldn't afford to piss off my wife right now. I had enough to deal with.

Without knocking, I opened the door. Eli was at his desktop computer, his fingers frantically clicking the WASD keys. He'd always liked to game . . . but he'd also liked sports, and his friends, and going to movies. This seemed to be his singular interest now. "Dinner," I said over the gunfire.

He kept playing. "In a minute."

"Your mom wants you to set the table."

His eyes never left the monitor. "'Kay."

Frustration clenched my jaw. "Now," I barked, closing the door before I said something I'd regret.

I used the bathroom, then changed into jeans and a sweatshirt. When I joined my family downstairs, the table was set with both chopsticks and forks (by whom, I didn't know). Tarryn was scooping stir-fry out of the wok and into her bowl, and Eli was filling glasses with water. Viv stood by, nursing a glass of white wine, her arms folded in a mildly perturbed stance.

"Yum-yum!" I said, rubbing my hands together. It was a bit over the top, since we ate this meal practically every time Viv was trying to smooth things over with Tarryn, so a lot. But my wife wore that *I'm being taken for granted* expression, so I wanted her to know I appreciated the meal.

When we were all seated, I liberally squeezed sriracha onto my heap of vegetables. "How was everyone's day?" I asked, pinching a piece of tofu with my chopsticks.

The kids muttered *fine* or *good*. Viv said, "I met with my first commercial client today."

Something in her tone told me I should already know this. "That's right. I was going to ask. How did it go?"

"It was okay." She popped a piece of carrot into her mouth. "Except she changed her entire aesthetic on me. I'll have to start over."

"That's frustrating."

Viv chewed. "It won't take me too long."

"Good. Good." My eyes moved to my son, shoveling food into his mouth. "Nice job on the window, buddy."

"Thanks."

I wanted to ask about the job hunt, but we weren't supposed to pressure him. "You been going to the gym? You don't want to get out of shape over the summer."

Viv's head jerked toward me, and she looked

like she wanted to stab a chopstick into my eye. What? Now we couldn't talk about fitness, either?

Tarryn came to her brother's defense. "God, let him relax. He just got home."

"He's been home for—"

*BANG!*

The sound that cut me off was the crack of a shotgun, the boom of a cannon, a meteor crashing to the earth. It made my heart lurch and I was on my feet, my chair tipped over behind me, in an instant. I looked at my family to see if someone had been hurt. They were shaken, their eyes wide, but they were fine. Everyone but Tarryn was standing.

"What the hell was that?" Viv's voice trembled.

"Something hit the window," Tarryn said weakly.

"Stay inside," I instructed, hurtling toward the front door with Eli on my heels. I should have stopped him from following me, but if someone was out there, my tall, athletic son would be a deterrent. And I wouldn't let anything happen to him. I would protect him.

"Be careful," my wife's voice called behind us.

I yanked open the front door and rumbled down the steps, my boy behind me. We were both in sock feet, too full of adrenaline to bother with our shoes. By this time, I'd realized that we hadn't been shot at, but that something had hit our sparkling-clean front window. And hard. Had it been a rock? A brick? And who had thrown it? It was still light out; the May sun wouldn't set for at least another hour. If the perpetrator had lingered, we would find him. Or her. Or them.

Our tidy front lawn was bordered by a few low hedges, but no one was hiding behind them. We hustled down the short driveway in our socks. I looked up the street, Eli down. There was no one in sight. The entire neighborhood was indoors, enjoying a peaceful dinner. Still, I paced the asphalt, peering around as my heart rate returned to normal.

Eli walked onto the lawn, oblivious to the grass stains on his white sport socks. He looked up at the window he'd cleaned earlier that day, then down at the ground beneath it. As he bent to retrieve an object, I hurried to join him.

"What is it?" I asked.

Eli stood up. In his palm was an apple, smashed to a pulp.

Viv and Tarryn materialized on the porch. "What's going on?" my daughter asked.

Eli replied, "Someone threw an apple at the window."

"Should we call the police?" Viv asked.

"For an apple?"

"It scared us half to death. It could have broken the window."

"No, it couldn't," Tarryn replied with her usual eye roll.

"It's just kids. Just mischief," I said, even though my pulse was still pounding in my neck.

"Little brats," Viv muttered. "Where are their parents? Why aren't they home eating dinner?" Tarryn shook her head and went back inside.

I turned to my son. "Hose this off before it dries."

"You'll have to get the ladder and the squeegee," Viv added. "We don't want streaks and water spots."

I saw the irritation in Eli's eyes, but I ignored it. His mother and I had worked all day, his sister had been at school. By all appearances, Eli had lounged around playing computer games. This was the least he could do.

Viv and I went back inside before our dinner got cold.

# *Eli*

THE SQUISHED APPLE came off the glass easily with the hose, but that wasn't good enough for my parents. God forbid there were a few water spots on the window, or worse, *streaks*! I stomped to the back of the house to the small detached garage. No one ever parked in the single-car space. It was chock-full of bikes that we rarely rode, camping equipment that never got used, sporting goods left over from my high school career, and stuff for the lawn and garden. There was also a freezer full of five-year-old meat that would probably never get eaten. The ladder hung from rungs on the far wall. I'd put it back there this morning after cleaning the egg off the glass. If I'd known I would be using it again soon, I'd have left it near the door.

I carried the ladder around to the front, still grumbling to myself. Was I the only person in this family capable of cleaning up these messes? Everyone else got to finish their dinner while mine got cold. And I was freaking starving. Propping the ladder against the window frame, I climbed up with the squeegee in hand. My family was at the table, finishing their meal. No one seemed to notice me hovering in the window like a ghost, even though they could clearly see me. They were too busy eating and talking, likely discussing the little vandals who'd been throwing food at the house.

The egg assault had clearly been premeditated. The kids had to have swiped a carton of eggs from their parents' fridge or gone to a convenience store and bought a dozen. But the single apple seemed spontaneous, as if someone was walking by, decided the fruit was too tart or too mealy, and threw it away. Hard. At our picture window. Maybe the two events weren't even connected? Or maybe they were and, as my parents seemed to suspect, we were being targeted.

When I'd scraped away the water, I climbed down the ladder and carried it to the backyard. This time, I propped it against the wall just inside the garage. Hopefully, I wouldn't need it anytime soon. Hopefully, *I* wouldn't need it at all. Despite my lack of effort, I'd gotten a call from the manager of a gastropub in Goose Hollow, inviting me for an interview. I felt ready now . . . ready to get out of the house, to meet some new people, to make my own money. A job in the service industry would be ideal. I could work nights and sleep during the day, thus avoiding my family completely. I wouldn't be here to clean up after these brats who were attacking the house. And best of all, working at a bar would piss off my parents.

They wanted me to get an internship at a bank or a brokerage. When I first got home, my dad had made some calls, passed on a few connections. "Send them an e-mail," he'd said. "They're looking for summer students." But I hadn't e-mailed. I wasn't emotionally stable then. I'd needed some time to hide out and decompress, to try to process what had happened back at Worbey. And I didn't want to work in finance for one of my dad's golfing buddies. So, I did nothing. And the window had closed.

He was pissed. "I went out on a limb for you," he said. "How do you think that makes me look?"

"That's what matters." I'd walked out of the

# *Tarryn*

I SAT IN my basement bedroom, listening to the house settle down above me. My parents went to bed religiously at eleven, but they were still wound up about the apple. Yeah, it had scared the shit out of us. Yeah, it was weird and annoying. But it was just a piece of fruit thrown by some kids. My parents were acting like a maniac had lobbed a grenade at us.

I didn't know who had thrown it, but I knew the type. There were plenty of kids at school who got off on bad behavior. Kids with divorced parents, kids whose parents worked a lot, kids who struggled in school—any excuse to be pissed off at the world. The culprits would be boys, in eighth or ninth grade, who smoked weed, cut class, and wandered the quiet streets at

room then, leaving him spewing and sputtering behind me. My parents were snobs, and they had no right to be. They were fakes, posers. They'd barely even gone to college, both stumbling into their careers, and yet, they expected my sister and me to become captains of industry, just so they could have bragging rights.

As I was about to enter the basement door in back, my phone vibrated in my pocket. On auto-pilot, I pulled it out and opened Messenger. Maybe hunger had clouded my brain, or irritation had erased my memory, but for that split second, I forgot that I was screening. With that one tap, I had opened the group chat with my soccer team—sixty-two unread messages. And now they knew I was there, knew I had seen their conversations, knew they could get to me.

I read only the messages sent today—seven of them. The first one was from Oscar, a cocky forward getting a business degree. Oscar could be loud and obnoxious when he was drinking, but we'd always gotten along fine at school.

> Eli, is it true that you're dropping out of Worbey?

How did he know? I hadn't told anyone. But I hadn't signed up for classes, hadn't renewed the lease on my dorm room. Could Oscar have found out through the college's administration?

The next message was from Connor, a rich kid who lived close to Worbey's Connecticut campus. He was a mediocre soccer player and there was speculation that his parents had bought his way onto the team.

What the fuck bro? Why?

Manny, a stocky defenseman studying economics like I was, cut to the chase.

Is this about that night? You said you could handle it

Oscar added:

I knew you were a fucking pussy

Pablo, another forward on a soccer scholarship from Mexico, tried a different tack.

Talk to us man. What's going on?

But Manny was aggressive.

Don't pretend you weren't a part of it, Eli
You did it too

He was right. I hadn't actively participated in the hazing ritual, but I had stood by and

watched it happen. Even as the boy t[...] screamed and begged them to stop, [...] ing. I was just as guilty.

The final message was from Noah, [...] just a short drive away in Vancouver, [...] ton. He was less arrogant than the ot[...] goofy and fun-loving. He seemed eager [...] and fit in, but I didn't hold that agains[...] fact, I liked him. We'd even talked abou[...] together over the summer. But his messa[...] not lighthearted. It was an outright threat[...]

Keep your fucking mouth shut Eli. I know where you live.

night looking to get into mischief. Suburban kids trying to be *street*. Some of them might end up in real trouble one day, but most of them were just trying it on. It wasn't a big deal.

My mom clearly disagreed. She'd had a third glass of wine while we cleaned up the kitchen, keeping up a running monologue about "lax parenting," and the "epidemic of boredom and entitlement." She wanted to call the principal at the middle school, but I talked her out of it. The attacks so far had to be random. If she snitched on the culprits, we'd become targets.

When the dishwasher was loaded and the wok hand-washed, I escaped downstairs, leaving my mom and dad chatting on the sofa. It was rare to see them talking to each other in the evenings. They used to watch TV together after dinner, but now my dad mostly worked, and my mom watched design shows that didn't interest him. My mom was pissed off at him, I could tell. She was cool and aloof, sometimes snappish. Dad never snapped back at her, so he must have done something wrong. But tonight, I could hear the steady buzz of their conversation. I guess being attacked by vandals was bonding.

Finally, around eleven thirty, my dad's heavy footsteps told me he was checking the locks and

I heard the creak of the bottom step as he and my mom headed upstairs. It wasn't easy staying up past midnight on school nights, but I had to make sure my family was asleep. There was no lock on my bedroom door and installing one would have looked suspicious. Eli was a risk— the loser couldn't find a job, so he gamed into the night, and then slept late in the mornings. But he wouldn't come down here. I'd been a complete bitch to him since he got home. He wasn't about to join me for a late-night sibling chat.

To build community—and make money—I had to be consistent. Even when I was exhausted, or I had an exam the next day, I had to show up. There was too much competition, there were too many options to become complacent. And I'd grown to need these people as much as they needed me. Not all of them. Some were randos, some were perverts. But I had a core group that I considered friends. They cared about me. They *adored* me.

When the house was silent, I sat cross-legged on my bed with my makeup mirror. Winged eyeliner required bright lighting and a steady hand; I was getting pretty good at it. I paired the dramatic eyes with glossy, hot-pink lips. It was a sexy, burlesque kind of look that made me appear older . . . but not too old. Finally, I dug under my bed and pulled out the lavender hatbox I kept there. Inside nestled an auburn wig cut into a chin-length bob. I twisted my dark hair into a bun at the back of my head and placed the wig over it. Adjusting it in the mirror, I took in my reflection. My transformation was complete.

It was just after midnight, and the house was silent. It was time. I was ready. With my blackout curtains drawn, I flicked on the two directional lamps that lit my set. I logged onto the website, and then I slipped out of my sweatpants and unbuttoned my top. Tonight, I wore a plunging, lacy fuchsia bra and matching panties.

I turned on the webcam and smiled into it. "Hey, guys. Did you miss me?"

# *Viv*

IT COULD HAVE been the extra glass of wine, or the stress of the hooligans throwing food at the house, but my husband and I made love that night. We'd stayed up talking well past our usual bedtime. I'd felt tense and on edge as we discussed the assault. "There's no respect for personal property anymore," I expounded. "Kids never have to work for anything, so they have no concept of value." Tarryn would have argued with me, would have said I was generalizing, insulting an entire generation based on a few bad apples, but thankfully, she was in bed.

Thomas took a sip of wine and smirked.

"What?"

"Nothing. I was just thinking about the stuff I got up to when I was a kid."

"Like what?"

"I don't think I should tell you." His hazel eyes were twinkling. There was an eternal youthfulness to my husband, that little-boy smile. No wonder other women found him attractive. Despite everything, I still did.

I took a sip of wine. "I'll tell you mine, if you tell me yours."

"You were a vandal?" He looked thrilled with the prospect.

"It was a short-lived career. You go first."

He set down his wineglass. "First, let me say that my high school vice principal was a real dick."

"Oh my god," I gasped. "What did you do to him?"

"He'd suspended my friend Stephen for something totally stupid. I can't even remember what, but we were mad. Mr. Mathers had to be punished."

"Tell me," I urged.

"We found out where he lived, just a few streets over from Stephen's house. Four of us went there one night." He shook his head at the remembrance. "He'd left his car window open a couple inches, so . . . we pissed into his car."

"That's disgusting." I laughed. "And a bit homoerotic."

"I feel bad about it now. But we got away with it, thank god." He picked up his wineglass and gestured toward me with it. "Your turn."

"Mine is nothing compared to that."

"You still have to tell me."

I smiled at him, enjoying our banter and connection. "When I was about nine, they were laying a new sidewalk in front of our house. We were told not to touch it until it dried. But a few of us got Popsicle sticks and wrote our initials in the wet cement."

"That's it?"

"Yeah . . . except I wrote my brother's initials instead of mine. My parents grounded him for two weeks."

"That's psycho, Viv. Seriously."

"I didn't want to get caught." I giggled. "And I never did."

We were having fun together, despite the tensions and secrets between us. And confessing our past bad deeds had placed the recent assault into perspective. Kids did stupid things for stupid reasons. Or for no reason at all. These attacks weren't personal, they weren't about us. They were just an annoyance, nothing serious.

And then, when we went up to bed, Thomas kissed me good night. And I kissed him back.

The next thing I knew we were touching each other, and he was so warm and comfortable; he knew how to please me, and I him. Soon, he was inside me, and it felt good and natural and right.

When it was over and he lay spent on top of me, he whispered into my ear, "I love you. You know that, right?"

I wanted so badly to believe him, and part of me did. But even if he loved me, I knew he was lying to me. I knew he was keeping something from me. And loving me didn't mean he couldn't be in love with someone else, too. Men could do that—compartmentalize: the comfortable old wife at home, the sexy babe at the office.

I should have confronted him then, should have questioned him. But instead, I murmured, "I love you, too." Because I was afraid. Afraid of losing the man I had loved my whole adult life, the man I *still* loved. Afraid of starting over at forty-seven, with two unhappy children and a glorified hobby as a job. I wasn't ready to know the truth and deal with the aftermath.

And, as it turned out, I had other things to worry about.

THE E-MAIL CAME in on Friday morning, just in time to ruin my weekend. I was in my office,

the spare bedroom between our room and Eli's.
I was costing some very cool rattan barstools
for the ice cream shop when the ping of an in-
coming message distracted me. It was from my
client, Alicia.

Hi Viv,

I won't be needing your decorating
services after all. I'll be happy to pay you
for your time so far, but I've decided to
go in another direction. Please send an
invoice for what I owe you.

Regards,
Alicia

Even in an e-mail, the frosty tone was unmis-
takable. What was going on? Alicia was the one
who had changed direction. She'd told me she
wanted *beach shack* and then did a one-eighty to
*Miami chic*. But I had promised her new mood
boards by next week, had been perfectly pleasant. I'd been a complete professional. This had
to be about something else.

Oh god . . . the lipstick.

She knew. Somehow. Alicia must have had in-
ternal security cameras installed to spot shoplift-

ers or staff dipping into the till. She'd have seen footage of me reaching into her expensive bag and plucking out her lipstick. I was so stupid, so impulsive, so fucked up. Alicia had made me feel jealous and inadequate and I had lashed out in the most inappropriate way. And now . . . I would be ruined. My career, my reputation, my entire goddamn life! Thomas and the kids would be angry, disgusted, mortified.

But what the hell could I do to stop it?

# *Thomas*

I SAT ON the toilet, scrolling through my phone (don't pretend you never do it). It was not the most scenic or hygienic locale, but the toilet stall was the only place I could go to guarantee privacy in the real estate office. If anyone peered over my shoulder and saw the images I was looking at, they would be horrified. *I* was horrified. They were violent and disturbing. And they were meant to destroy me.

My pants were around my ankles for veracity, but I was just sitting, just staring. The e-mail had come in while I was in my office cubicle pulling comps. When I saw the name, my heart had skipped a beat: Chanel69. I'd hurried to the men's room, locked myself in a stall, and dropped my pants. Only then did I open the missive.

This was the third e-mail I'd received from Chanel69. The first had arrived a few days after I'd returned from the bachelor party, still puffy and bleary and full of drinker's remorse. I hadn't been that wasted since college. It was embarrassing. And unsettling. Because most of that night was a blank.

I'd almost deleted the message without opening it, thinking it was spam.

Hi Thomas,

I met you at the Golden Dunes golf resort. I gave you a lap dance and you took me back to your room. When we were alone, you were violent with me. I want you to see what you did.

Chanel

At first, I thought it was a prank. Leo and Roger had to be behind it; they were taunting me for getting so messed up. I'd opened the first photo and I had to laugh. The image was comical! I was seated in an Eames-inspired armchair that I recognized from Roger's suite. My hands gripped the arms, my expression a mixture of embarrassment and sheer terror, as the stripper (was her name really Chanel? Leo and Roger had probably made it up) gave me a lap dance. "Chanel" had long dark hair, large fake breasts, a tattoo of a phoenix snaking its way from belly to collarbone. Her ample butt cheeks were rubbing the front of my blue linen shirt. I looked like I was going to piss myself from fear. Or, possibly, start crying. It was funny. Viv might not have seen the humor in it, but my discomfort was comedically obvious. But the next photos were not humorous. Not at all.

The first shot was dimly lit, but I'd recognized the masculine bedroom. I recalled the double bed with its gray bedspread and two red throw pillows, the funky lamp on the nightstand. My black carry-on suitcase was on the chair in the corner. On the bed lay a man with a woman astride him. It was me. And it was Chanel.

I was fully dressed—that's how I recognized myself. Viv had bought me the linen shirt, an aqua blue that worked with my skin tone, she said. Though my face was indistinguishable, the color was visible even in the faint lighting. I had a vague memory of the lap dance in the living room, but I had no recollection of being alone with Chanel in the bedroom. But there I was, flat on my back, being straddled by a naked stripper. I felt embarrassed and ashamed and frightened. Because if this photo ever got out, I'd be humiliated. My wife would kill me. But when I'd clicked on the next image and it filled the screen, my stomach dropped.

This photo showed the damage: Chanel's delicate neck was black and blue, the bruises revealing the distinct shape of four fingers. Her throat had been gripped, roughly, brutally, by a man's large hand. Someone had tried to choke her, to strangle her. The next image was even worse. On the top of Chanel's ample breast, just above the phoenix's flames, was an angry red bite mark.

I couldn't have done it. I'd never been rough with a woman in my life. Yes, I'd been blind drunk that night, but tequila didn't turn a mild-mannered dad into a violent misogynist. Even if I'd been drugged (some of the guys had taken MDMA), I would not have hurt the exotic dancer. There was just no way.

Was there?

I shouldn't have responded. Or I should have responded differently. By apologizing, I'd incriminated myself. And my words made it clear that I had no recollection of my time with Chanel.

> I'm very sorry this happened to you. But I didn't do it. I couldn't have.

The second e-mail came a few days later.

> I expected you to deny it, but these photos
> are proof. I can send them to your wife,
> your kids, and your boss. I can post them
> on your social media. Then everyone can
> decide for themselves.

It was clear. Chanel was looking for much more than an apology.

> What do you want?

She'd demanded $50,000 in bitcoin, sent instructions for setting up a cryptocurrency wallet that would allow the smooth and anonymous exchange of funds. Now this third e-mail had added a timeline.

> I'm sick of waiting. You have two weeks, or
> these photos will be sent to everyone you
> know.

I couldn't let it happen. Being photographed in bed with a stripper was bad enough, but the bruises and the bite mark . . . Jesus Christ. They must have been staged. Viv and the kids had to know that I would never, *ever* strangle a woman, never ever bite her. But even if they believed me, they'd be humiliated.

If the photos were posted on social media, there would be at least a few viewers who would doubt my claims of innocence. The agency would drop me. I'd lose clients, friends . . . my reputation. Somehow, I had to make this go away.

There was no way I could pay Chanel $50,000. Viv and I had curated the appearance of wealth, with our big house, the luxury cars, and our son's fancy college. But I'd bought the house for a song when it was in foreclosure, and the cars were leases. We were still paying off the bathroom and closet renovations my wife had insisted upon. I'd married a woman who excelled at making things look pretty and perfect, even when they weren't. It was her special skill, and she'd turned it into a career. We were just two of millions of Americans living beyond our means.

But I knew how to negotiate. It was my job. And I'd read numerous books on the subject. The best way to deal with a ridiculous offer was "strategic umbrage," remaining calm and poised while clearly taking offense. My response would make Chanel see that her request was ridiculous, completely outrageous. I e-mailed her back.

I don't see how that would ever work.

My blackmailer would be offended, pissed off, but she wasn't going to release the images of me. Why would she? Then it would be over, and she'd get nothing. If this was really about money, she'd come back with a lower number. I'd counter. There would be some back-and-forth, but eventually, we'd agree on a more reasonable figure. I could pull from our line of credit if need be, and hope Viv didn't notice. It was a risk I had to take.

I stood, pulled up my pants, and dropped the phone into my pocket.

# *Eli*

I TOOK AN Uber home from my job interview. The account was attached to a credit card my parents had given me when I was at college—*for emergencies.* This wasn't an emergency; it was a celebration. I'd taken the bus to the gastropub in Goose Hollow, but I deserved a ride home. I'd nailed my interview and gotten the job. My first training shift was on Monday. I felt a weird combination of relief, elation, and a perverse sense of triumph. My parents had wanted me to get a job and now I had one. But they weren't going to be happy about it.

The brewery/restaurant was totally hipster. It served roasted brussels sprouts and deep-fried pickles and thirty-seven kinds of beer. My new boss, Peter, was in his late thirties and had a handlebar mustache. The gastropub had pool tables upstairs and live music on weekends. The main floor was family-friendly, offering a kids' menu with mac and cheese and chicken strips. That's where I would start (unfortunately) busing tables in the evenings. But when I turned twenty-one, I'd move to the upper level. I wanted to be around the action—and the money. Eventually, I could become a bartender: make big tips, meet cool people, grow a beard. It wasn't the kind of future my parents wanted for me. And that made me want it all the more.

If they knew I viewed my busboy job as a launching pad for a career, they'd freak out. I had two years of an economics degree under my belt, and now I wanted to walk away from it to sling beers. But this was *my* life. I was sick of my mom and dad living vicariously through me, taking out their educational regrets on their kids. I was sick of my family in general. My parents were so tightly wound, and my sister was a bitch on wheels. Once I started making decent money, I'd get my own apartment. Until then, this job would at least get Mom and Dad off my back. And give me a reason to get out of the house.

The Uber pulled up in front of our home and I saw the driver glance at it, heard his low, appreciative whistle. Our house wasn't the fanciest in the neighborhood, but I knew it was impressive. And my parents took excellent care of it. They were always renovating something, always updating the furniture or rugs. They were "house-proud," a term I heard them toss around when talking about their real estate or decorating clients. To me, a house was just a building.

My dad wasn't home. His weekends were spent driving clients around to look at properties or hosting open houses. He had associates who sometimes did it for him, but I think he enjoyed it. When I told him about my busboy job, he'd make a sarcastic comment, something like: *I didn't realize you liked picking up dirty dishes so much. That sounds much better than working at a bank!* My mom wasn't going to be thrilled either, but she'd hide it better.

I jogged up the front steps, digging my key out of my pocket, and let myself in. For a second, I thought the house was empty, but then I heard my mom moving around in her upstairs office. She worked from home but was sometimes at a client site, or an exercise class. I decided to tell her about my job now, to get it out of the way. I knew what to expect: a fake smile, some mildly encouraging words. If she told me I was *settling*, that I could have done better, I'd point out that they'd wanted me to find work and I had. But my mom was nonconfrontational, unlike my loud and blustery dad. She would probably try to hide her disappointment.

Kicking off my shoes, I climbed the stairs. My mom must have heard my footsteps because she swiveled in her desk chair to face me. "Hi, honey."

"I've got some news."

"Oh?"

"I got a job."

A broad smile spread across her face and she stood. "Good for you, Eli. Where?"

"The Thirsty Raven. In Goose Hollow."

I saw her face fall, just a little, but she covered. "I've been there. They make a great Cobb salad."

"They have thirty-seven types of beer."

"What will you be doing?"

"Busing tables to start. But I can move up."

"Busing is a great summer job. You'll make a few tips and meet some new people." She looked genuinely pleased. Maybe I'd misjudged her. "And you'll be happy to get back to school after a few months of clearing dirty dishes."

My jaw clenched. I would tell her again, in no uncertain terms, that I was not going back to

Worbey College. If my parents tried to make me, I would leave. I would move out, stay with friends, even sleep on the streets. But then she reached a hand toward me.

"You have something on your cheek." She wiped at it as if I were a toddler.

"What is it?"

"Chocolate maybe? What did you eat for lunch?"

"A turkey sandwich."

My mom sniffed her fingers. "Oh my god, Eli. It smells like poop!"

"On my face?" I didn't wait for a response but stormed to the bathroom down the hall. In the mirror I saw the faint brown streak on my cheek. I turned the faucet on and that's when I noticed the smudges on my hand.

Mom had followed me. "Did you fall in some dog doo?" she asked, elbowing her way to the sink.

"I didn't fall. It's on my hand." I was vigorously pumping liquid soap with my left hand, scrubbing my right hand and face.

"Did you take the bus home?"

"I got an Uber."

"It could have been on the car door handle."

"I would have smelled it." As I continued to

scrub, a thought struck me. I turned off the faucet, quickly dried my hands and face, and rumbled down the stairs.

"Where are you going?" My mom was on my heels, but I didn't answer, didn't pause. I yanked open the front door and went onto the porch. I looked at the hand railings, freshly painted last summer, clean and white because my dad wiped them down every weekend when he did his yard work. Then I looked at the front door.

The handle was smeared with a sticky brown substance: shit.

# *Tarryn*

ON WEEKENDS, I hung out with Georgia and Luke. We went for walks, to the mall, sometimes we smoked weed. Our friendship was comfortable to the point of being dull, like a pair of worn-in sneakers that still felt good, but we all craved a pair of six-inch stilettos. At least, I did. Sometimes I was tempted to tell them about my camming life, just to shake things up. Georgia would have been shocked. Luke would have been impressed. But I'd decided that my alter ego, my second life, was mine alone.

When I got home around four o'clock, my dad's car was in the driveway. He was rarely home on the weekends, busy at open houses or chauffeuring potential buyers around. Still, it wasn't unusual for him to pop home and then go out again later, so I didn't think anything of it. But when I opened the door and saw my mom, dad, and brother seated in the living room deep in conversation, I felt a prickle of foreboding. They immediately stopped talking and looked at me.

"What's wrong?"

"Nothing," my mom said quickly. "We just wanted to talk to you."

I kicked off my shoes. "About what?"

My parents exchanged a quick look that filled me with dread. Something bad had happened. Had my grandma died?

Mom patted the sofa beside her. "Come sit."

But I selected the designer chair in the corner, farthest away from them all. "What's going on? Is Grandma Joyce okay?"

"She's fine," my dad assured me. "Everyone's fine."

My brother leaned forward in the armchair, his face dark and scowling. "Those kids put dog shit on the door handle!"

I laughed. I couldn't help it. It was just so bizarre. And clearly, Eli had touched it. The thought of the little prince with dog poop on his hands was too much.

"It's not funny," my brother snapped. "It's fucking sick!"

"It is," I said, forcing a serious expression. "But how do you know it was *dog* shit?"

"Shut up," Eli muttered.

"It could be cat shit. Or human shit."

"That's enough!" my dad bellowed, as my mom scolded, "This is serious, Tarryn!"

Dad cleared his throat. "Someone had the nerve to come onto our front porch, in the middle of the day, to put feces on the door handle. Who would do that?"

I felt the weight of their eyes and realized the question was not rhetorical. They expected *me* to answer. "You still think I know something about all this?"

"The eggs and the apple could have been random," my dad replied. "But painting poop on our front door? That's personal."

"Is there something going on at school?" my mom said gently. "Or with your friends?"

"What about on social media?" Eli said. "Do you have beef with someone?"

"Maybe a younger boy?" my dad suggested.

"Oh my god," I snapped, "this is so chauvinistic."

"What?" Dad looked completely befuddled.

"It's like . . . *that boy pulled your pigtails because he likes you.* As if males don't have to take responsibility for their bad behavior. I'm so fuck-ing over this bro-culture bullshit."

"Tarryn. . . ." Mom was admonishing me for my swearing, missing the point altogether. At least my dad looked a little sheepish.

"And how do you know *kids* did this?" I threw in.

"Because it's childish," Dad responded. "Adults don't act that way."

"Don't they?" I looked at him. "Maybe it's some psycho from your work. Maybe he doesn't like the house you sold him." I addressed my mom. "Or it's some woman you pissed off at spin class. Or she hates your decorating." And then I turned to my brother. "Plenty of kids hated you in school, Eli. *Mr. Popular. Mr. Perfect. Mr. Soccer Star.*"

I saw them take this in, saw the doubt flicker in their eyes. But only for a second.

"If you're not willing to be open and honest with us," Mom sniffed, "then I guess we'll just have to suffer this abuse."

"I don't know anything!" I snapped, standing up. "And I can't believe you're trying to guilt-trip me when this is not my fault!" I stormed out of the room and hurried down the basement stairs.

Alone in my bedroom, my anger bubbled over. I got that they were upset. Shit on the door handle was next level, totally taking things too far. But these assaults were not about me. I didn't have enemies. I didn't have beef. I was basically invisible to my peers. Why would they attack me when they didn't even notice me? It was only when I was camming that I felt seen and important. And no one in my chat room knew who I was or where I lived.

And then I remembered, about a week ago, there had been an odd comment.

I like the red hoodie you wore today.

The words sounded innocuous, and they would have been if they had been posted anywhere else. But I never wore more than a bra and panties when I was camming. Not to mention a wig and heavy makeup. None of my online fans knew my real name, my identity, or even that I lived in Portland, Oregon. The camming website had extreme privacy controls. So, none of my viewers knew that I had recently bought a red hoodie that I wore to school, out for coffee with friends, and on errands.

The commenter's handle was unfamiliar, but I always had guests popping into my chat room. If they made a rude comment or request, I blocked them. If they liked what they saw, they'd become regulars. The mention of my hoodie had to be a coincidence. Or spam. But I'd blocked the viewer, just to be safe. And then I put it behind me. Because no one in my real life knew that I was camming; I'd made sure of that. I hadn't even told my closest friends. And even if some-one discovered my cam page, they'd never sus-pect that the sexy, erotic Natalia with the auburn hair and dramatic makeup was plain old Tarryn Adler.

Would they?

# *Viv*

MY SPIN CLASS started at 9 A.M. I was dressed in my Lululemon tights and a pink tank, my hair pulled back in a ponytail. I'd applied a dab of blush and one coat of mascara, so I looked presentable but not made-up. Normally, I looked forward to this Sunday class. A good sweat set me up for the whole week. But as I stared at my reflection in the full-length mirror, I saw the tension in my shoulders, the set of my jaw. My complexion was ashen under the rouge, and my eyes had a haunted appearance. I looked frightened. Because I was.

If Alicia Fernhurst knew that I had stolen her lipstick, she would undoubtedly tell her friends. Likely, she'd share the camera footage with them, too. A couple of Alicia's confidantes attended my cycle class. There was a good chance

I'd see Marcelle McHale in class today. She and Alicia had known each other for years. And Dolly Barber's attendance was more sporadic, but she and Alicia were close. If these women knew what I had done, I couldn't face them. The humiliation would be too much.

I had a vivid memory of reaching into Alicia's bag and grasping her lipstick. I recalled the racing of my pulse, the shallowness of my breath, the adrenaline high when I walked away with her property in my possession. But I didn't always remember the act. Sometimes, I just found an item in my purse or pocket when I got home. It was almost as if I entered a trancelike state when I stole some objects. Or maybe my guilty conscience blurred the memory, softened the edges.

The lawn mower was buzzing outside the window. Thomas was busying himself with yard work as he did every Sunday morning. He could easily have skipped a week—the yard looked perfect— but curb appeal was important to him and he enjoyed his noisy little gadgets. With my husband otherwise engaged and both my children sleeping in, I slipped into my closet and went to my hosiery drawer. Removing the false bottom, I stared at the collection of pilfered items.

I picked up the bottle of nail polish, such a

dark shade of plum it was almost black. I tried to remember where I had gotten it, but I couldn't. It might have been in a medicine cabinet in a condo I'd staged for one of Thomas's colleagues, but I wasn't sure. The corkscrew, I remembered taking. It had come from a dinner party at our neighbors' house—Camille and Warren. The conversation had turned political, the biggest faux pas when entertaining. I'd felt uncomfortable as heated opinions flew across the table, had excused myself to get a glass of water from the kitchen. Somehow, the heavy corkscrew had found its way into my bag.

The Zippo lighter was a mystery. Who used a lighter like that anymore? I couldn't think of anyone in my orbit who smoked regularly. It must have come from a home I'd staged or decorated. But I recalled taking the single gold hoop earring. It had belonged to Trina from my book club. I'd used her bathroom during our wine-soaked discussion of *Educated*, and saw the earrings sitting there in a little glass dish. I'd felt tipsy and reckless. It was the first item I had stolen from a friend. It wouldn't be the last.

The bag of pills . . . I had stumbled across them in a linen closet, hidden behind a stack of towels. They were clearly pilfered, stolen, or otherwise illicit, or else they would have been in a prescription bottle. I peered through the plastic at the small blue circles, stamped with the numeral 30. These pills looked slightly rough around the edges and had a dull finish, which seemed odd. But I wasn't familiar with medications. Neither Thomas nor I took anything stronger than Tylenol. Or the occasional Ambien.

While I couldn't recall whose home I'd been in, I remembered reaching for a clean hand towel and finding the stash. The discovery had given me a thrill. And I'd felt an even greater thrill when I'd liberated the bag from its hiding place. I'd felt justified, even noble. Someone was using these pills recreationally and I was removing the temptation.

And then there was the lipstick. Alicia's lipstick. The slight exhilaration I'd felt sifting through my treasures was replaced by a deep sense of self-loathing. And of shame. What was wrong with me? If word got around that I was a thief, even a kleptomaniac, I'd be a pariah. And I deserved to be. My throat clogged with emotion, and I blinked back the tears that threatened.

Replacing the false bottom, I closed the

drawer filled with my ill-gotten treasures. Then I stripped off my workout clothes and pulled on a pair of jeans. I realized that I couldn't go to spin class—I couldn't go *anywhere*—until I figured out how to deal with what I had done.

# *Thomas*

EVERY SUNDAY, I got up early and puttered in the yard. I enjoyed doing chores, as long as they involved some kind of power equipment. That morning, I mowed the front grass and edged it with the weed-whacker. Then I power-washed the front steps and the driveway. Viv had cleaned the shit off the front door with a heavy-duty bleach cleaner, but I gave it a blast with the power-washer, just to be sure.

When I was done, I headed for the shower. As I washed my hair with a thickening shampoo, I thought about my daughter's words last night. She'd been adamant that the recent attacks had nothing to do with her, had even tried to deflect the blame onto us. Her defensiveness only made her look more responsible. This had to be about Tarryn. I didn't know much about her life, or her friends, but I knew she was a cute girl with a huge chip on her shoulder. She was bound to attract some negative attention.

Tipping my head back, I rinsed the soap from my hair, my mind drifting to more pressing matters. I still hadn't heard back from my blackmailer. How could I negotiate if she wouldn't come to the table? The deadline to pay the fifty grand was looming. Obviously, I was going to miss it. I still felt certain—fairly certain—that Chanel wouldn't release the incriminating photos, that she would come back with a lower, more reasonable figure. I had the line of credit, if need be, but if I could sell the house on Hancock, that albatross around my neck, my commission would help my problem go away.

A thought struck me then. Could Chanel be behind the recent attacks on my house? I knew nothing about the woman I'd supposedly assaulted. Did she live in Portland? Was she taking out her anger at me on my home? It seemed unlikely . . . but maybe she had kids or younger siblings who were doing the dirty work?

No. No way. Blackmailers didn't egg houses, throw apples, and wipe shit on door handles. This was kid stuff. It had to be about Tarryn. Or maybe Eli. I turned the water off and reached for a heated towel. I had the Hancock open house at two. My hopes had been dashed when the last potential buyers settled on a bungalow in Laurelhurst. Today was the day, I told myself as I rubbed my hair. A buyer was going to walk in the front door.

THE HOUSE WAS a dated split-level with a *Brady Bunch* vibe, minus the charm. The owners, a disagreeable couple in their late sixties, had refused to pay for Viv's staging services. I'd recently brought it up again as a way to freshen their listing, but they would not fork out for it. I could have asked my wife for a discount, even a freebie, but I didn't want this property on her radar. And I didn't relish a speech about her professional value, and women being taken for granted. Luckily, my assistant, Emma, was eager to help out and make a little extra money for her upcoming nuptials. On occasion, I paid her cash to tidy, declutter, hide the appliances in the oven, and make coffee.

When I arrived at the Grant Park house, Emma was in the kitchen, arranging a vase full of pink tulips. The place looked spotless and smelled like fresh coffee and the box of warm doughnuts that was sitting on the counter. On the fridge, brightly colored magnetic letters spelled WELCOME HOME.

"It looks great in here," I said. I pointed at the fridge. "Nice touch."

"Thanks." Emma looked pleased with herself. "I picked up the fridge magnets at the dollar store, and some of those cord wrapper thingies to tidy up behind the TV."

Emma was better at staging than she was at administration and seemed to enjoy it more. She had really gone above and beyond today with the extra touches. Maybe she could sense how badly I needed to sell this place? I pulled a few bucks from my wallet. "Thanks for your help."

She looked at the money for a second, and then up at me. "Your wife has a staging business, right?"

"Yep. Staging and décor."

"I was wondering if you could mention me to her. Maybe set up a meeting? I'd like to move in that direction, eventually."

"Sure," I said, though I hated the thought of losing my assistant. Good help was hard to find, and there was too much going on in my life to have to train someone new. And my last assistant had been hungover at least three times a week.

"Thanks, Thomas." Emma took the money and stuffed it into her pocket. "I've got to run. Paul and I are trying wedding cakes this afternoon."

"Lucky you," I said, grabbing a doughnut.

She was shrugging on her jacket when she said, "Are you okay? You seem kind of . . . tense lately."

I met her gaze, saw the concern in her dark-brown eyes. Emma was a nice kid, had a good camaraderie with all the agents. She and Leo Grass had a teasing sort of banter that entertained the whole office (even me, until he became my nemesis). But could I open up to a twenty-seven-year-old woman about what I was going through? What would I even say?

*Well, Emma, I'm being blackmailed for assaulting a stripper; my wife thinks I'm cheating on her; my son's dropping out of college; and anonymous delinquents have been throwing food at my house and wiping dog, cat, or human excrement on my front door handle. So, yeah . . . a little tense.*

Emma was young and carefree, focused on her wedding and her future. She wouldn't understand. And I wouldn't burden her. "I just really need to unload this house."

"I know," she said with a sympathetic smile. "It's going to happen today. I can feel it."

I forced a smile as my stomach twisted. It had better.

# *Eli*

MY DAD WAS in a good mood at dinner. He'd picked up pizza on his way home from wherever he'd been. I thought maybe it was a celebration for my new job, but apparently my mom just didn't feel like cooking. The news was on TV as we ate. My parents kept up a running commentary on the stories of the day, moaning about politicians and policies while my sister and I chewed in silence. No one mentioned that tomorrow was my first shift at the Thirsty Raven. Not until the end of the meal when I excused myself.

"Will you be home for dinner tomorrow night?" Mom asked, stacking the plates.

"No. My training shift starts at four."

"Here." My dad handed me the pile of dirty plates. "Your first training shift."

From anyone else, it might have been funny. From him, it was condescending and belittling. I stomped to the sink and dumped the dishes, then headed up to my room. Behind me I heard Dad say, "What? It was a joke."

Collapsing onto my bed, I pulled out my phone. Tomorrow marked a new beginning for me and the end of the Worbey chapter. I now knew that my college soccer teammates were not my friends. I'd thought they were good guys, a bit cocky, a bit rowdy, but decent human beings overall. Something had come over them that night—booze, group contagion, excess testosterone—that had turned them into monsters. I'd learned about it in a sociology elective. They'd done something horrible, but they were boys, just like me.

But they weren't like me; that had become clear when I opened their messages and read their taunts and threats. They were mean and ruthless, cared only about saving their own skins. I didn't want to destroy them like they thought I did. I just wanted to forget the whole fucked-up incident. But I was the weakest link and they were afraid of what I might say. And they were not going to let me bring them down.

Luckily, cutting them off was easy. I blocked

all their numbers from calling my phone. Then I went through Instagram, Snapchat, and Facebook, systematically eliminating my former friends. I also deleted the Messenger app. I probably should have done that when I first got home, before they could turn on me. But better late than never. And then, as I did on occasion, I checked up on Drew Jasper.

It appeared that he'd blocked the rest of his abusers, but somehow, I had slipped through the cracks. Maybe he remembered that I was just a bystander, not a participant in his assault. More likely, he'd forgotten about me altogether. Drew hadn't posted much since the incident. If I was fucked up about it, I could only imagine how he was coping. But there was a new photo on his Instagram, a picture of a sunset over a lake surrounded by thick forest. The caption read simply:

Home

I couldn't remember where Drew was from, but it was clearly somewhere rural. Or maybe his family had a lake house? There was a sense of relief in that single word: *Home*. Drew would not be going to back to college, either. I wondered what he had told his family. Was he able to tell them the truth? Or had he felt the need to lie to them, too? Had they grilled him, demanding

answers? Accused him of being selfish and ungrateful, the way my parents had? Normally, I
observed his page undetected, not wanting to
draw attention to my lurking. But I decided to
like his post. Because I got it. I understood.

Drew had come to Worbey in the winter se-
mester. I'd barely met the guy before that night.
He hadn't seemed like a victim; a strong forward
with an outgoing personality. Drew had had no
problem chugging the drinks the team forced on
him, wearing the bra and panties that were the
hazing tradition. We'd all gone through it; it
wasn't that bad. But Drew was a late arrival and
forced to do it alone. Maybe that's why things
had taken a bad turn?

He'd been handling it fine until the paddle
came out. It was about eighteen inches long including the handle, the letters ƧƆW tooled into
the black leather. We'd all been spanked with it,
hard enough to emblazon the acronym for Worbey College Soccer onto our pink backsides. It
was painful, ultimately degrading, but bearable.
What happened next, wasn't.

Drew had tried to call it off, had tried to stag-
ger away, but the guys wouldn't have it. There
was some shoving, some grabbing, and the next
thing I knew, they had him pinned down on the

floor. Manny ripped the panties off and Oscar smacked Drew with the paddle. Hard. Too hard. The letters were already visible on his red ass, but Oscar kept spanking, even as Drew twisted and writhed and screamed for him to stop. When Manny took the paddle off Oscar, I thought the abuse was over. But it wasn't. Manny turned the instrument around, and he used the handle.

The memory made me feel sick, made me hate myself, so I went to my desk and turned on my computer. Gaming was the only thing that let me forget the past, even the present. If I was better at it, I'd get on Twitch and never do anything else. Everything disappeared when I was playing League of Legends. Memories, even time ceased to exist. So I was surprised when there was a knock at my door. My mom poked her head inside.

"It's late. Maybe you should shut it down?"

I glanced at the time in the corner of my screen: 10:36. "I will. Soon."

"We're going to bed. Can you put your headphones on?"

"Sure. Good night, Mom."

"Good night, sweetie."

I placed the headphones on my ears and turned

up the volume. I stayed up for another hour, probably closer to two. If I played long enough, I could fall into an exhausted sleep, unbothered by dreams about Drew and Oscar and Manny.

I was so immersed in my game that I barely heard the explosion on our front lawn.

# *Tarryn*

I WAS IN my wig, bra, and makeup when the blast interrupted a camming chat about fish oil supplements (you'd be surprised how many viewers were completely satisfied to discuss health and wellness with a girl in her underwear). My first instinct was to run from the room in my camming ensemble, but thankfully, I thought better of it. I closed the laptop, tore the wig from my head, and flicked off the lamps I used for lighting my set. Only then did I peek out the corner of my heavy curtains. Gray smoke snaked across our front lawn, and my heart jumped into my throat. What the fuck had happened?

A few seconds later, my parents' feet entered the frame. I saw my dad's sweatpants and untied running shoes, heard him mutter, "Jesus Christ. It's a smoke bomb."

"Call the police," my mom said, her voice tense and shrill above her fluffy slippers.

Eli's bare feet joined them. "It's harmless, Mom. Just noise and smoke."

"It's not harmless," she cried. "These lunatics threw a bomb on our front lawn in the middle of the night! I want to find out who the heck is behind this and why."

The smoke was starting to dissipate now, so I moved away from the window. Would my parents really call 911? Would the police show up over something so innocent? I wanted to go upstairs to find out, but I'd have to remove my makeup first. And throw a robe over my sexy lingerie. And I had to let the camming community know that I was okay. They cared about me. They'd be worried.

Opening my laptop, I left the camera off and typed into the group chat box.

> Sorry guys. I have to sign off now, but I'll see you tomorrow!

I watched a few comments come in from my regulars.

> Hope everything's okay.

> Did Daddy catch you?

Take care, Natalia.

And then, a comment from an unfamiliar name . . .

Careful little girl. Someone could be out there.

Someone who knows what you're up to.

# *Viv*

THE NEXT MORNING, shaky and exhausted, I drove downtown rehearsing my spiel in the privacy of my Volvo. I had figured out a way to save face while returning Alicia Fernhurst's expensive lipstick. She no longer wanted to work with me, I understood that, but I had to try to salvage my career. And my reputation. I was confident that my story sounded plausible, but my armpits were sweaty, and my hands felt slippery on the wheel. The stress of last night's smoke bomb attack had me wound up and on edge.

I'd insisted that the police needed to be informed about the assault, because that's what it was: an *assault*. The officer who eventually came had been sympathetic, but ultimately useless. There was nothing she could do without evidence, and no way to identify the assailants. She recommended installing a camera that would act as a deterrent and potentially ID the culprits.

"But it's probably just bored kids," she said, as if that made it okay, as if that meant we should just ignore it. It was not okay. Our home was our sanctuary. Having it attacked by faceless hooligans was frightening and distressing. These kids needed to be caught. They needed to be taught a valuable lesson about kindness and respect. Their parents needed to realize that their job wasn't over as soon as their kids were out of diapers.

My daughter's strident words flitted through my mind. *How do you know* kids *are doing this*? But it *had* to be children. Even if Thomas or I had enemies, no adult would stoop to throwing eggs or smearing poop on our door handle. No grown-up would wake us in the middle of the night with a smoke bomb. This was clearly the work of adolescents, maybe immature teens. Grown-ups dealt with their problems head-on. As I was about to do with Alicia.

The thought struck me then . . . Alicia's son, Magnus. And the other one, the son who was going to MIT. Could they be behind the recent attacks? Had Alicia showed her boys the footage of me taking her lipstick, and now they were punishing me with eggs and fruit? Dog shit and smoke bombs? Would a Columbia student resort to vandalism to avenge his mother? The other son was younger, still in high school. Maybe he was the one assaulting us?

But the timing didn't fit. The eggs had been thrown the night before I met with Alicia and took the lipstick. The odds that we had two different attackers were slim to none. We'd never been targeted like this before. No . . . this had nothing to do with me.

It had to be about Tarryn. She was a pretty girl in her own unique way, but she wasn't exactly approachable. The culprits were probably younger boys with a crush, or possibly a spurned flirtation. Tarryn told me less than nothing about her personal life, so she could have broken some kid's heart and now he was lashing out. Or this could be about Eli. But he was older and, frankly, more amiable than his sibling. My money was still on my daughter.

I parked in front of the ice cream shop and paid the meter. As I turned, my reflection met me in the plate glass window. The woman who stared back at me looked so normal, so professional and pulled-together. This was not a woman who stole small objects for the thrill of it or took personal items out of spite. How could she live with such a shameful secret?

When I approached the glass door, I could see Alicia inside. She wore jeans and a T-shirt that were more expensive than my entire outfit including my shoes and bag, and she was staring at her laptop set up on the counter. I rapped on the glass to get her attention. She looked over and I saw the distaste on her pretty features: *The thief returns to the scene of the crime*. My cheeks burned as she walked over to unlock the door.

"Hi, Viv." Alicia sounded confused, slightly disturbed by my presence. But she stepped back and ushered me inside. I could hear hammering in the back; a builder was installing bathroom cupboards or a counter. It drowned out the sound of my thudding heart.

I stopped a few feet in, lingering in the entryway. "How are things coming along?" My voice sounded high-pitched and strained.

"Getting there."

"Great. Great." I looked around the space. "I don't want to intrude, I know you're busy, but—"

"Look, I'm sorry about the e-mail," Alicia interrupted. "I'm sure it was a shock. And I hope I didn't sound rude. It's just . . . I've completely blown my budget and Dennis has laid down the law."

Dennis was her wealthy husband, the man who was funding this project. It quickly became clear. Dennis had *made* her fire me.

"He told me I didn't need a professional decorator, that it wasn't worth the money. No offense."

"It's fine."

"I told him that you're really good. And that you have a lot of experience. But he refuses to pay for decorating services." Her attractive face darkened. "This is supposed to be *my* business, but he still holds the purse strings."

Relief flooded through me like warm oil. "Don't worry. I understand."

There was emotion in Alicia's dark eyes as she continued. "Maybe I should have been content going for lunches and working out and walking the dog. But with the kids off to college, I felt like I needed something more." She looked around at the unfinished space. "The shop's not even open yet and I already feel like I've failed."

"You haven't," I said quickly, reaching out to pat her arm. "This place is going to be great."

"I don't know." Her chin crinkled. "I'm just so tired."

I wanted to hug her, but that would have been too intimate, too familiar. We were only acquaintances, after all. And I knew that embracing her would open the emotional floodgates. So I gave her shoulder a supportive squeeze. "It's normal to feel overwhelmed. But you can do this."

Alicia pulled herself together. "I'm sorry. I didn't mean to fall apart." She gave me a small smile. "What can I do for you?"

My carefully rehearsed speech flitted through my mind: *I think I took your lipstick by mistake. I have the same one and when I saw you put it in your bag, I thought you'd taken mine by accident. When I finally opened it, I knew I could never pull off that color.*

But she didn't know I had her lipstick. There was no camera, no footage of me taking it. There was no point in confessing, and no point in returning it.

"I wanted you to know that there are no hard feelings. And you don't need to pay me for the mood boards."

"I insist."

"Honestly, it was only a few hours. Don't worry about it."

Alicia looked misty again. "That's so sweet of you. And I'll be sure to recommend your services to my friends. I saw your work at Dolly Barber's house."

"Yes," I said, "I decorated the children's bedrooms."

"You did an amazing job. Dolly was so happy."

As I strolled back to my car, I felt weak with relief. I'd gotten away with it . . . again. But this had been too close for comfort. The stealing had to stop, should have stopped ages ago. I'd never understood the uncontrollable impulse. It was like an itch that had to be scratched, a thirst that had to be slaked. I knew it was wrong, but in the moment, I always told myself that I wasn't hurting anyone.

And yet, Alicia Fernhurst had let me glimpse her vulnerable side. She might have tons of money and two exceptional children, but she suffered the same self-doubt and insecurities that I did. Of course, a missing lipstick was nothing more than an annoyance to her. She could easily afford to buy another one. Still, I felt bad for hurting her, for lying to her, for taking what was hers.

Just not bad enough to return her lipstick, apparently.

# *Tarryn*

HISTORY USED TO be my favorite class, but I couldn't focus that day. It was clear that someone online knew that the redheaded sex kitten Natalia was really frumpy high school student Tarryn Adler. And that *someone* knew that our house was being attacked in the night. Was the same person sending me the creepy messages behind the assaults on our home? Even though I was virtually invisible at school, had opted out of the pathetic teen social scene, my parents were right: this had to be about me. Because only kids would smear shit on a door handle. Only kids would throw food at the house, toss a smoke bomb on the lawn. Did someone hate me enough to harass me online and come after my family? There was only one possibility . . . and he was seated two rows to my right.

Bryce Ralston was cute, effortlessly popular, *and* he played basketball, so I'd never given him a second thought until Madame Lanois paired us up to write a skit for French class. I saw the envious look from Lanie McGregor when the names were read. Lanie had had a crush on Bryce for years. So had Milly Bevan. But not me. I was completely unaffected by his looks and athletic prowess. I wanted someone dark and edgy, a pensive outlier. Bryce was a normie.

We were given some class time to work on the project, but Madame Lanois suggested three extra rehearsals. At first, Bryce and I were all business, writing up a simple skit about grocery shopping. (We only knew a handful of French verbs, plus the names of fruit and vegetables.) It was pretty boring, so Bryce and I started cracking jokes. He was funnier than I had expected, but I still wasn't attracted to him. He kind of reminded me of Eli.

That's going to make what happened between us sound pretty gross, but I soon stopped looking at Bryce in a sisterly way. To my surprise, he was into me. It was obvious. When we met at a local coffeehouse to work on our project, he laughed—hard—at all my jokes. When we rehearsed our skit in his basement, he found excuses to touch me in a playful way. And then he started to text me. At first, it was always about "Pierre à L'Épicerie," and then we started to talk about other things. Some nights, we texted for hours, talking about everything and nothing.

You're different than other girls, he'd texted.

I know

And then things got messy. Really fucking messy.

The bell rang, and everyone stood up on cue. I tried to catch Bryce's eye as he strolled out of class, tried to see if he looked guilty or angry, but as usual, he ignored me. He hated me, he had for months. But did he hate me enough to vandalize my house? To find me on a camming site and send me a creepy message? I didn't think so. Because if he got caught, then everyone would know that this cool, popular guy had been brought to his knees by weird, chubby Tarryn Adler.

And that would kill Bryce Ralston.

# *Thomas*

CAMERA NUMBER ONE was screwed into the top right corner of the doorframe. I'd affixed camera number two to one of the porch posts. I adjusted the motion zones to ensure maximum coverage of the property. When I opened the app on my phone, I had a full view of the steps and the entire front yard. If anyone approached our house—from the street or from either side of the lawn—bright lights would turn on and the cameras would start to record. It was a simple project, but I felt distinctly masculine. I'd installed the small cameras with my bare hands. I was working with the cops, taking measures to protect my family. And once I got the little shits who were harassing us on video . . . well, I wasn't sure what I would do, but it wouldn't be pretty.

The policewoman had suggested that a camera might be a deterrent. And if we could positively ID the culprits, the cops would take action. I understood they were busy, that serious crimes were happening all over the city, but I'd been hoping for a stakeout. I wanted these kids caught, charged with trespassing and mischief. They'd get no more than a slap on the wrist, but at least they'd think twice before targeting another innocent family.

We'd had two more attacks since the smoke bomb had exploded on our lawn. On Tuesday night, we'd been pelted with tomatoes. I'd run onto the porch, hoping to catch the little buggers, but they had scurried away like vermin. There were six to eight kids—a pack—and they paused at the end of our block.

"Too late, faggot!" one of them yelled.

It was not my finest moment, but I had yelled back: "I'll rip your fucking heads off if I catch you!"

On Thursday, lacking in originality or produce, the kids had gone back to eggs. I'd gone outside with the hose (Eli was at work), and when I came in, I found my wife near tears. The knowledge that there was a gang of hooligans watching our house in the night, waiting for

their moment to strike, rattled Viv's nerves. And
mine. Every time a foreign object hit our window, we jumped out of our skins.

"I just don't understand," Viv said. "Why us?"

"I'll take care of it," I promised her. And now,
with these cameras, I was.

If the boys dared to return, we would have
them on film. Maybe Tarryn would be willing to
finger the perps, but I was doubtful. She wouldn't
want to turn in her schoolmates. I got that. What
I really wanted was to grab one of them, take
him out back, and tune him up. I'd alluded to as
much with the police officer.

"You don't want to do that," she'd said. "Assaulting a minor is a serious crime. And it might
just escalate the abuse from the other kids."

"I was just kidding," I said, even though I was
only half-kidding.

The officer was right, though. And I wasn't
about to beat up a fourteen-year-old. But I could
scare the shit out of him without physical violence. I could make sure he and his wannabe
hoodlums never walked down our street again. I
stepped back and surveyed my handiwork. I
hoped the bright lights and the two cameras
trained on my lawn would do the trick.

I glanced at my watch. I was meeting poten-

tial buyers at the house on Hancock. Thanks to Emma's cheerful staging, a couple with three young kids was interested. It was the most enthusiasm I'd had on the place since it went on the market six months ago. If I could close the deal, my share of the commission would be roughly twenty-five grand. With that, and a little room to play in the line of credit, I could make my blackmailer a reasonable offer. The deadline was just a week away now. I needed Chanel to lower her price and I needed to buy some time. But I could manipulate her into doing both. I was ready.

And then, I'd make the whole mess go away. No one, including my wife, would ever know what had happened that night.

# *Eli*

THINGS HAD BEEN going pretty well at the Thirsty Raven. I was trained by an eighteen-year-old named Lucius who treated his busboy job like neurosurgery. There was a system to collecting the dirty dishes, to placing them in the plastic tubs, but obviously it wasn't rocket science. We had other duties, too, like filling salt and pepper shakers, unloading the dishwashers, and setting the tables between seatings.

"The sauces are key," Lucius told me, wiping a bottle of ketchup with a damp cloth. "If someone orders a meal and their favorite sauce is empty, the whole experience could be ruined."

"Totally," I said, and it almost sounded sincere.

By the second week, I was out from under Lucius's protective wing and working on my own. My manager, Peter, was impressed with me. I was polite, quick, and efficient. Lucius still tried to boss me around, but I pretty much ignored him. I was two years older than he was, and totally capable of performing my duties. As soon as I turned twenty-one, I'd move upstairs, and he'd be left behind.

That night, a section of the restaurant had been commandeered by a fiftieth birthday party for a woman named Kelly. They'd ordered a set menu, so I was running food in addition to clearing dishes, filling water glasses, and replenishing soft drinks. I was so busy that I didn't notice them at first, seated in a large booth in the back corner: my high school friends Sam, Tyrone, and Derek.

They had definitely noticed me. Three pairs of eyes followed me from kitchen to table, their lips moving as they analyzed my presence. I hadn't seen Sam since that day he'd ridden by on his bike, hadn't seen Derek and Tyrone since Christmas break. Sam had invited me to Sarah Ephremova's party, but I hadn't gone. He'd sent me a couple of texts after, but I ignored them. I hadn't known what to say.

But I couldn't ignore them now. I headed over to their table. "Hey, guys."

They replied in unison, a muttered, "Hey."

"How's it going?"

"Great," Derek said coolly, taking a chicken wing from the pile in front of them.

"How about you?" Tyrone asked, an edge to his voice. "What's new?"

"Umm . . . not much. Working a lot. Hanging with the family."

Sam played with a fry on his plate. "When I saw you washing your window, you said you'd just got home the week before."

"Uh . . . yeah."

Derek tossed a bare chicken bone onto his plate. "But Curt saw you getting coffee two weeks before that."

"Really?" I scratched my head. "Is he sure it was me?"

"He's sure."

I could feel my cheeks getting hot. They'd caught me in a lie, and I wasn't sure how to wriggle out of it. "Finals were intense," I tried. "I was pretty out of it when I got home. I guess I messed up my dates."

Sam snorted to himself, but Tyrone looked me in the eye. "Don't worry about it, Eli. You're too good for us now. We get it."

"That's not it," I said.

"Then what is it?"

How could I explain that I was a different person now, but not in the way they thought? That I had witnessed something, *participated* in something that had affected me on a cellular level. It had changed my academic and professional future, my thoughts, feelings, and actions. I wasn't ready to go out for wings and talk about YouTube videos and girls and gaming. I just couldn't.

Before I could stammer a lame response, I heard a girl's voice behind me: "Hey, guys." I turned to see Gabby Sullivan, a girl from our high school. She was all tight jeans and dewy makeup and stick-straight hair. I'd only had a couple of classes with her, but I'd known her a bit through my ex, Arianna. And that's when I noticed the girl trailing her.

My heart started to pound in my chest. I'd only seen Arianna a handful of times since we broke up. It had been awkward, a little painful, but I was strong then, not like now. I was the one who had ended it, so I should have been over her. I should have moved on. But the sight of the girl I had loved, had confided in, had felt closer to than anyone else in my life made my stomach twist and churn.

We'd dated through half of junior and all of senior year of high school. Maybe it was childish, but I really thought we'd be together forever. My parents had never liked her, though. They hadn't articulated it, but it was clear in the condescending way they spoke to her, in the way my mom looked her over and my dad looked through her. Arianna wasn't like us. She lived in an apartment with her single mom. They didn't have a lot of money, but her mom worked hard as a caregiver at an old folks' home. Arianna was pretty and sexy, with long dark hair and eyelash extensions, and she wore tight, revealing clothing. But all the girls at school dressed that way—except my sister, who preferred sweatpants and a snarl. Arianna wasn't academic, but she was wise. And she was sweet. She understood me.

Before I left for Worbey, my parents sat me down in the living room. "What are you going to do about Arianna?"

"We'll do the long-distance thing," I said. "I'll be home for Thanksgiving and Christmas. And she's going to come visit me." Arianna was taking a gap year to work at a clothing store and save up for college.

My parents had launched into a lecture on expanding my horizons, being open to new experiences, embracing a new chapter. They didn't *tell* me to break up with her, but it was clear that they thought I should. And I was a kid then. I thought my parents knew what was best for me. I trusted them. And they were right about one thing: balancing college and soccer and a long-distance relationship was hard. As a goalie, I was under extra pressure, and economics was a challenging program. So, when I came home for Christmas break, I ended it.

But now, here she was, so pretty, so warm and familiar. "Hey, Arianna."

"Eli . . ." She was surprised to see me. "I didn't know you worked here."

"I just started." My voice sounded funny, tight and constricted. "How are you?"

Her demeanor changed then, like she'd just remembered how I'd hurt her. "I'm great. Thanks."

I watched her slide into the booth, and I watched Derek's arm slide around her shoulders. They both looked at me for a moment, watching me absorb this information. I knew Arianna had moved on, that she was seeing someone, but I hadn't expected it to be one of my best friends. Make that *former* best friends. The flicker of guilt on their features was soon replaced with a *fuck you* stare. Because I deserved this. I'd left them both behind, and they had found each other.

Grabbing a couple of empty plates, I headed back to the kitchen. I focused on the birthday party, tried to ignore the table at the back. But I could sense them watching me, talking about me, could hear them laughing at me. There was a hollowness in my belly, a pit of emptiness. Because now I knew. . . .

The guys at Worbey College weren't the only ones who hated me.

# *Viv*

FOCUSING ON GRATITUDE had been challenging *before* we were targeted by vandals; I hadn't even tried since. But now, I closed my eyes, breathed through my nose, and attempted to summon it. It had been a difficult few weeks. The cameras Thomas had installed had not been a deterrent. We'd suffered more eggs, tomatoes, even water balloons filled with red paint. (What kind of psychopath took the time to fill up those tiny balloons? How had they even done it? Had they used a funnel? A squeeze bottle? An eyedropper?) And the rough footage of faceless figures at the end of our driveway was useless. We couldn't tell the height, age, complexion, or hair color of our attackers. All we knew was that they took great delight in assaulting us.

Watching them do it only made me feel more vulnerable.

I slipped deeper into the warm water, the bubbles tickling my chin. Despite my stress, there were still things to be grateful for . . . like the deep soaker tub we'd installed last fall. And a successful staging project I'd just completed for a top realtor in town. I was truly thankful that I'd smoothed things over with Alicia Fernhurst, and that she didn't know I had taken her lipstick. And I felt gratitude—and pride—that I'd been able to stop my little habit cold-turkey.

I hadn't stolen anything for more than two weeks. Not from the six-bedroom home I'd staged. Not from the penthouse apartment where I'd done a consult. Stopping had been easier than I'd anticipated. All it required was mindfulness. When I got the urge to pocket an item, I brought my attention to the present moment and breathed through the yearning. And then it would pass. This awareness also allowed me to examine why I had done it in the first place.

It had all started when Thomas first became distant and secretive, and escalated when Eli announced he wasn't going back to college. It was about control—or, more accurately, my loss of it. But I was working on acceptance . . . while trying to figure out what the hell was going on with my husband and attempting to convince my son to return to school. At least Tarryn was consistent. She was her same moody and disdainful self.

I was becoming a better person, and for that, I was truly grateful. In addition to breaking my stealing habit, I was going to be kinder—more loving toward my difficult daughter, understanding of my troubled son. As for my husband . . . well, that would be more of a challenge. Because now I knew, without a doubt, that Thomas was cheating on me. And I knew with whom.

The text had come in while he was in the shower. Thomas had left his phone on the dresser, had forgotten to put it on Do Not Disturb. The message had popped up in the preview window. It was from Emma.

Have you talked to your wife?

I knew Emma was Thomas's assistant. She did administrative work for my husband and a number of agents. He'd mentioned that she sometimes helped him with small staging jobs when I was too busy to assist him. But I had never met her. I thought it was just due to circumstance: we hadn't attended the company softball game because Eli was coming home from college that weekend. The staff barbecue had been canceled due to rain. But now I realized that Thomas had been intentionally keeping us apart. And now I knew why.

The water was cooling off, so I turned on the hot tap with my foot. The stream came out cold at first, but it soon heated up. I let the scalding water pour into the bath, my thoughts on my husband's mistress. I recalled Thomas telling me that Emma was engaged, busy with preparations for her upcoming wedding. It was probably a way to throw me off the scent. Emma wasn't getting married; she was in love with my husband. Or perhaps she *was* getting married and her unsuspecting fiancé was a victim, just like I was. The thought made me feel queasy and sad. I turned the hot water off.

Have you talked to your wife?

What was Thomas supposed to talk to me about? Was he going to tell me he was leaving me for Emma? Walking away from his wife and children so he could start over with his assistant? God, it was such a cliché, but clichés existed for a reason. Thomas was just one of millions of men who'd decided to trade in the wife for a newer model.

Downstairs, I heard a key in the front door. It was after ten—too early for Eli to be home from the gastropub, so it had to be Thomas. He'd texted to tell me he'd be late. Paperwork, he'd said. A few months ago, I would have thought nothing of it, but now I knew. . . . It was an excuse to be with her. *Emma*.

I listened to him go to the kitchen and open the fridge, and I made a deal with myself. If he came upstairs, if he popped his head in to say hello, I would confront him. I'd tell him that I had seen the incriminating text. I would demand to know what was going on between him and his secretary. And then . . . and then what? Would I kick him out of the house? Or fight for my marriage? I still didn't know.

But Thomas didn't call my name, didn't come upstairs, didn't say hello. He must have gotten something to eat and gone into the family room to watch TV. My husband wasn't ready to talk about this either. So I could live in denial for a little while longer.

I pulled the plug, and all my gratitude went swirling down the drain.

# *Thomas*

ON FRIDAY NIGHT, I'd stayed at the office until almost eleven. That couple had made an offer on the Hancock place, giving me a reason to work late. But I was really waiting to hear from Chanel. I had officially missed the deadline for the bitcoin transaction. She now knew I wouldn't pay—not the fifty grand, anyway. At any moment, the mortifying photos of the two of us could be sent to everyone in my life. I'd been confident that she wouldn't play her hand so soon, but I'd sat alone in the office, checking my phone compulsively, my chest tight with dread.

At around six, Leo Grass had popped his head over my cubicle. "Coming for a beer, mate?"

I hadn't joined the other brokers for beers

since I'd received the blackmail threat. I still couldn't be sure that Leo and Roger weren't behind it . . . although Leo's casual demeanor was convincing. Even if they weren't blackmailing me, I knew they weren't my friends. Friends didn't let friends get blackout drunk and take a stripper back to their hotel room.

"Can't. Got an offer on Hancock."

Roger walked up. "You coming, Adler?"

"He can't," Leo said. "He's finally going to unload the Hancock house."

"Did you have an exorcism?" Roger quipped. "Get rid of the evil spirits haunting the place?"

I forced a weak chuckle. "Emma did a mini-staging. I guess it did the trick."

"Emma?" Leo said. "Your wife's going to be jealous."

"My wife's not fucking jealous of Emma," I barked.

The guys exchanged a look, and then Leo spoke tentatively. "I meant because Viv does most of your staging. But you used Emma and sold the place."

"Oh. Right."

"Join us later if you want," Roger said. "You seem like you could use a drink."

But I hadn't joined them. I'd waited and I'd

fretted. Why wasn't Chanel giving me a chance to work this out? Didn't she understand how blackmail worked? I had all my figures prepared, I'd factored in my timeline, but then . . . she didn't contact me. Finally, I'd gone home. Viv was in the bath. I didn't want to disturb her. She'd had a busy week, and she deserved to unwind. And I hated lying to her, but I couldn't tell her the truth. I heated up some leftovers and ate them. When I went upstairs, my wife was already asleep. Or at least pretending to be.

THE NEXT MORNING, Viv slept late. Even though she'd gone to bed before me, she had tossed and turned all night. I knew, because I'd been awake for most of it. At seven, I rolled over and checked my phone. Nothing from Chanel. Nothing to indicate that the incriminating photos had been sent to my contacts, no friends or colleagues telling me I was a piece of shit, asking why I'd violated an innocent woman. It was too much to hope that this would all just go away, that Chanel would decide it wasn't worth the trouble, but still . . . a small part of me did.

Without disturbing my wife, I got up, went downstairs, and made coffee. As I waited for it to brew, I checked the camera app on my phone.

This had become routine since I'd installed the surveillance equipment the week before. The cameras were activated by movement, recording the things that go bump in the night. Those *things* were often shadowy figures congealing at the edge of our lawn, hurling whatever food they could smuggle out of their parents' fridges. They were wise to the cameras, never getting close enough to be identified.

Last night's footage showed Eli coming home at 11:45 P.M. He never went out after work, never went to a party or got pizza with friends. He hadn't been socializing at all since he got home from Worbey. I hoped he'd come out of his shell soon, get over whatever had upset him at college. He'd been moping long enough.

The video log showed no more movement until 1:17 A.M. That was awfully late for teenagers to be out looking for trouble. The other night, the camera had caught a family of raccoons crossing the lawn. I pressed the PLAY button and then poured myself a cup of coffee. But what I saw on the screen was not a gaggle of furry critters. What I saw sent a frisson through my body, nearly made me drop the coffeepot.

A male figure in dark pants and a dark hoodie pulled tight to conceal his face walked purposefully up our driveway. Without context, it was difficult to tell his size and height, but he moved like an adult, with determination and confidence. He was not fourteen; he had to be an older teen . . . if he was a teen at all. The figure held an object in his right hand. I looked closer at the screen.

It was a knife.

With my heart in my throat, I watched him scurry around my vehicle, then run off into the night. At the edge of our property, he stopped, raised a middle finger to the camera.

*Fuck you.*

I slammed the coffeepot back on its base and hurried outside. The video footage was too grainy to see what the vandal had been up to, but it was clearly nothing good. I ran toward my BMW, sitting out in the drive like a sacrificial lamb. I should have told Eli to empty out the garage. I should have parked my car in it, away from danger. Viv's Volvo was parked on the street, a safer spot, ironically. Stumbling down the front steps, I prayed for something as benign as wiping shit on the door handles.

No such luck.

All four tires were flat. Punctured with a blade.

# *Tarryn*

MY DAD BARGED into my bedroom without even knocking. "Tarryn, wake up."

"No," I grumbled. It was Saturday. I always slept late on the weekends, my only chance to catch up on the sleep I missed all week.

"I need you to look at something."

His tone made me lift my head groggily. My dad sounded upset, but not in the usual blustery way he got upset. He sounded . . . small.

He sat next to me on the bed, his phone in his hand. "Can you watch this video?"

I rubbed my eyes and watched, the nape of my neck prickling with anxiety. The dark figure in our driveway at night was unnerving. The time stamp read 1:17 A.M. I'd been camming while this guy was just outside my window, vandalizing my dad's car. Luckily, I had the blackout curtains, so he couldn't see my lights on, couldn't peek in to see what I was doing.

My dad asked, "Do you recognize him?"

"I can't see his face."

"But he looks about your age, doesn't he? He's not a little kid."

He wasn't. The culprit appeared to be my age, or even Eli's. He could even have been an adult from what I could tell from this video. I glanced up at my dad and saw his worry and stress, the lines around his mouth and eyes. I realized how rarely I actually looked at him. He had changed, gotten older, more vulnerable. "Give it here," I said.

With the phone in my hands, I replayed the video. Could the shadowy figure be Bryce Ralston? He was the only person I could think of who would want to hurt me. Of course, Bryce might not do the dirty work himself. He had plenty of douchebag friends who'd be more than happy to harass me. But as hard as I stared, I couldn't identify him.

"I'm sorry. I don't recognize him."

My dad took his phone back. "Tell me honestly, honey. Do you have any idea why these kids are doing this to us?"

I couldn't tell my dad what I had done to

Bryce, why he despised me. It was not the kind of thing you shared with your father. And I definitely couldn't tell him about the overly familiar comments on the camming site. Another one had come in last night, just before I signed off at three. It was from another name, another fake. Every time I blocked this guy, he came back with a new name, a new account.

You look hot as a redhead. But I think I prefer you as a brunette.

I'd blocked the commenter again, but it was clear that he wasn't going away. Someone knew who I was. . . . But what would they do with that knowledge? Would they expose me? If my parents found out, they would lose their minds. They didn't understand sex-positive feminism and sexual agency. And I was their underage daughter. They thought they had to protect me.

"Maybe Eli knows something about it," I said. "This guy could be his age."

Dad nodded, then patted my shoulder. "Thanks for trying, honey," he said. "Go back to sleep."

I lay back down, my eyes wide open.

# *Eli*

I WATCHED THE video in bed that morning. Dad had e-mailed the footage to me with the words:

Do you know this asshole?

It was impossible to see his face in the low-quality footage, but I could tell the *asshole* was at least Tarryn's age, even maybe mine. In fact, it could have been a forty-year-old from what I could tell. The figure didn't scurry and skitter like an excited little kid; it walked up the driveway with purpose. And with a knife. This guy was not simply a hooligan out for kicks. This guy meant business.

I might be on the outs with my high school friends, but they wouldn't vandalize our home or our car. They weren't like that. And they knew my parents, liked them even. My college friends were pissed at me too, but they lived all over the country. Even if they'd wanted to harass my family in the night, they couldn't. Except for Noah Campbell. He lived in Vancouver, only a half-hour drive from our home.

Keep your fucking mouth shut Eli. I know
where you live.

But I *had* kept my fucking mouth shut. Even when Drew Jasper reached out to me, after I'd liked his photo of the lake. Even when he asked for my support, I'd remained mute.

It was one line, sent through my DMs on Instagram.

Will you back me up?

I hadn't responded. I felt like a fucking coward, but I couldn't do it. I couldn't make myself a target. So there was no reason for Noah to show up at my house, to walk down our driveway and slash my dad's tires. The secret of what happened the night of the hazing was still festering inside of me, unspoken. No, this was not about me.

There was a tentative knock at my door then, and it opened a crack. I was expecting my mom, but my sister poked her head through the doorway.

"You awake?"

"Yeah."

She slipped into the room. "Did Dad send you the video of that shithead slashing his tires?"

I sat up on my elbows. "Yeah. It's pretty psycho."

"Dad has to get his car towed to a garage. He's freaking out."

"I'll bet."

"Mom's really losing it, too. She keeps talking about the *escalation*." Tarryn rolled her eyes. "She's acting like he was walking down the driveway with a machete. Like he's going to burn the house down next."

I smirked. My mom tended to blow things out of proportion. Slashing Dad's tires was really bad, but we weren't in serious danger.

My sister moved farther into the room. "Do you know who it was?"

"I could barely see him," I said. "I thought he looked about your age."

"Don't blame me for this," Tarryn snapped. "Mom wants to send the video to Principal Gorman. If she does, I'll drop out. I'm serious."

I snorted a laugh. "If you dropped out of high school, Mom would spontaneously combust."

Tarryn allowed a hint of a smile. "If Mom goes to Gorman, this will get a million times worse. I'll be targeted. The house will be targeted."

"Yeah."

She perched on the end of my bed. "They won't listen to me. Can you tell them?"

"I can try."

She said nothing, just toyed with the string of her pajama pants for a moment. I'd grown used to my snide, scowling sister, but she looked younger. And sweeter. Like she was when we were kids. Then she looked up at me.

"Why aren't you going back to Worbey?"

My sister and I had never been confidantes. I was three years older, sporty and academic: Tarryn was alt, a social justice warrior, a nonconformist. But she was my little sister and that connection was there, would always be there. I could tell her what had happened, how I had stood by and watched it all. She would listen, with sympathy, without judgment.

But the truth could also be weaponized. Tarryn was desperate to deflect the harassment away from her, terrified that my mom would go to the school and destroy her reputation. My sister might tell my parents about the hazing to distract them. They'd contact the college. I knew they would. And then things would really blow up.

"Nothing happened," I said with a shrug. "I just hated it there."

# *Viv*

ON MONDAY AFTERNOON at two fifteen, I sat in Principal Gorman's utilitarian office. I'd timed this meeting to avoid seeing my daughter—or any students—in the school hallways. Tarryn would have killed me if she found me there. She had begged me not to meet with her principal. My "meddling" would only make things worse—for Tarryn. For all of us. She'd even enlisted Eli's help in convincing me that no good could come from involving the school. I understood her concerns, but I was sure I could do this without anyone knowing. And I had no other choice.

The attacks were escalating; the police agreed with me. Two different officers—both male—had come to the house, wandered around the driveway, taken photos of Thomas's tires, and viewed the videos. Their presence had made me feel conspicuous and embarrassed. Everyone in the neighborhood would be peeping through their windows at the squad car, gossiping about us, speculating on what we'd done to instigate this harassment. The police took the offense seriously—or so they said. They would file a report. If the perpetrators were caught, they would be charged. But with no way to identify them, the cops were powerless to stop them. Tarryn and Eli couldn't—or *wouldn't*—tell us who these kids were, or why they were attacking us in the night. The police had suggested the school might be able to help. Mitchell Gorman was my only hope.

"I'm sorry this is happening to your family," the principal began. He was in his forties, slim, and well-dressed. On his desk was a framed photo of his partner and two fluffy dogs. I'd had minimal interaction with the administrator, but I knew that he ran the school with a firm but fair hand. His air of calm capability was reassuring.

"Thank you," I said. "It's been really stressful."

Mitchell gave me a sympathetic nod. "I watched the video you sent of the figure in your driveway. And I e-mailed it, without context, to the teachers of grades ten through twelve. Unfortunately, we weren't able to identify the culprit. We can't even be sure he attends this school."

"But he must," I said. "This has to have something to do with my daughter."

"Have you tried talking to Tarryn about it?"

If Mitchell Gorman thought getting to the bottom of this was as simple as *talking* to Tarryn, he clearly didn't know her. "I've tried," I said, my voice wobbling with exasperation. "But she won't open up to me."

"Her attendance record has been spotty lately. She's been missing a lot of morning classes."

My shoulders sagged. "She told me she had a free period. I'm so naïve."

"Sometimes it's hard for teens to be honest with their parents. She might be more forthcoming with her counselor. Or even with me."

"Please," I said quickly, "she begged me not to come to you. She can't know I was here."

"I'll talk to her counselor. Barb Harris is really tactful. She can call Tarryn in to discuss her senior year's timetable. She can gently prod her to open up about what's going on."

"Could you talk to some of the boys in her grade? This kid had a knife. He could be dangerous."

"It was difficult to see what he was carrying."

"He was carrying a blade! The tires were slashed!"

The principal steepled his fingers together. "If

this were happening on school property, I'd have more power. But until we can confirm that *our* students are harassing you, this is probably a matter for the police, and not the school."

Principal Gorman couldn't help me after all. I'd risked my relationship with my daughter to come here, and now he was dismissing me. The police had sent me to the school. The school was sending me to the police. I felt frustrated, powerless, and scared. My face flushed and, to my chagrin, tears welled in my eyes.

"I'm sorry," I stammered, fishing in my bag for a tissue. "I didn't mean to get emotional."

"It's understandable," Mitchell said, but he looked a little uncomfortable. He grabbed a tissue box off his credenza and slid it toward me. As the tears spilled over, I gratefully reached into it.

"It's empty," I said.

"Gwen always has tissues. I'll get some." He seemed eager to leave, relieved to get away from the sniveling mess in his office. The mother who didn't know her daughter was cutting classes, who couldn't even talk to her own child. The woman who fell apart, blubbering over eggs and tomatoes and tires, who hallucinated a knife into the hand of a mischievous child.

That's when I spotted his pen, a Montblanc

ballpoint. It was an awfully fancy pen for a public-school principal, worth about $700. I'd considered buying one for Thomas's birthday, but thought it seemed a bit excessive. But apparently it wasn't too much for Principal Gorman. I plucked it off the pile of papers and felt its weight, the sleek black surface. Did an ineffectual principal like Mitchell Gorman deserve such an expensive writing instrument?

My hand was already moving toward my purse even as my brain shouted at me to stop. The pen was too exposed, too expensive. And I couldn't steal from my daughter's principal. If I got caught, Tarryn would be humiliated. She would never forgive me. I would never forgive myself.

But my arm was inside my bag when Mitchell returned, holding a tissue box. I couldn't pull the pen out now and return it to the desk. I had no choice but to let it drop and reach for a tissue.

"Thank you," I said, dabbing at my eyes and blowing my nose. And then I stood. "I'll let you get back to work."

"I'll keep my ear to the ground. Let you know if I hear anything."

"Thank you for your help." It almost sounded sincere.

But it wasn't.

# *Tarryn*

EVERY DAY AFTER school, I had a standing date on Northwest Twenty-Third with Luke and Georgia. We went for coffee, or smoothies, or doughnuts, and bitched about school, or gossiped about the popular kids. Luke's favorite topic was our sort-of-hot English teacher, Mr. McLaughlin, who'd supposedly had a fling with a student two years ago. Georgia had an enduring crush on my brother, which was pretty disturbing. Eli was best friends with her cousin Sam . . . or at least he used to be. I looked forward to our post-school debriefs, but today I had other plans. Today I was meeting Bryce Ralston at a park a couple blocks from the school.

"Why?" Luke asked, ever protective. "Do you think Bryce has been throwing the eggs and shit at your house? Do you think he slashed your dad's tires?"

Georgia's hazel eyes were wide. "Oh my god. Would he do that?"

"Who else?" I asked. "He might get his friends to do it for him. But if these attacks are about me, it has to be Bryce."

Luke's brow furrowed. "I don't see it."

"He hates me. He was a total dick to me."

"Yeah . . . ," Georgia said tentatively, "but just because you hurt him."

I *had* hurt him. But not intentionally. Our French study sessions had turned flirtatious, and eventually, they'd turned physical. Bryce's mom was a dentist, his dad was a lawyer. They were never home, allowing us ample time to kiss and play in his disheveled bedroom. No one knew what we were up to—except Luke and Georgia. Bryce hadn't told any of his friends. They were cool, popular, shallow—they'd taunt and tease Bryce if they knew he was hooking up with Tarryn the weirdo, Tarryn the art ho. I was Bryce's dirty little secret, but I didn't mind. In fact, I thought it was kind of hot.

Going all the way was my idea. We had chemistry. We had opportunity. And the drawer in Bryce's bedside table was stuffed with condoms provided by his dad. I'd thought Bryce was a fuck boy, but it turned out he was a virgin, just like I was. I felt ready, physically and emotionally. I liked him. I trusted him. It just made sense.

We'd been hanging out for a couple of months, hooking up for about three weeks, when he made the pronouncement. We were pressed together in his single bed, our bodies damp and sticky. "I'm ready to tell my friends about us."

"You don't have to."

"I don't care what they think. I like you. Like . . . I really like you."

I wriggled out of his arms so I could face him. "I like you, too, but—"

"Just because we're in different social circles, doesn't mean we can't be a couple. Fuck what everyone else thinks."

Maybe I could have been kinder, but I was shocked. So, I was honest. "I don't want to be a couple. I just want to have sex with you."

Bryce was incredulous. He had *deigned* to have feelings for me, and I was turning him down. How could I reject his square-jawed, muscular perfection? Why didn't I want to bask in his aura of popularity? He'd been willing to take the teasing and disdain of his dickhead jock friends, and I was telling him thanks, but no thanks.

My cheeks burned at the memory of his pain that had quickly morphed into anger and then hatred. He'd stopped speaking to me. He barely even looked at me, but I felt his loathing all the same. I turned to Luke and Georgia. "Just because I bruised his ego doesn't give him the right to harass my family." I walked away before they could try to change my mind.

I WASN'T SURE Bryce would show up. He'd read my text but hadn't responded. Still . . . I had a feeling he'd come. I'd made it sound urgent. And serious. Because it was. Slashing my dad's tires was next-level fucked up. And trolling me on the camming site was totally obsessive. I perched on a park bench as far away as I could get from the squealing toddlers on the playground equipment. If Bryce didn't turn up soon, I was going to have a pounding headache. Then I saw his tall, athletic form approaching.

"Hey," I said, when he joined me.

"Hey." He didn't sit down. "What do you want?"

Now that he was here, I wasn't sure how to begin. If he wasn't responsible, I didn't want to draw attention to the attacks on my house. They were oddly embarrassing. And there was no way I would admit to camming if Bryce didn't know.

Finally, I said, "Do you still hate me?"

"I never hated you, Tarryn. I just think you're a bitch."

My cheeks burned. He was angry and lashing out, but I had done nothing wrong. I stood up. I didn't like the power differential of him looming over me. "I'm sorry that you got hurt. But that's not my fault."

"You're right. I was stupid to think you had feelings."

"I have feelings," I snapped. "They were just different than yours. That doesn't make me a bitch."

"No," he said, eyes narrowed. "It makes you a *slut*."

I would not be slut-shamed by this crybaby asshole. "Fuck you. Just because I rejected you doesn't mean you can fuck with me and my family."

He gave a derisive laugh. "How am I fucking with you and your family?"

I looked into his face, saw his hurt and his hate, but he wasn't lying.

*Shit.*

"Forget it," I said.

As I walked away from him, I berated myself. I'd gotten it all wrong. Bryce was not the one attacking me. Someone else was taunting me online, harassing me at home. Someone else hated me that much.

But I had no idea who.

# *Thomas*

THE E-MAIL FROM Chanel came in while I was at the garage, picking up my car after having all four tires replaced. My comprehensive insurance had covered the cost, but I'd still had to fork out a sizable deductible. And then there was the hassle of having the car towed and borrowing Viv's car for three days while we waited for the work to be done. My car was my livelihood. That damn kid had hit me where it hurt. Maybe this *was* about me?

I was in a pretty foul mood when my phone vibrated in my pocket. Even though the device buzzed constantly, somehow I knew. Thanking the tire guy, I hurried to my car. Only when I was alone inside did I open the message.

50K. Now. Or the pictures are going out.

Empathy. That was the key to getting the other side to lower their ask. Finding different, softer ways of saying no. Taking a deep breath, I wrote back.

I'm afraid that's just not possible.

Dropping the phone into the console, I backed out of the garage's parking lot. Chanel would blow up, posturing and threatening, but she wouldn't send out the photos. If she did, she'd get nothing . . . nothing except my humiliation. And what satisfaction would that give her? If she'd wanted me to be punished, she should have called the police. But she hadn't. Because *I* hadn't hurt her.

Time had provided no more clarity on the events of that night. No snippets of memory had revisited me. But I was still confident that I hadn't choked and bitten that woman, that I was incapable. I would never grab a woman by the neck—*ever*. And as for the biting? That just wasn't me. I'd never even playfully nipped a lover; it had never even crossed my mind. If I'd tried it with Viv, she would have smacked me upside the head.

Even though I was confident in my innocence, proving it was another matter. So, I would have to pay Chanel—or whoever was behind this blackmail bullshit. I'd set my limit at $25,000. It was my commission on the Hancock place. The buyers wanted a quick closing. I'd get the money in a month, and it would slip through my hands as if I'd never had it.

Half an hour later, I pulled up to a luxury home in Lake Oswego. It had just come on the market and the listing agent was giving realtors a preview. I saw Roger Bains's Mercedes across the street, saw him standing in front of the house, chatting with another agent. I wasn't in the mood to make pleasant small talk with him. If I stayed in my car long enough, he might leave.

Grabbing my phone, I checked my e-mail. I'd expected Chanel to take longer to respond, but, finally, she seemed eager to negotiate.

> 40K. Next week.

We were getting closer. But we weren't there yet.

> I'm sorry. I really wish I could pay, but that's too much.

I sent the e-mail with my heart lodged in my throat. This had to work. My negotiation skills could not fail me, not now. Not for this.

Then I turned off my phone and headed for the house.

# *Viv*

I WAS IN my home office when I heard the front door open and then slam shut.

"Mom?"

It was Tarryn. She never called out to me when she got home from school, preferring to skulk down to the basement until summoned for dinner. Usually, I accosted her, just to check in, to ask how her day had been, but she rarely, if ever, sought me out.

"Up here," I said brightly. My daughter's tone had been unreadable. Was it possible that she had some good news she wanted to share? Maybe she'd done well on a test. Or gotten a role in the school play. But the gooseflesh on my arms elicited by her heavy footsteps on the stairs did not bode well. As usual, my daughter was not happy.

I spun in my chair to greet her. "Hi, honey," I said to the dark cloud that filled my doorway.

"You went to Principal Gorman," she spat. "I specifically told you not to."

Panic rendered me speechless for a moment. Was denial my best strategy? Or had Gorman or the counselor outed me? Finally, I stammered, "Wh-what?"

"Ms. Harris called me into her office. She pretended she wanted to talk about next year's timetable, but after about five minutes, she started grilling me about my *problems*."

"What problems?"

"Exactly! But she was all like . . . 'Do you have issues with kids at school? How are your romantic relationships? Any problems there?' "

"It's her job to check in with the students."

"Don't lie to me, Mom. Did you go to Gorman? Did you send him that video?"

I was cornered, caught.

"These boys are scaring me, Tarryn. They're out there in the night with weapons. They're doing serious damage now." I stood, moved closer to her. "You won't tell me what's going on with you, and I'm worried. I love you."

She took a step back. "That kid attacked Dad's car. Maybe it's about him! Or Eli! Or you!"

"That seems pretty unlikely, don't you think?"

"No. I don't, actually. But now everyone at school will be talking about this. About me."

"How would they know?"

"Ms. Harris pulled me out of class! When I came back, I was upset. They'll figure it out."

"Kids get pulled out of class for all sorts of reasons."

"Yeah. And somehow, we always find out the truth." Her eyes were shiny, and I wanted to hold her, but I knew she'd push me away. "Why didn't you listen to me? Everything's going to get worse. A million times worse."

She thundered down the stairs, back to her basement lair.

THAT NIGHT, I lay in bed listening to the rain on the roof and replaying my decision to speak to my daughter's principal. It was what any concerned, caring parent would have done. Tarryn was sullen and secretive and she was being harassed by menacing boys in the night. It was terrifying, for all of us. It was my job to protect her.

She felt betrayed. I understood that. But there was no way for other students to know what was said in her counselor's office unless Tarryn told them herself. Ms. Harris was a consummate professional, used to dealing with delicate matters. Although . . . she hadn't done a great job of hiding her intent with Tarryn. And the video *had* been circulated amongst several teachers. . . .

Thomas was snoring softly beside me. He'd backed up my decision to visit Tarryn's principal, told me not to worry. "She'll get over it," he'd said. "You did it because you love her. She knows that." But I wasn't so confident. My relationship with my daughter couldn't handle much more strife.

My mind was still racing when the rock smashed through the window.

# *Eli*

THE THIRSTY RAVEN was so slow that night, that my boss let me go a half hour early. It was pouring when I caught the bus, but when I hopped off at the Wildwood Trail stop on the edge of Washington Park, the rain had slowed to a drizzle. The heavily forested section of the park was scenic during the day, but spooky at night. Its looming trees and dense foliage could cover all sorts of nefarious activity. A girl's body had been found there when I was a kid. But I didn't feel unnerved. I was tall and strong. And Arlington Heights was quiet, safe, and asleep.

I walked through the silent streets, past the unlit mansions and upscale homes. Our house would be dark, too. It was eleven twenty, past my parents' strict eleven o'clock bedtime. My sister might be awake, but any light shining from her room would be extinguished by her blackout curtains. She stayed up late, like me, but she wasn't gaming. She was probably on Reddit or watching YouTube videos that made her hate society. But as I neared my house, I saw that the porch light was on. And my dad, in pajama pants and a T-shirt, was nailing a board across the windowpane in our front door.

*Shit.* . . .

"What happened?" I asked as I walked up. But I knew. My mom should not have gone to see Principal Gorman. Tarryn had been right.

"They came back," Dad muttered, banging in the last nail. "This is getting way out of hand."

"What did they throw?"

"See for yourself." He pointed with the hammer at a stone the size of a child's fist. "It went right through the glass. Thank god no one was standing there."

"Jesus."

He dropped the hammer to his side. "Listen. I need your help with something."

"What?"

"Do you work tomorrow night?"

"Yeah. I work all week . . . I have Saturday night off."

"We'll do it Saturday, then."

"Do what?"

He leaned in and lowered his voice. "We have to make this stop, Eli. That rock could have seriously hurt someone. Your mom or your sister."

"You can't beat these kids up," I responded.

"We're not going to *beat them up*. We're just going to scare them. Make them think we'll hurt them if they don't stop bothering us." He saw the reluctance in my eyes, so he continued, "These kids have no respect for the police. Or for their principal. They think they're untouchable."

"They *are* untouchable. Because they're kids. They're not going to go to jail for throwing eggs and rocks. And they can't be expelled for behavior off school grounds."

My dad's voice was even lower "They're minors . . . and you're still a minor."

He wanted me to do the dirty work so that he didn't get into trouble. He was using me, and I said as much.

"God, no, Eli. I wouldn't let you get into any trouble. I swear." He ran his free hand through his hair. "I don't know what else to do. Your mom is really stressed. Your sister's upset. Enough is enough."

In the porch light, I could see how old and worn down he looked. He'd always been confident and gregarious, so sure of himself. But these kids were beating him. They were winning. And he didn't like it.

"I'm going to bed," I said, "I'm exhausted."

But I knew I wouldn't sleep.

# *Tarryn*

IT WAS WRONG to feel smug when I heard the glass breaking, but I did. Maybe not smug, just validated. I'd told my mom she had made things worse by going to the school, and I'd been proven right. Kids from Centennial High were attacking us, that much was clear. But who was putting them up to it? And why?

I'd gone upstairs to survey the damage . . . and my mom's sheepish expression. But when I saw her standing there in her robe, her face pale and drawn, I'd felt no satisfaction. She was clearly stressed—and frightened, staring intently at her phone. As I walked up behind her, I saw the attack playing out on her tiny screen: a group of faceless boys at the end of the driveway; several of them stepped forward and hurled rocks; the sound of breaking glass as one stone hit its mark. When Mom sensed my presence, she'd turned toward me, her eyes shiny.

"Tarryn, I'm sorry." It was barely a whisper.

I didn't need to say *I told you so.* She felt bad enough.

My dad walked in from the garage, wearing pajama pants and work boots. He was carrying a hammer and a square of wood. He looked as exhausted as my mom did.

"Viv, can you call the cops? We need to file a report." And then to me, "Go back to bed, honey. They're gone."

There had been a knot of emotion in my throat as I descended the stairs. It was guilt. My mom and dad were upset, weary, falling apart. Dad was a bit overweight; what if he had a heart attack? Would it be my fault? If this harassment was about me, I'd find out who was behind it. And I'd make it stop.

Even if I hadn't been trying to stay awake, I couldn't have slept. Adrenaline was coursing through me from the attack and, of course, my dad was hammering a board over the broken window. I watched TikTok videos until I heard my brother come home. He and my dad spoke in soft voices on the front porch. When I finally heard the creak of the stairs, it was after midnight. That's when I got ready.

My regulars would be waiting for me; they always were. I got over a hundred views a night. There were about ten clients who spent the entire session with me and paid for the privilege. They were the ones I felt obligated to, they were the reason I showed up. Even when I was tired. Or grumpy. Or when sociopathic shitheads were attacking my house. My community needed me. We had real conversations, and they asked real questions. Yeah, I knew that they probably had their dicks out of their pants while they asked about my math test, or my favorite ice cream flavor, but that didn't mean they didn't care.

In my wig, makeup, and lingerie, I turned on the camera.

"Hey, guys. Did you miss me?"

It was my standard greeting. And I liked watching the affirmative messages roll in. Bender50 was there, and yes, he had missed me. A lot. He was a caregiver for his elderly mom and didn't get out much. DeeDee1 and DeeDee2 were online, as usual. They were a married couple who'd suffered several heartbreaking miscarriages. Zon5 was wheelchair-bound and had a platonic relationship with his wife (or so he said). Our time together was the highlight of his day, he'd told me, more than once. Pardyguy was a new immigrant from Bangladesh and having trouble meeting women. And then, an unfamiliar name.

**LitLad:** I missed you. You cut too many classes.

The message provoked a queasy feeling in my stomach combined with a perverse sort of excitement. It was him. I knew what I had to do.

Private conversations were the best way to make money in camming, but I rarely had them. The one-on-one chat rooms were where you were expected to do the kinky stuff: masturbate, pee on camera, and much, *much* worse. I wasn't into it. And my viewers were my friends, my community. I didn't want to know about their perversions. Like, I knew they had them—they spent every night chatting to a seventeen-year-old girl in a bra—but I didn't want the gory details.

Swallowing my apprehension, I direct-messaged LitLad.

Want to go private?

The normal response to that invitation would have been: *How much?* A private session could cost from one hundred to ten thousand tokens

($10 to $800), depending on what the hostess was willing to do. I wasn't going to do anything but interrogate this asshole, but he didn't know that. His response came quickly.

OK

He didn't even ask about money.

Assuring my viewers that I'd be back soon, I shut down the group feed. I was alone with this person who knew me, who was harassing me. "Do you want to turn your camera on?" I asked.

No

No surprise there.

"So," I said, folding my arms across my scantily clad chest, "you seem to know me. . . ."

The response was instant: Maybe

"Where did we meet? Do we go to school together?"

The same word appeared on the screen:

Maybe

I took it as a yes. "Tell me who you are."

No

"Why not? What are you afraid of?"

The cursor blinked at me for a few seconds. And then . . .

I could get into a lot of trouble.
And so could you.

"What does that mean?" I snapped. "Are you threatening me?"

Ur playing a dangerous game, baby doll.

The condescending words enraged me. Who was this creep to tell me I was in danger? From what—him? The delinquents outside? And then my parents' wan, exhausted faces flitted through my mind. This guy could be toying with me and my family.

"Are you behind the attacks on my house?"

Nothing.

"We're fucking over it, okay? You'd better stop, or we'll catch you, and my dad and brother will beat the shit out of you."

Still no response. I leaned into the camera, spoke through gritted teeth. "Don't be a fucking coward. Tell me who you are."

I waited, my pulse pounding, my face hot and red and twisted with rage. And then the name disappeared.

LitLad was gone.

# *Thomas*

IT WAS NOT a good day to be meeting with potential new clients. I'd had about three hours' sleep, my nerves were shot, and I was in a foul mood. But I was in no position to turn down a referral. A tech executive was relocating to Portland. She was looking for a large family home for herself, her husband, and their two kids, who would be joining her at the end of the summer. I was the perfect realtor for her. As a dad, I knew all the best schools, the safest and friendliest communities, the best sports fields and recreation centers. We were meeting at a café near her office in twenty minutes. I had just enough time to print an exclusive realtor contract. Might as well be optimistic.

The e-mail came in as the last page was printing. I looked at the notification in the bottom right corner of my screen and told myself to ignore it. I had just enough time to grab the contract and get to my meeting. But my hand was already moving my mouse, already opening the message . . . just in case it was from Chanel. And it was.

> Thomas,
> 35K. Today.
> Or this goes to your wife.

Beneath it was Viv's company e-mail address.

I opened the attached photo on my phone. (I couldn't have my shame filling my monitor, visible to anyone who passed by my cubicle.) It was the picture of me, flat on the bed, with Chanel astride me. There was a chance I could explain this to Viv. I would tell her I'd passed out, that I hadn't participated in that moment, that I'd been set up. It was all true. And the photograph backed me up. It meant I could continue my negotiations.

The best tactic, according to my business books, was to offer 65 percent of your target price. They also recommended using precise, non-round numbers to add credibility to the offer. So, I wrote back:

I'm afraid that's impossible. I'll give you
$16,259.
In one month.

Chanel would be insulted, and rightly so.
She'd fire back with a figure like $30,000. I'd go
up to $22,000. It would seem like a significant
jump, but it was all part of my strategy. Eventually, after my meeting with the tech executive,
we'd get to $25,000, paid to her in three weeks.
I would have achieved my goal. I got up and
headed to the shared printer.

My phone vibrated in my pocket. Pulling out
the device, I opened the message, prepared to
read Chanel's angry counteroffer. But to my chagrin, I found that she had not revised her offer
at all.

35K. Today.
Or these photos go to your kids.

There were two photos attached. Glancing
around to ensure I was alone, I clicked on the
first one. It was the same photo she planned to
send to Viv. If I could explain it to my wife, I
could explain it to my children, as horrible and
shameful as that would be. But when I opened

the second attachment, I saw the close-up image of that angry red bite mark.

My stomach churned, sending a sour taste into the back of my throat. What would my children think when they saw that injury? Would they believe that their father was capable of such vile abuse? That he would violate a woman in such a brutal and disgusting way? Could I convince them that I had not hurt Chanel? That I was being set up and framed? Eli might listen to reason, but Tarryn wouldn't. I knew that for sure. I felt a wave of panic, sweat pricking my forehead and the back of my neck. But then I noticed what Chanel had not included.

The kids' e-mail addresses.

Viv's contact details were easily accessible. She had her own business with all her information on her website. But how would Chanel be able to send the photos to my children? They rarely used e-mail, except for school projects. I didn't even have those addresses. We communicated strictly by text. Chanel was bluffing. And I would call her on it.

> How will you send these to my kids?
> Do you have their e-mail addresses?

She responded instantly. With Tarryn's and Eli's Instagram handles.

Even though we'd instructed the kids to keep their accounts private, Chanel could still direct-message them. All my son and daughter would have to do was accept the message request. And then, they would be able to see the shameful photos of their father.

*Fuck*.

Suddenly, I heard a familiar voice coming from the front of the open-plan office. "Hi, there. You must be Emma."

It was Viv. What was my wife doing here? It's not like she never came to the office unannounced, but—wait a minute, she never *did* come to the office unannounced. My schedule was so erratic that it would have been pointless to visit me here without calling first. But she was here now. I hurried toward the reception area.

"I've been wanting to meet you," Emma was saying, as I barreled up to them. "Your staging work is really inspiring. I told Thomas—"

"Hi, hon." My voice sounded high-pitched. "What are you doing here?"

"I was in the neighborhood," Viv said, her smile cool. "I thought we could have lunch."

"God, I'd love to, but I'm meeting a potential client."

"That's a shame."

"It is, yeah." I swallowed my anxiety. "Let me grab some stuff from my desk and I'll walk you to your car."

"Sure."

At my cubicle, I pulled out my phone, my hands clammy, slippery with stress. I looked at the last e-mail from Chanel, with my kids' Instagram handles, and I knew what had to be done. All the negotiation books said not to cave in. They said to hold firm, wait until the other side countered before increasing your offer. But these authors weren't trying to save their marriages and their relationships with their children. Their personal and professional reputations weren't on the line. Business negotiations and blackmail, I realized, were two very different things.

I can send you 10K now, I wrote, my
thumbs trembling on the tiny keyboard.
I'm closing on a house in three weeks. I can
give you the other 25K then.

Please, Chanel. It's the best I can do.

With shaking hands, I grabbed the contracts, my wallet, and my keys, and hurried out to meet Viv.

In the elevator, my wife said, "Emma seems nice."

"Emma? Yeah, she's great."

"Getting married soon."

"Yep."

What was going on with my wife? Her demeanor was cool and suspicious. But how could she know about the negotiations taking place on my phone? And if she already knew, why was I giving Chanel any money at all? The elevator door opened, releasing me from the subtle but distinct tension. We walked to Viv's Volvo, parked on the street.

"Let's go for dinner one night this week," I said. "Just the two of us."

"I don't want to leave the kids alone with those hooligans out there."

"Right, of course." I rubbed my nose with a knuckle. "Rain check on lunch then?"

"Sure."

She allowed me to kiss her cheek, and then she got into her car and drove away.

I was going to be late. It was unprofessional, to say the least, and I needed this new client more than ever now. As I hurried into the parking garage, my phone vibrated in my pocket. I pulled it out and checked the email. It was from Chanel.

**Deal**, she said.

A small noise escaped my throat, something between a strangled sob and a sigh of relief. It was done. Handled. Chanel had got what she wanted, but at least I had protected myself.

Now I could focus on protecting my family.

# *Viv*

MY VISIT TO Thomas's office had revealed nothing. Emma had acted so friendly, so normal. She'd have to be a complete sociopath to be that pleasant while she was sleeping with my husband. I'd also managed a glimpse at her screensaver—a photo of Emma kissing a muscular young man with a shaved head, holding her left hand out to highlight a simple solitaire diamond. It confirmed what Thomas had told me about her upcoming nuptials. My suspicions might have been assuaged if Thomas hadn't acted so strangely. He was sweating and stammering, making excuses for not being able to join me for lunch. Something was up with him; I was sure of it.

But the tension I was feeling now, the tightness in my shoulders and jaw, could be attributed to the upcoming weekend. Our tormentors came on Friday or Saturday nights, often both. They sometimes plagued us with midweek visits, but they never missed a weekend. This time, Thomas said, he would be prepared for them. That morning, over a strong cup of coffee, he told me his plan.

"You can't," I said automatically. "They're just kids."

Unlike the lone figure with the knife, the video footage of the culprits hurling rocks at our house confirmed their youth, if nothing else. Their age made them all the more menacing, in my opinion. Because I knew that the frontal cortex—the part of the brain that controlled risk-taking and impulse control—was undeveloped in these kids. They had a higher tendency toward violence and rash behavior, were more susceptible to group contagion. And they had difficulty understanding that actions had consequences.

"We've tried to do this by the book, Viv. The cops can't help us. The school can't or won't help us. It has to stop."

"We could move."

My husband scowled. "We're not going to be run out of our house by a bunch of brats."

"It's not just about that." I toyed with the handle of my Worbey College mug. "Maybe it's time for a change? Maybe it would be good for us?"

"It's not the right time in the market. And we just renovated. Why do you want to leave?"

I didn't answer. Bringing up the text from Emma, the distance between us, felt overwhelming on top of everything else. I stood and took my mug to the sink. "You can't rough those boys up."

"We won't hurt them. We'll just scare them."

"You could get into serious trouble. You could get Eli into trouble. And it's just wrong."

"Fine." Thomas's chair scraped the floor as he got up. "We'll just let these kids terrorize us and damage our property until they get bored. How long do you think that will take? Six months? A year?"

No answer was required. My husband stomped out of the room.

I SHOWERED, DRESSED in jeans and a soft mauve T-shirt, and went out to the front yard. I had no meetings today, and my garden was in need of attention. Thomas took meticulous care of the expanse of green velvet that was our lawn, but the small plot of pink winter heather, white buxifolia, and the miniature Jap-

anese maple was mine. I'd planted bulbs between the evergreen plants for a pop of color,
but they were now droopy and spent. They
should have been deadheaded weeks ago, but
I'd been distracted. Now, with shears in hand, I
snipped the faded blossoms, losing myself in
the meditative monotony of manual labor.

"Hi, Viv."

Shading my eyes with a gloved hand, I saw
Camille, my neighbor two doors down. She was
a bigwig in human resources, a decade older
than I was, but fit and youthful. Her husband,
Warren, was retired, and her three daughters
were grown, all doing impressive things in exotic
locales. Camille was in charge of all social activ-
ities on our street. She wielded her power lightly,
but there was no doubt she had it. My thoughts
flickered to the corkscrew I had stolen from her
kitchen, and I felt my cheeks flush.

"Hi, Camille," I said. She was walking her
Australian shepherd, Banjo, who came over for a
pat. I scratched him behind the ears. "How are
you?"

"Good," she said vaguely. "So . . . what's
been going on over here? We couldn't help but
notice the police have been visiting you."

I straightened so we were on eye level. "Some

kids have been bothering us," I said breezily. "Throwing eggs and tomatoes. It's so childish."

"Nadine heard a group of boys yelling and swearing late at night." Nadine lived across the street from Camille. "They woke her up."

"They're annoying," I said with an eye roll. "But they'll get bored soon."

"And Warren said he heard Thomas one night, screaming at the top of his lungs."

"He lost his temper. It's been really frustrating."

Camille pulled Banjo away from a shrub he looked about to eat. "I don't mean to pry, but . . . why are they targeting *you*?"

I pulled my gloves off, finger by finger. "We have no idea. Tarryn and Eli swear they don't have any enemies. And Thomas and I certainly haven't done anything to instigate it."

"There must be *some* reason."

"I think it's just random."

"That doesn't make sense. No one else on the street has been attacked."

I could feel my face getting red, could feel a fluttering in my chest. "I-I don't understand it either, Camille."

My neighbor thought I was lying, I could see it in her eyes, in the purse of her lips. She thought I was hiding something. She'd take this conversation back to Nadine, and they would gossip and speculate. Which of the Adlers was responsible for the harassment? What had they done to provoke these children? Was the rest of the neighborhood in danger?

"Well, I'm sorry you're going through this," she said, but she didn't sound sorry. She sounded irritated.

I responded through the thickness in my throat, "Thanks."

I watched her walk away, Banjo trotting beside her. She was already digging in her pocket for her phone, already going to call the neighbors to debrief. Dropping my gloves with my gardening tools, I hurried into the house.

Thomas was dressed for work, tying his shoes in the front entryway. He looked up when he heard me enter. He saw the embarrassment, even shame, in my eyes.

"Do it," I said. "Don't hurt anyone, but make it stop."

# *Eli*

WE ATE DINNER like it was a normal night. My mom had made eggplant parm. I preferred chicken parm but then Tarryn wouldn't eat it. She didn't appear to be wasting away, but Mom usually tried to accommodate her. The TV was on, as always; no one wanted to make conversation. My mom sipped a glass of wine, and my dad was on his second beer. Everything seemed completely normal, on the surface. But it wasn't.

The food was not sitting well with me. I wasn't exactly nervous about what we were about to do, but it didn't feel right. It was risky. Even dangerous. But I couldn't opt out. My dad was not in the best shape. If he tried to intervene with these kids on his own, they might turn on him. They could swarm him and beat the crap out of him. I couldn't hide in my bedroom gaming while my dad was mauled in the front yard.

Tarryn and I cleaned up the kitchen and then I went up to my room. Most of the attacks happened after eleven, so I had some time to kill. I checked Drew Jasper's social media pages and found nothing new. And then I went to Arianna's Instagram page. She posted mostly selfies, her eyebrows arched, her lips puckered—young, sweet, and sexy all at once. There was a pic of her and Derek. #bae. It made me feel hot and sick, so I tossed my phone on the bed, and went to my computer. Gaming never let me down. I got so immersed that I forgot everything until my dad knocked on the door.

"Ready?"

I wasn't. But I got up and followed him downstairs.

We set ourselves up on a picnic blanket behind the hedge. My dad had brought a couple of beers and he held one out to me. I was almost legal, but Dad had never offered me a beer before. It was an attempt at bonding. Too late.

"No, thanks."

"Suit yourself. More for me."

The weather was mild, but I felt a chill sitting on the cold ground wearing jeans and a hoodie.

The neighborhood was quiet, despite it being Saturday night. A couple of Ubers drove by, taking people to more vibrant parts of the city. Or maybe bringing them back. Dad chatted about a sports documentary he'd watched about a famous soccer player. I should definitely watch it, he said. "Cool," I mumbled.

I don't know how long we sat there, but he had finished both beers when we heard the gang approaching. They were talking at full volume, so confident in their invincibility that they didn't bother being quiet. My dad leaned close and I could smell the alcohol on his breath. "On my cue . . ."

This was such a bad idea, but he was already on his haunches, ready to pounce. I crouched too. I had to back him up.

The boys' voices got quieter as they got closer. Maybe they did fear getting caught? More likely, they just preferred a surprise attack. There was the shuffling of sneakers on the asphalt at the end of our driveway—it sounded like six pairs at least—and the zip of a backpack. Then a voice said, "Throw it, Will."

That's when my dad suddenly burst out from behind the hedge. If he'd given me a signal, I'd missed it, but I was quick, an athlete, and I was on his heels. The boys were stunned by the sight of a heavyset, middle-aged man and his tall, athletic son barreling toward them. If the circumstances had been different, the looks on their faces would have been hilarious. At least a couple of them let out frightened shrieks, a bottle hit the pavement, and the boys turned and ran. They were fast, but I was faster. Before they'd reached the next driveway, I was on top of one of them. His black hoodie was within my grasp. I reached out my hand, touched his shoulder, and then let him slip through my grip. Because nothing good would come from grabbing a kid and scaring the shit out of him until he told us the truth. These boys wouldn't stop until *they* wanted to.

I slowed to a jog and halted, watched the boys sprinting off down the road.

And then I heard my dad's voice behind me.

"I caught one!"

# *Thomas*

"WHAT'S YOUR NAME?" I growled. The kid was as tall as I was, but his body was soft and doughy. Puppy fat. He wore a navy-blue jacket with a hood (of course), and sweats. I guessed he was probably fifteen or sixteen. The fear on his face made him look younger.

"Will," he muttered.

"Will what?"

He wriggled his arm in my grip. "Let me go. You can't keep me here."

"I want your name and your phone number. I'm calling your parents."

"No! Don't! My dad will kill me."

Eli was beside me now. He was probably pretty impressed that I'd managed to grab one of these kids when he couldn't. He was holding a broken beer bottle. "Is this what you were going to throw at our house?"

"No," Will said. "We were going to drink it. In the park. And then you ran out and attacked us."

"Give me a fucking break," I grumbled. I held my hand out. "Give me your phone."

"Fuck you. You can't take my personal property."

The bravado was already returning. I felt a surge of rage at this kid's lack of respect. His lack of fear. "You little shit," I growled, patting his jacket pockets.

"Stop touching me! I don't have my phone."

"Uh, Dad . . ." Eli said. "We might want to take this off the street."

"Good thinking."

Each taking an arm, my son and I hustled Will into our yard. "Take him around back," I said.

"Why? What are you going to do to me?" Will didn't sound so cocky now.

"That depends on you, Will," I said, and I liked how I sounded like a hard-boiled cop or a grizzled PI.

The backyard was dark, but the motion-sensor lights flicked on as we entered. Will squinted in the glare, and I got a good look at him. He had tawny skin sprinkled with acne, dark hair, a dusting of fuzz on his upper lip. He was a boy, a son, probably a brother. But he was also a hooligan, and a vandal.

Eli kept a grip on the kid's shoulders while I faced him. "Why are you doing this to us?"

No response.

"Answer me," I barked.

Will squirmed, but Eli held firm. "Let me go," Will said.

"Tell me why you've been attacking us, and I will."

He looked down at the grass. "I don't know."

"So, you throw shit at our house, slash my tires, break our window, but you don't know why?"

He shrugged.

"Stop fucking lying!"

He twisted violently then, wriggling out of his jacket. He tried to run, but Eli and I were on him. I lunged for the kid just as Eli did and the three of us toppled onto the grass, landing with a thud.

"Help! Help me!" Will screamed before I clapped my hand over his mouth. If Viv thought we were hurting this boy, she would come out here and put a stop to it. That could not happen until I got some fucking answers.

"Shut up," I snarled at him. "We're not even hurting you." He stopped struggling, but I could see the terror in his eyes. "Answer our fucking questions and you can go home to your mother."

Will was crying now, or almost crying. He looked really scared. I hate to admit it, but it was incredibly satisfying to see him cower like this.

"Dad," Eli said, and I could tell he was freaked out. "Maybe we should let him go."

"Not yet."

Eli stood, and dragged Will to his feet. I got up more slowly. My knee was throbbing. "Now," I said, when we were all standing. "No more screaming like a little bitch. What's your last name?"

"N-Nygard," he stammered.

"And all these attacks on our house, the eggs, and rocks, and bottles . . . is this about Tarryn?"

"Who?" He looked genuinely perplexed.

"Never mind," I said. "Just tell us why you've been attacking us."

"Finn asked us to do it," Will mumbled. "He gave us some weed."

"Who the hell is Finn?"

"He used to go to Centennial High, but he got kicked out. I see him at the skate park sometimes. He asked if we wanted a job. We'd get paid in beer and pot."

"A *job* throwing shit at our house. A *job* slashing my tires."

Eli sounded calm in comparison. "Why did *Finn* want you to attack us?"

"I don't know. . . ." The boy sounded sincere. "I barely know him. I don't even know his last name. But some of the guys thought it was fun. They wanted to keep doing it."

"Damaging property is fun?" I boomed. "Scaring the shit out of my wife and daughter is fun?"

Will looked up at me. "Getting a reaction out of *you* was fun."

I thought about the times I'd run out onto the porch in my robe or scuttled down the driveway in my socks. How I'd yelled and threatened, thinking I was intimidating. But they'd been laughing at me. My bluster had egged them on.

"Can I go home now?" Will said. "Please?"

Eli and I exchanged a look. We'd gotten all we could out of this kid.

"I'll call your parents," I said. "They can come get you."

"No. I snuck out. They'll lose it." His voice was trembling, and I felt the first stirrings of pity for this soft boy. "I'll give you my phone number," Will said. "You can call them tomorrow. Just let me talk to them first. Let me tell them what I did."

I looked at Eli, who shrugged and nodded. Will Nygard recited his parents' phone number, and I punched it into my phone. "This better not be fake."

"It's not." The resignation in his voice made me believe him. "Can I go now?"

"Only if you promise not to come back here. Ever."

"I-I promise."

I nodded to Eli, who let go of Will's arm. The boy took a tentative step, looked at us both, and then turned and ran away.

We watched him go, like a little fish we had caught and released.

# *Viv*

"HELLO?" IT WAS a man's voice, deep and rather brusque. I had hoped Will Nygard's mother would answer the phone. We could have talked boy-mom to boy-mom. But it didn't feel appropriate to ask for her. Maybe the poor kid didn't even have a mother. Maybe that's why he was sneaking out of his house and getting up to no good. Surely, Mr. Nygard would be receptive to what I had to say. He was probably a very reasonable man. . . . Most people were when approached correctly.

Thomas had wanted to make the call, but he could be confrontational. And aggressive. I was calmer and more diplomatic. I'd sent my husband off to the office while I contacted Will Nygard's family. I would make them see that we were nice people, struggling with the fear and anxiety caused by their son and his cohorts. The Nygards could contact the parents of the other boys involved. How these parents dealt with their kids was up to them. (If I'd gotten a similar phone call from a distressed mother, Eli would have received a stern lecture on respect and consideration. And then he would have been grounded for the rest of his teen years.) But we weren't going to press charges. We didn't want any sort of compensation. We just wanted it all to stop.

"Hi. Am I speaking to Will Nygard's father?"

"Yes. This is Jack Nygard."

"My name is Vivian Adler. I live in Arlington Heights on—"

He cut me off. "I know where you live. My son told me."

So, Will had told his father about last night's encounter. But Jack's tone implied that perhaps he hadn't gotten the full story. "Did your son tell you that he and his friends have been harassing us for several weeks now?"

"*Harassing you?*" Mr. Nygard snorted. "They're boys. Boys get into mischief."

I kept my voice steady. "They've caused serious damage to our property. They've slashed my husband's tires. They've broken our window."

"My son and his friends threw eggs at your

house. And tomatoes. That's all they've done. It was harmless."

Harmless? My nerves and insomnia begged to differ, but this man wouldn't care about that. He'd call me hysterical, or some other chauvinistic term. I could feel sweat at the nape of my neck, dampness in my armpits, but I pressed on. "We have them on camera throwing rocks. And puncturing the tires on our car."

"Can you identify my son?" he sneered.

"Well, no. . . . But we caught him in front of our home last night. He was about to throw a beer bottle at us."

"Will and his friends were going to drink some beer in the park," the man stated, "and then your husband and son came out of nowhere and attacked them."

An incredulous laugh bubbled out of me. How could Jack Nygard believe such a preposterous story? How could this conversation be going so wrong? "These boys have been bothering us, almost nightly, for weeks. We just want it to stop."

"So, your husband and son thought they'd beat my kid up?"

"No one beat your kid up, Mr. Nygard. They just talked to him. They just tried to get some answers."

"Is that what they told you?"

"I was there," I lied. Because I knew that Thomas and Eli would never, ever have hurt this boy. "I saw the entire conversation."

"Will has bruises on his arm and on his shoulder. He said your husband swore at him and berated him until he was in tears. They tackled him to the ground and twisted his arm."

"They did no such thing," I cried. But I wondered: *Had they?* Thomas was so angry. And Eli was just a kid himself. He could have gotten carried away.

"I've already talked to a friend of mine at the police department. You can expect a visit from the cops."

"We just want to be left alone," I said, my voice trembling. "There's no need to get the police involved."

"Your husband should have thought of that before he dragged my son into his backyard. That's unlawful confinement. That's assault."

"It wasn't like that," I said, but my voice was weak.

"My kid is traumatized. Your husband and your son are going to pay."

And then he hung up.

# *Thomas*

I HAD BEEN eager to call Will Nygard's parents, to tell them exactly what I thought of their delinquent little brat, but Viv's instincts were right. I was too angry, too riled up. My wife would handle the call to the Nygards better than I could. She was calm, and reasonable, and also seriously rattled by all the shit that had been happening to us. Viv would make them understand that they needed to get their kid under control. Hopefully they'd ground him for the entire summer. If they refused to punish him . . . well, the poor kid had been terrified last night. He wouldn't come within ten miles of our property. Eli and I had taught him a serious lesson.

I'd gone into the office to do some *research*. It was Sunday, so I had all the privacy I needed.

Tarryn had denied anything more than a cursory knowledge of a kid named Finn who had been expelled from her school. She said they had barely interacted before he'd been kicked out for good. Still . . . I knew how kids "collected" people on social media. My daughter would have freaked out if she caught me scrolling through her Facebook friends list, but I wasn't doing anything wrong. She'd accepted my friend request years ago, before she decided her mother and I existed only to annoy her. I had full access to all her connections.

Like most people her age, Tarryn rarely used the platform, but she still had over six hundred friends. She must have added most of them back when she was social and actually liked people. I scrolled quickly through the alphabetical list, pausing at the letter *F*. This Finn kid was the key to understanding why we were being attacked. Will was just a pawn, a foot soldier. While Viv handled his parents, I would get to the bottom of this abuse.

Tarryn had two Facebook friends named Finn. I clicked on the first name and went to his profile. This boy lived in San Diego. He must have moved away from Portland, or else Tarryn had met him on a school trip or something. I

clicked on the second Finn—Finn Dorsey. Like
my daughter, his school was listed as Centennial
High, and he had not been active on Facebook
for a few years. His profile pic showed a pale,
skinny boy, about thirteen years old, with a mop
of blond hair. It was a dated photo. He would be
older now, probably about Tarryn's age. Could
this slightly nerdy kid with the shy smile be behind the harassment? Could he provide the answers I sought?

I clicked through his photos, the most recent
taken almost three years ago. Most were pictures
of Finn and his friends doing skateboard stunts,
corroborating that I probably had the right kid.
Will Nygard had said that he saw Finn at the
skate park. That's where Finn had asked the boys
if they wanted a *job* attacking us. But why? Why
did this kid hate us so much? It didn't make any
sense. But if I could find him, I could ask him.

There were a few photos of Finn on a family
camping trip—or so I assumed from the ubiqui-
tous blondness of the other campers. I clicked
through the scenic shots: a glassy lake, a small
boy resembling Finn holding up a fish, a blond
woman roasting a marshmallow. And then, there
was Finn, standing in front of a canoe, with my
colleague Roger.

What the actual fuck? How did Roger know this boy? There didn't appear to be any biological connection—Roger was of South Asian descent— but his hand rested on Finn's shoulder in an avuncular way. What the hell was going on?

I massaged my temples, an effort to ease the crushing tension in my skull. Was it just a coincidence that Roger Bains was close to Finn Dorsey, the kid who'd convinced his friends to torment us? It had to be. . . . But then, Roger had also brought Chanel into my orbit, the woman who was now blackmailing me. Could there be some connection between my two nightmares?

My head was swimming. It didn't make sense, but then . . . what if it did? Ever since Roger's bachelor weekend, I'd been avoiding him as much as possible. So, if he had a problem with me, how would I know? Maybe he was angry, intent on destroying me? But why? What had I ever done to Roger Bains? Nothing. I'd done nothing. Unless . . . there was more to that blank night at the golf resort.

Grabbing my phone, I searched my contacts for Roger's number. I would find out where he was, and I would confront him. I would finally get to the bottom of all this shit. If Roger had put Finn Dorsey up to this mischief, I would find out why. And then I would . . . well, I didn't know what I'd do, but I would make it stop. Even if I had to get physical. At that moment, my phone rang in my hand.

When I saw Viv's name on the call display, I felt a sense of foreboding. As soon as I answered, I could hear her quiet, repressed sobs. "Viv, what's wrong?"

Her voice sounded so small, and so far away.

"What did you do to Will Nygard?"

# *Tarryn*

IT WAS THE end of English class and everyone was filing out, when Mr. McLaughlin said, "Tarryn. Can I talk to you for a second?"

He didn't look up from the pages he was marking, and his voice didn't provide any clue to the reason he needed to speak to me. Luke caught my eye and raised his eyebrows, but I ignored him. I didn't share his infatuation with Mr. McLaughlin. He *was* kind of good-looking—for a teacher. He was in his late twenties, fit, with cool glasses. Maybe it was the rumors that had always swirled around him, but he gave me the creeps.

"Yeah?" I said, standing in front of his desk. Mr. McLaughlin waited until the last kid had left the room, and then he said, "Take a seat."

I grabbed a chair from the closest desk and sat across from him, arms folded.

"I read your essay on 'The Yellow Wallpaper.' "

It was a short story written by early feminist Charlotte Perkins Gilman, first published in 1892. In it, the narrator had been diagnosed with "temporary nervous depression" after she had a baby. Her physician husband insisted on a rest cure, where she was forced to leave her writing and home behind and stay alone in a room with hideous yellow wallpaper. Ultimately, she'd gone insane. My essay argued that social media platforms were a similar trap for women. They kept us focused on our appearance and our sexuality, discouraged us from serious discourse. But then, when we gained power from our looks, we were dismissed and slut-shamed.

"It's an excellent essay," Mr. McLaughlin said. "Thought-provoking and well-written. But there was one line that concerned me."

I knew instantly the words he was referring to. I'd written them, then deleted them, and then typed them again. Because it was the truth. It was how I felt. But I'd worried it might grab the wrong kind of attention. Apparently, my instincts were right.

*If I want to use my body or my sexuality to make money or to gain attention, that is up to me. I shouldn't be shamed for it. I shouldn't have to hide it. But I do. . . .*

Mr. McLaughlin cleared his throat. "I have to ask. . . . Are you engaging in any sort of risky behavior, Tarryn?"

I unfolded my arms and gripped the sides of the chair. "I was being hypothetical. I was making a point."

His cheeks looked red and he shifted in his chair. "Are you sure? Because if there's anything you'd like to talk about . . . with me or with your counselor, we're here to listen."

"I'm good."

"Okay . . ." He sat back in his chair, his eyes still on me. "You know I'm open. If you ever want to tell me anything." He crossed a foot over his knee. "I'm a lot more chill than your other teachers. I think I kind of *get* you, Tarryn Adler."

I took in his lazy posture, the hint of a smile on his lips, his slightly glassy gaze. The hairs on my arms stood up and a chill ran through me. What I saw on Mr. McLaughlin's face was not concern, but *interest*. He wasn't worried about me, he was *curious*. Maybe even a little aroused by the prospect of me using my sexuality for money.

*Ew.*

A couple of years ago, the school had been abuzz about Mr. McLaughlin and a senior named Jordan Henry. She was smart and pretty, but everyone said she was really stuck up. I was only in ninth grade, so I barely knew who she was, but by the end of that year, I did. Everyone did.

They said Mr. McLaughlin had offered to help Jordan with her college admissions essays. They said they'd spent time alone in his classroom, and eventually, he invited her to his house. It was a small bungalow, just a couple blocks from the school. It had become a sort of tourist attraction for curious students, or students (like Luke) with crushes.

Jordan Henry's friends claimed to have seen text messages between the two of them. Jordan told her friends they were in love. We'd all heard that Mr. McLaughlin had almost gotten fired, but because Jordan was eighteen, the school couldn't get rid of him. It was all rumor and speculation, but right now, it felt true. And the way he was looking at me felt icky. And wrong.

And then it struck me.

*LitLad.*

Mr. McLaughlin was my lit teacher.

Holy shit. Had *he* sent the creepy messages? I couldn't remember the other names the commenter had used. Were they related to literature too? Was my own teacher watching me camming in my bedroom in a wig and underwear?

I stood. "Can I go now?"

"Only if you promise to come to me, if you ever need to talk. About *anything*."

But I didn't promise. Without a word, I hurried out of the room.

# *Eli*

I WAS JUST crawling out of bed when I heard the doorbell. It was almost 10 A.M., but my parents were both at home. Their tense voices had drifted up from the kitchen, their words muffled by the sound of coffee cups being refilled, breakfast dishes being loaded into the dishwasher. I didn't know who was at the door, but it wouldn't be for me. I didn't have any friends left.

As I was pulling a T-shirt over my head, my mom appeared in my doorway. "The police are here," she said, her voice low. "They want to talk about the other night. With that boy, Will Nygard."

"Okay."

She stepped into the room, pressing the door closed behind her. "They want to make sure you and Dad didn't do anything illegal." She coughed slightly. "You didn't, right?"

"I don't think so."

"Eli"—she looked flustered—"this is important. Your dad could get in serious trouble if he hurt that boy in any way."

"I know."

"Because Dad is an adult. And Will is a minor."

"I get it," I snapped. She was asking me to cover for him, to take the blame. She didn't have to articulate it any further.

"It'll be fine," she said, touching my cheek. "You didn't do anything wrong, sweetheart. Just . . . tell them what happened."

She turned and hurried out of the room.

As I descended the stairs, I saw my dad sitting in an armchair facing two uniformed officers, one male, one female, who were seated at opposite ends of the sofa. They both looked stern, and strong and intimidating. And I had to lie to them.

"Look, these kids have been harassing us for over a month," Dad was saying. "They're out there in the night with knives and rocks. It's been terrifying."

"Sounds stressful," the male officer commiserated.

"I just wanted some answers. I'd never harm a child."

My mom introduced me as I entered the room. "This is our son, Eli."

"Hi, Eli," the female cop said. "We'd like to ask you a few questions about Saturday night. About Will Nygard."

"Okay."

The other officer said, "Can you take me outside, Thomas? Show me where everything happened?"

My dad's eyes darted to mine. They were separating us, making sure our stories lined up. My throat suddenly felt thick and clogged. I wanted to swallow, but that would make me look nervous, and guilty.

"Of course." My dad stood, his smile too big, too practiced.

As he and the male officer left the room, I took Dad's chair. My mom perched on the seat vacated by the other cop.

"So," the police officer said, with an encouraging smile, "can you tell me what happened on Saturday night?"

"These kids have been harassing us for a while," I said. "It's been scary for my mom. And stressful for all of us. They were going to throw a bottle at our house, but my dad and I stopped them."

"How did you stop them?"

"We just jumped out and scared them."

"Jumped out of where?"

I glanced at my mom, who was trying not to look panicked. She wasn't doing a very good job.

"We were sitting behind the bushes."

"Waiting for the boys to show up?"

It sounded like a stakeout. Like an ambush. "We just wanted to talk to them. To ask them why they were bothering us. To ask them to stop doing it."

"So, what happened when they showed up?"

"They dropped the beer bottle and ran away. But we grabbed one of them."

"Grabbed him, how?"

"Just . . . by his jacket."

"Who grabbed him? You or your dad?"

My cheeks and earlobes were burning. I could feel anxiety coming off my mom in waves, but I kept my cool. "I think my dad sort of blocked his path, and then I held onto his arm."

"Will Nygard says he was thrown to the ground."

So, the kid was lying about us. That made what I had to do easier. "He slipped when he was running away. We never threw him down."

"And then what happened?"

"We took him into the backyard."

"Why?"

"He was yelling and swearing at us. We didn't want to wake up the whole neighborhood."

"And what happened in the backyard?"

"We asked him some questions. My dad wanted to call his parents, but Will said they'd kill him. So, we let him go."

"Did you or your father hit Will?"

"No. Never."

"Did you threaten him with any sort of weapon?"

My mom said, "God, no! We don't have weapons in this house."

The officer turned to her. "A weapon can be a piece of wood. A phone. Anything like that."

"No," I answered. "Nothing like that."

"What about verbal threats?"

"I don't think so. Like I said, we just asked him some questions."

"Do we need to get a lawyer?" My mom's voice was shrill.

The officer said, "I'll need to talk to my partner, but I don't think you have anything to worry about." She stood up. "But you can't touch these kids. I know it's frustrating. I'm sure it's scary. But it's not worth it."

"We won't even look at them," Mom answered. "Right, Eli?"

"Right."

I stayed alone in the living room while my mom escorted the officer to the door.

# *Viv*

BY THE TIME the police officers left, my stomach was twisted into painful knots. I went into my office and tried to do some invoicing, but I couldn't focus. I sat on the floor, cross-legged, tried to breathe away my anxiety, to no avail. My nerves were already on edge from the near-nightly assaults, and now the police had come into our home to interrogate *us*.

"Relax," Thomas had said, rubbing my shoulders a little too vigorously. "We dodged the bullet." Did that mean he and Eli *had* hurt that kid? That they had lied to the police? If that was the case, I didn't know the man I was married to. And my son was turning out just like him. Thomas kissed my forehead before he hurried out the door. "We're safe."

But I didn't feel safe, not at all. Because now we knew, definitively, that there was no way to stop these hooligans. They were untouchable. We couldn't take matters into our own hands without getting arrested or sued, but the police wouldn't help us catch them. The school refused to aid us without a positive identification, but my daughter either couldn't or wouldn't ID them. No one was taking this seriously. No one but me.

Eli was in his room gaming. Or watching YouTube videos. Or maybe porn . . . Whatever he did alone in his room for hours on end. He didn't hear me slip down the stairs to the basement; if he had, he wouldn't have cared. He'd think I was doing the laundry, or cleaning the downstairs bathroom, or organizing the storage space. But I went directly to Tarryn's room and tentatively opened the door.

Will Nygard did not know my daughter—at least, that's what he'd told Thomas and Eli. They had believed him. But that didn't mean that Finn, the boy at the source of these attacks, didn't know her. Even if he wasn't on Tarryn's radar, that didn't mean she wasn't on his. Finn could have watched her, loved her, loathed her, from afar. If I could find out the reason behind these assaults, maybe I could make them stop.

Unlike most girls her age, my daughter was tidy, a minimalist. She didn't collect trinkets or keep sentimental notes or ticket stubs. She didn't have notebooks filled with sappy poetry or lyrics to love songs never written. But somewhere in this room, there had to be insight into Tarryn's life, a clue to why these boys were targeting her. I was almost certain these assaults had something to do with my daughter. And yet, I hovered in her doorway, my heart pounding in my throat.

It wasn't just respect for my youngest's privacy that stopped me. It was fear. Of Tarryn, and what she would do if she found out I'd been snooping through her stuff. And of what I might find there. What if Tarryn wasn't simply going through a surly, grumpy phase? What if she was on drugs? Engaged in some other risky activity? Something . . . sexual. Something dangerous. Then I would know that Thomas and I had failed her.

But this was not the time to be a coward, to bury my head in the sand. I pushed through my trepidation and entered the room. I went straight to Tarryn's dresser and rifled through her drawers. I found no stash of weed, no pills, no weapons. The only surprise there was all the lacy lingerie sets my daughter owned. They were incongruous with the shapeless T-shirts she bought at thrift stores, the stained sweatpants she preferred, but the pretty underwear was not incriminating in itself.

The closet provided nothing of interest, but under her bed, I found a round hatbox covered in lavender fabric, and a simple shoe box from a sporting goods store. I opened the smaller box first. In it, I found an array of makeup: dramatic eye shadows, bold liquid eyeliner, vibrant lipsticks. I'd never seen my daughter paint her face, certainly not with these bright colors. Removing the lid from the hatbox, I discovered an auburn wig, cut into a stylish bob.

Tarryn must have been experimenting with traditional femininity. Despite her ardent feminist principles, she wanted to try being a girly-girl. It was completely understandable, and no cause for concern, unless . . . there was more to it. What if she was taking pictures of herself wearing the wig, the makeup, and the sexy lingerie and sending the photos to a boy? Or *boys*? Or *men*? Without looking at her phone and laptop, I couldn't know for sure. And Tarryn made sure her devices were never left unattended.

I slid both boxes back under the bed, then surveyed the room to make sure there was no evidence of my visit. Slipping out, I gently closed Tarryn's door and leaned against it, my eyes closed.

What was going on with my daughter? What she was up to, and what she was *into*? I had no idea. And I knew just as little about my husband and his secrets. And then there was Eli, who still refused to tell me why he had dropped out of college. My husband and children were all keeping things from me. No one felt comfortable enough to open up to me. No one trusted me enough to confide in.

Then the stash of items hidden in my walk-in closet drifted through my mind: the plum nail polish, the lighter, the hoop earring, the corkscrew, those tiny blue pills, the lipstick . . . and now, Mr. Gorman's Montblanc pen.

I realized that everyone in my family had secrets. And mine might be the worst of all.

# *Thomas*

WHEN OVER A week passed without an attack on our home, I considered the matter handled. It hadn't been pretty, but Eli and I had taken care of it. Without doing any physical damage, we had scared the crap out of Will Nygard. His father had told Viv the boy was *traumatized*. If that was true, I felt badly, but I had my doubts. And at least he'd think twice before he came anywhere near our house again. Soon, word would spread to all his horrible little friends.

When the police had shown up at our door, I'd been rattled. It was bullshit that the cops had allowed those boys to harass us for so long, but when we took matters into our own hands, they were all over it. Apparently, Jack Nygard had a friend on the force. Luckily, I'd been able to talk my way out of it, and Eli had backed me up. It was over. We could relax.

Except, I couldn't.

"I don't care why they did it," Viv said, "as long as it's stopped."

But Viv didn't know that I'd found Finn, the instigator of the attacks, online. She didn't know that this Finn kid went on camping trips with my colleague Roger. The same colleague who'd gotten me embroiled in this mess with Chanel. The more I'd thought about it, the more I'd realized: it could not be a coincidence. Roger's involvement was key. He was out to get me. And I was going to find out why.

Luckily, he was in the office that day, talking at volume eleven into his wireless earbuds. "You don't need to thank me," he was saying, as I walked up to his cubicle. "It's my job to make sure you're ecstatic."

"Hey, buddy," I said, when he'd disconnected. "Buy you a burger?"

It wasn't unusual for us to grab a bite together. At least, it hadn't been prior to his most recent bachelor party. But ever since Roger had returned from his honeymoon on Maui, I'd been aloof . . . toward him, Leo, and the other agents who'd attended the debauched golf retreat. Now I had to be charming, unassuming, and pretend I hadn't been pissed off at him. When we were alone at lunch, I would convince him to open up to me. I would get him to tell me everything he knew about Finn Dorsey.

Roger's eyebrows knit together, for just a second; then he looked at the $14,000 watch on his wrist. "Why not?"

"SO . . . ," I began, when we'd ordered our sandwiches and beer, "my daughter met this kid named Finn. Apparently, he knows you."

"Finn Dorsey?"

"I think that was his last name. Blond kid . . . she said."

"Yeah, that's him." Roger sighed. "I was his stepdad for a couple of years. How's he doing?"

"Tarryn didn't say. She just said she met him."

"He's a troubled boy."

"Troubled how?" The beers arrived, and I took a grateful gulp from the bottle.

"He got kicked out of school. Beat the shit out of another boy. Badly. When they searched his locker, they found a knife. And some weed."

"Jesus. Is he dangerous?"

"I'd tell your daughter to steer clear. He's a good-looking kid. And he can be charming, but he's got a really dark side."

"He sounds like a psychopath."

"He's had a tough time." Roger took a drink of beer. "When his mom and I broke up, I tried to be there for him, but he hates me. We lost touch."

"So, you haven't talked to him lately?"

"No. Connie turned her boys against me. Yeah, our marriage ended badly, but I was a good dad to those kids. Better than their own father ever was."

It came back to me then. Connie, Roger's Scandinavian-looking second wife. We'd met at a company barbecue. Or maybe a picnic. I remembered Tarryn playing with two little blond boys while Eli competed in the sack race, the egg and spoon toss. Had one of those sweet kids grown up to be our tormentor?

I looked at Roger and saw that he was a little misty-eyed. He cared about this boy, Finn. He missed him. Or maybe Roger felt guilty for leaving Connie and turning her son into a psycho. But had he put Finn up to harassing us? It seemed unlikely.

We chatted about work until our burgers arrived. Then I asked, "How's newlywed life?"

"Good." He chuckled through a mouthful of meat. "I've had some practice."

"You should write a how-to."

"Maybe a how-not-to." Roger washed his

burger down with the rest of his beer. "But I'm not going to fuck this one up. Ex-wives are expensive. And Tina is great." He dipped a fry in ketchup. "I had a close call with the bachelor party."

My cheeks burned instantly. "That was quite a night."

"Too bad you missed most of it. Only *you* could fall asleep during a lap dance."

I chuckled. "What?"

"The dancer was pretty offended. She was really working it, and you just nodded off. It was hilarious."

"I'll bet."

"Didn't you see the photos?"

"Who has photos?"

"Leo took them. But they've been all around the office. You were comatose, dude. It was like *Weekend at Bernie's*. They were putting hats on you and stuff. They were posing you in compromising positions with the strippers." Roger feigned concern. "I told them not to do that. I told them it could get you into trouble with your wife, but they were having too much fun."

I set the medium-rare burger on my plate, the pink flesh suddenly turning my stomach. It all made sense now. I hadn't assaulted Chanel; I had *insulted* her. But was she really angry enough to make up the whole thing? To fake those injuries to get some money out of me? I'd already paid her ten grand from our line of credit. So far, Viv hadn't noticed, but I lived in fear that she would. The Hancock house was hurtling toward closure. It had passed inspection and subjects had been removed without incident. In a week or so, I could get my commission. And I was supposed to turn it all over to my blackmailer.

A picture was coming together in my mind: me, passed out, with Chanel astride me, and Leo taking pictures, laughing his ass off. Either Chanel had got the photos from Leo, or someone else had taken photos, someone with a motive in mind. One of Chanel's colleagues, perhaps. Then Chanel had faked her injuries, had them photographed, and sent the incriminating images to me.

I looked at Roger, shoveling fries into his mouth, and thought about telling him about the extortion. He was a savvy guy. He might know how to handle this. And he could back up my claims of innocence. But he'd watched me get blackout drunk, laughed as I was photographed dressed up like a fool, straddled by a naked woman. He'd let the pictures circulate through my place of work without telling me. I didn't want to be the butt of another joke.

"I've got to get back," I said. "I'm expecting a call."

"Sure." He waved for the check, even though I'd invited him. I didn't object when he dropped his black card.

AS SOON AS I walked into the office, Emma scurried toward me. "Thomas . . . this guy's been waiting for you for over an hour."

"Which guy?" But I didn't need to ask, because he was already heading my way. He was a slim, bearded millennial. I'd never seen him before in my life, but there was no doubt he knew who I was. When I saw him reach into the inside pocket of his jacket, my heart began to hammer in my chest: a primitive fight-or-flight response. He pulled an envelope from his pocket.

"Thomas Adler?"

"Yes?"

He thrust the package into my hands. "You've been served."

# *Eli*

I WAS IN my room, changing into my work uniform—black jeans and a white button-down shirt—when I heard my dad come barreling into the house. He was always like a bull in a china shop, stomping around on his heels, slamming doors and cupboards; every movement designed for maximum noise and disruption. But there was extra force behind the door slam today, and his footsteps sounded even heavier than usual. I felt a prickle at the back of my neck. Something bad had happened.

When I stepped onto the main floor, the tension was palpable. My parents were in the kitchen, my mom's face as white as the papers she held in her hand. "What's going on?"

"Will Nygard's father is suing us."

"For what?"

"Fifty thousand dollars!" my mom cried.

My dad knew what I meant. "For Will's emotional distress. His mental suffering. Supposedly, Will can't sleep, can't play with his little friends, can't go to his fancy private school because he's *traumatized* by what we did to him."

"What did you do to him?" Mom asked, not for the first time.

"Nothing!" Dad and I replied in unison.

"We barely touched him," I added. "He's a pussy."

"Eli, don't be vulgar," she chided.

"He's right," my dad said. "The kid's a crybaby. No wonder, with a daddy who sues people for giving his son a lecture."

"I don't understand this," my mom said, scanning the document. "The police said there was no case. How can Jack Nygard sue us?"

"Civil cases don't require the same burden of proof as criminal cases," I explained. "It's fifty percent plus one in a civil case. Criminal cases require ninety-nine percent consensus."

My parents looked at me. "How do you know that?" Dad asked.

"I took a prelaw class at Worbey."

"Look at all the useful things you're learning there," Mom said with a smile.

"I'm late for work."

"Take an Uber if you want," she offered. I saw my dad flinch, like we suddenly couldn't afford an eight-dollar car ride because we were being sued. Maybe we couldn't? Maybe Will Nygard's dad was going to destroy us? Even more reason I couldn't get fired.

"Thanks," I said, already hailing a ride on the app.

THE UBER DRIVER had tried to make conversation, but he quickly got the message that I wasn't in the mood to chat. I stared out the window, my mind running through recent events. How had everything gotten so messy and out of control? Kids threw eggs and shit; it wasn't a big deal. But serious damage had been done to our property. And now, my parents were being sued. My mom didn't look like she could handle much more drama. She was really pale and looked like she'd recently lost weight.

When the Camry pulled up at the Thirsty Raven, I checked my watch. I was seven minutes early for my shift. I climbed out of the car with a mumbled thanks, as the driver sped away. I was about to head inside, when my gaze was drawn to a white Mercedes-AMG parked on the street.

It was just two spaces away from where I stood, and I could clearly see the driver, sitting in his seat, watching me.

It was Noah Campbell. My former soccer teammate. My former friend.

He didn't look away. He didn't slink down in his seat or try to hide. He just stared at me: *I see you.* His presence was a warning. A threat. The guys from Worbey College could get to me.

Or maybe they already had?

# *Tarryn*

"THERE'S SOMETHING I have to tell you. . . ."

Luke turned to look at me. We were on his queen-size bed, propped up by a mountain of neutral-colored throw pillows, watching YouTube videos on his laptop. We'd smoked some pot after school, but the effects had mostly worn off by now. We were just feeling lazy. And thirsty. And apparently, my inhibitions were lowered, because I said:

"Promise me you won't freak out."

"I won't."

"You won't promise? Or you won't freak out?"

"Just tell me!" Luke demanded.

I had kept my secret for so long, but I couldn't do it anymore. Not since the creepy messages. "I've been . . . camming."

Luke blinked a couple of times. "Seriously? Since when?"

"For a few months. Well, more than a few. Ten months."

"Oh my god! Why did I not know this?"

"I just wanted it to be my thing." I shifted on the bed to face him. "You can't tell Georgia. She'll think it's slutty."

"No, she won't. But I won't tell her."

"Thanks."

"So, what's it like?" he asked. "Is it hot? Or is it creepy?"

"Camming isn't what people think it is. My viewers are nice people. They're my friends."

"*Friends* who stare at your tits and watch you masturbate?"

"I don't masturbate on camera. And I always wear a bra and underpants."

"What do you do, then?"

"We talk. About TV. Or school. Or our favorite foods. Most of them are lonely. They want that connection."

"But they pay you?"

"Yeah. I'm making decent money. I'd make a lot more if I did privates, but that's where you have to do all the crazy shit."

"Like sit on cakes? I heard that's a thing."

"It's a thing."

"Aren't you scared someone will recognize you?"

"I wear a wig. And lots of dark makeup. I thought there was no way, but . . . I've been getting some creepy messages."

"Creepy how?"

"Like, this guy knows things . . . that I wore a red hoodie to school. That I skipped class. Stuff like that."

"Oh shit."

"I know. And I think I know who it is. . . ."

"Who?"

I took a breath. "Mr. McLaughlin."

Luke tried, and failed, to suppress a laugh. "Umm . . . I'm not sure you're Mr. McLaughlin's type."

I socked him with a throw pillow. "Umm . . . fuck you."

"You know I think you're gorgeous, Tarryn. But remember Jordan Henry? She was so prissy. And squeaky-clean. Plus, I heard that they were really in love."

"He's a teacher. That's disgusting."

"But he was only twenty-six. She was eighteen."

"McLaughlin called me in to talk about my

paper." I could feel my cheeks flushing. "He was all like: 'I get you, Tarryn. I'm a lot more chill than your other teachers.' It made my hair stand on end."

"He does have a history. . . ."

"And the message came from LitLad. Like, literature lad."

Luke grimaced. "But why would Mr. Mc-Laughlin be on a camming site? He's young. And he's hot. Aren't the guys all lonely losers?"

"They're not *all* lonely losers," I grumped.

"Could Bryce Ralston be watching you on the site? Maybe you mentioned something about it when you guys were hooking up?"

"No way. I felt him out. He's not smart enough to lie that convincingly."

We sat in silence, both pondering who could have found me online. I was so irrelevant at school; I couldn't imagine anyone else searching me out. Or even caring if they stumbled upon my chat room. And then Luke spoke.

"What if it's not someone from your real life who found you on the camming site? What if someone from the camming site found you in real life?"

"But how?"

"They could have found your IP address.

Maybe they hacked into your computer. I don't know how that stuff works, but I'm sure it can be done."

"Oh my god . . . they could find out where I live. And where I go to school."

"Do any of them seem obsessed with you?"

"They all do. That's the point."

"Tarryn, you need to take this seriously. You might have a stalker."

"I should go," I said, as I scooched off the bed. I suddenly felt hot, and sweaty, and queasy.

"You should probably tell your parents. Or even the police."

"No way," I snapped instantly.

"Promise me you'll stop camming, at least."

"Just . . . don't worry about it." I opened his bedroom door. "I'll handle it."

I hurried out of Luke's bedroom before he could question me about what I meant. Because I really didn't have a plan. I had no idea what I was going to do.

# *Viv*

MY DAUGHTER AND I sat at the dining table, eating our chickpea curry in silence. Eli was at work, and Thomas was showing a house in Kings Heights. I hadn't questioned my husband about this evening meeting, hadn't pressed. If it was just an excuse to see Emma, or some other woman, I didn't have the energy to be jealous. And some time alone would allow me to process this mess we were in. Well . . . I wasn't technically alone, I was with Tarryn. But with the current state of our relationship, there wasn't much difference.

"I've got homework," Tarryn said, standing up from the table.

I looked at my youngest in her usual slovenly ensemble and thought about the sexy lingerie I'd found, the wig and the makeup. Was there a way

I could question her without revealing my invasion of her privacy? I didn't have the emotional bandwidth for a confrontation right now. Her righteous anger and indignation would undo me.

"Okay, honey. I'll clean up."

"Thanks." She pushed her chair back.

"You know I'm always here for you, right?"

Her eyes narrowed. "What's that supposed to mean?"

"Just . . . that I support you. And I love you."

"Great," she said. "Thanks." But there was no warmth in her words.

When she'd disappeared into her basement lair, I dumped the rest of my curry into the compost and loaded the dishwasher. My mind cycled through recent events: the faceless boys attacking us; Thomas and Eli accosting Will Nygard; the boy's father suing us for emotional distress and mental suffering. How had everything escalated so quickly? Gotten so blown out of proportion? As I wiped the counters, clarity began to seep through the jumble of thoughts. It was male bluster and bravado that had gotten us into this mess. Perhaps female tact and diplomacy would get us out.

The Nygards' address was right there on the lawsuit, a sixteen-minute stroll from our home, according to Google Maps. (How convenient for Will and his playmates.) The sun was heavy in the sky, but I decided to walk. It would allow me to gather my thoughts, to prepare my spiel. My shoulders and jaw were tense, but I was confident in my mission. I could fix this with compassion and reason. It wasn't too late.

Their home was a stately two-story, tastefully updated from its turn-of-the-century origins. It was slightly smaller than our house, but it would have spectacular views of Mount Hood off the back deck, increasing its value. It was built close to the road, a short path lined with stylish solar-powered lights leading to the front door. Parked out front were a Mercedes sedan and an Audi wagon. The Nygards were not short on money. The lawsuit was simply meant to punish us.

I hovered at the edge of their property for a moment. Was it a no-no for the defendant in a civil suit to show up at the home of the plaintiff? It seemed highly likely, but I had never been sued before so didn't know for sure. Still, I had come this far. With a fortifying breath, I strode to the front door and rang the bell.

If Jack or Will Nygard answered, I would assure him that I came in peace, that I was not trying to cause trouble, that I just wanted a quick word with his wife/mother. I didn't relish facing off against the Nygard patriarch. He'd been dismissive and belligerent on the phone, and I knew his type. He'd try to intimidate and bully me . . . and he might succeed. To my relief, the door swung open and I stood facing a woman, about my age. She was shorter than I was, heavier, with lovely dark hair and eyes. Her calm female energy gave me a good feeling.

"Hi there," I said, my voice warm and conciliatory, "my name's Viv Adler."

She folded her arms across her chest, instantly hostile. "What are you doing here?"

Her tone and body language made it clear that her son had filled her with misinformation. Of course he had. It was normal for a kid to lie to protect himself. But I was here to gently set the record straight.

"I thought we could talk this out, woman-to-woman. Mom-to-mom. I feel like things have gotten way out of hand."

"Things got *way out of hand* the night your husband and son attacked my boy."

Any vestiges of the sweet nature I'd first glimpsed were gone. Mama bear was coming out. I kept my voice level. "I'm very sorry for that. But your son and his friends had been vandalizing our house for weeks. It's been really scary and upsetting for all of us."

"All my son ever did was throw a few eggs. That's hardly *vandalism*."

"Our tires were slashed. Our window was broken."

"That wasn't Will."

"My husband caught him with a glass beer bottle. He was going to throw it at our house."

"Will and his friends were going to drink beer in Washington Park. They just happened to be passing by when your husband and son ambushed them."

Her gullibility was astonishing. This might be more challenging than I'd thought.

"Look"—I swallowed the lump of anxiety clogging my throat—"Thomas and Eli may have been a little . . . forceful—"

"*A little?*" she snapped. "They tackled my son to the ground. They dragged him into your backyard in the dark of night. Your son held his arms behind his back while your husband yelled abuse at him. Will is fifteen! He was terrified!"

"They just wanted to know why we were being targeted! They just wanted some answers! These endless attacks have caused us incredible anxiety."

"My son is suffering anxiety! He can't sleep. He's lost his appetite. His skin has broken out."

"I'm truly sorry that Will is upset. But I don't see how fifty thousand dollars is going to help him sleep at night. Or . . . make his pimples go away."

Her dark eyes narrowed at me. "You people need to learn that you can't treat a child that way."

"Your son needs to learn that he can't attack people's homes with impunity. He needs to learn about consideration and respect."

"Really? I'm getting a parenting lesson from a woman whose family engages in father-son child abuse. Do Thomas and Eli go out kicking puppies together, too? Knocking baby birds out of nests?"

"It wasn't child abuse! It was a stern lecture that should have been delivered by his own mother and father!"

She let out a humorless laugh, almost a bark. "You're nuts. Just like your husband."

"You're a . . . vindictive jerk, just like *your* husband."

"Get out of my yard before I call the police." She slammed the door in my face.

I turned and hurried along the path, now illuminated by the trendy solar lights. I had come here to fix things, and I had made them worse. So much worse. Would Mrs. Nygard really call the police on me? Would they add trespassing to the lawsuit? My heart was fluttering, and I was on the verge of tears, but I was almost at the street.

And then my gaze fell on the last light on the path, the stylish lantern stabbed into the lawn. It was about four inches above the ground, a tasteful orb with a brushed nickel finish. The Nygards could be watching me right now, making sure I was leaving. But I was powerless to stop myself. In one swift move, I plucked the light from the earth.

Concealing it between my body and my arm, I hurried toward home.

# *Thomas*

I'D SHOWN THE ultramodern house in Kings Heights to a twenty-eight-year-old app developer who'd quickly decided it wasn't right for him. After he left, I lingered in the empty home, all glass, beams, and concrete, my laptop set up on the quartz countertop. The current owners had given me an hour window for the showing. They wouldn't return for forty-five minutes, at least. This gave me the privacy I needed to sort out my next move.

Now that I was being sued for fifty grand, there was no way I could pay my blackmailer the remaining twenty-five. I was innocent, I had not abused Chanel. That had been confirmed after my conversation with Roger Bains. But the photos, if leaked, could still hurt me. Badly.

Those who didn't know me well might think I was capable of such violence. They might believe I was a monster who would strangle and bite a stripper. But the people who mattered—my wife, my kids, my real friends—would know that I'd never ever do such a thing. They would believe me.

They had to.

I examined the photos on my laptop screen. They still turned my stomach. Even though I hadn't done the damage, someone had. Maybe it had been done intentionally, maybe it hadn't. Either way, it was disturbing. Zooming in on the photo of the bite mark, I looked at the deep-red bruising, the spot of blood where a tooth had pierced the skin. Jesus. An injury like that could not be faked with makeup. Chanel had let someone hurt her that way for money. And then, I noticed something.

The bruises made by the bottom row of teeth were distinct. There were the usual indentations, and then there was a gap, just left of center. A tooth was missing. Whoever had bitten Chanel's breast had a gap in their smile, a lost lateral incisor. My teeth were close to perfect. I'd even had Invisalign a few years ago.

The proof was irrefutable. I had not hurt

Chanel, and her photograph was evidence! No one could doubt me now.

Excitedly, I composed an e-mail to Chanel.

> I'm not paying you any more money.
> You can't frame me for this.
> I didn't hurt you and you know it.
>
> Thomas
> P.S. I have all my teeth.

I hit SEND and heard the message swoosh away.

I packed up my laptop and headed home, relief lightening my step, lifting the corners of my lips. The attacks on our home had ceased, and now I had shut down my blackmailer. I even had a plan to deal with the lawsuit. Things were definitely looking up.

I tried to ignore the knot of anxiety that still twisted my stomach.

# *Eli*

NOAH DIDN'T COME into the restaurant that night. My eyes darted regularly to the front door, but he never materialized. Was he still sitting out there, waiting for me to finish? Did he know Drew Jasper had asked for my support? Was Noah here to make sure that I didn't give it to him? Noah Campbell was a messenger, sent to let me know that my teammates could still get to me, even though I'd blocked their phone numbers and social media access. His presence was an implied threat. On my break, I ate a burger in the kitchen, afraid of what might happen if I went outside.

I wasn't physically scared of Noah Campbell; I just didn't want to get into some kind of scuffle in front of the Thirsty Raven. I was bigger, stronger, and probably tougher. I had never been in an actual fight, but I was pretty sure Noah hadn't, either. But he'd always seemed so desperate to please everyone on the Worbey soccer team. He might do something crazy, like pull a weapon on me. After my shift, I steeled myself for a confrontation. But when I walked out into the crisp night air, Noah's Mercedes was gone.

My earbuds played ambient techno as I rode the bus home. I closed my eyes and lost myself in the music. I was exhausted, tired of thinking about the mess at Worbey, the mess at home, the mess that was my life. The music soothed me, swept me away. I was so immersed I almost missed my stop.

As I walked through the streets, I turned down the soundtrack and savored the stillness. It was almost midnight on a Thursday, and no one was stirring. Everything felt peaceful, content . . . normal. Like nothing was wrong and ugly and hateful. Maybe, if I just kept walking, I could stretch out this moment.

And then I saw the flames.

# *Tarryn*

IT WAS ALMOST midnight, but I hadn't even started putting my makeup on and I was still in my sweatpants and T-shirt. My regular viewers would be expecting me any minute now, but I didn't know if I could go online tonight. Someone out there in the ether had found me. They knew where I lived, where I went to school, what I wore, and when I cut classes. That person could be out in the night watching my house right now. And the thought scared the crap out of me.

At dinner, I'd been tempted to open up to my mom, but she was distracted and upset. She kept taking deep breaths and letting out small sighs. And she barely touched her curry. She'd told me we were being sued by Will Nygard's dad. It wasn't the right time to tell her that her daughter was a sex worker and that it had just turned dangerous.

I wanted my people, my tribe. The camming community would listen to me. They'd worry about me and offer to help. But one of them could be my tormentor. And what could the rest of them do for me? They didn't know me, not really. They couldn't protect me from someone who had found where I lived, where I hung out, where I went to school. Only my parents could do that. And maybe the police.

And then I heard my brother's voice. It sounded like he was on the front porch. "Mom! Dad! Wake up!"

Had those fucking kids come back again? What had they done now? It was so annoying. I was really over it. Then a fist banged on my window. "Tarryn! Get out of the house!"

I jumped off my bed, my heart pounding in my throat. What the hell was going on? I ran from my room and up the basement stairs to the main floor. My mother, in her nightgown, met me at the top. "Get outside, honey." The smell of smoke hit me, and I hurried toward the back door, my mom on my heels.

We moved around to the front yard, where my brother was holding the garden hose and my dad had a fire extinguisher, both trained on our hedge. It had burned halfway to the ground. The flames had licked up the sides of our porch, charring the white painted posts. What would have happened if my brother hadn't come home from work when he did? Would our house have burned down? Was someone trying to kill us?

My mom was on the phone. "We need the police and the fire department," she said, giving them our address. "Please hurry."

# *Viv*

WE SAT IN the living room, all four of us unable to sleep though it was now almost 3 A.M. I wanted to be strong for my family, but I was overcome, on the verge of tears. This harassment had suddenly become serious. Almost deadly. The fire inspector had told us that someone had used an accelerant on our hedge. Someone had tried to burn down our house, with us in it. Someone hated us enough to kill us. . . . But, why?

The police had dismissed it as another prank gone wrong: "Kids can be stupid. They don't think through the consequences of their actions." But this felt different, it felt calculated. And the security camera footage made my blood run cold. It had captured a hooded figure walking calmly around the edge of our lawn carrying a gas can. That person could have killed us. Had they intended to? Or were they simply indifferent to our survival? The police had the footage, but as usual, it was useless. It could have been a boy, a man, even a woman—it was impossible to identify the perpetrator.

"No more secrets," I said, my voice wobbling. "Does anyone know who's behind this? Why someone would want to kill us?"

Tarryn's eye roll was subtler than usual. "They didn't try to *kill* us, Mom. They tried to burn the hedge."

"The front porch was on fire!" Thomas backed me up. "The house would have gone up next!"

"These kids are stupid," Eli said. "But they're not killers."

"We can't minimize this," I said. "This isn't just mischief now. Someone is trying to hurt us. To seriously hurt us. . . . Who? Why?"

No one spoke for a moment. My family appeared to be considering the question. I had done so myself and come up empty. I had no enemies. . . . Yes, I'd stolen a few things, but they were small, meaningless. And their former owners remained clueless. Even if they knew, they wouldn't burn my house down in retaliation. It was far too extreme.

Thomas ran his hand through his hair. "Will Nygard said that a boy named Finn offered him beer to attack us. I think it was Finn Dorsey."

"Who is Finn Dorsey?"

"He was Roger Bains's stepson for a while. When he was married to Connie."

"He went to Centennial for a couple of years," Tarryn said, "but I barely talked to him. He was a total skid."

"What does that mean?" I asked.

"He smoked pot, skipped school, failed classes—a loser, basically."

Eli said, "I remember him from Dad's company picnics. He was really hyper."

"Roger says he's troubled," Thomas added. "He sounds mentally ill. Maybe even dangerous."

"But why would he want to hurt *us*?" I asked.

"I have no idea," my husband said.

"You need to call Roger," I said. "Right away."

"He's not even in touch with the kid anymore. Besides, it's the middle of the night."

"Well, he must know something! This can't just be a coincidence."

Thomas sighed heavily. "I already talked to Roger. I'll try again in the morning."

"And someone needs to talk to Finn Dorsey."

"I'll have a word with him," Thomas said.

"No, you won't," I snapped. "I think one lawsuit is quite enough."

"*You* talk to him then. Or talk to his mom."

I thought about my conversation with Will Nygard's mother, how it had devolved into a screaming match. I thought about her solar light, now wiped clean of dirt and just fitting, diagonally, in my hosiery drawer.

"Eli . . . could you speak to Finn?"

My son's head jerked up. "Why me?"

"He might relate to you. Even look up to you. He's more likely to open up to another kid."

"I barely know who he is. How would I even find him?"

"Will said he hangs out at the skate park," Thomas suggested.

"It's the one on Blaine Street," Tarryn added. "I remember seeing him there with a bunch of the skids from school."

"I'm working," Eli muttered. "I'm supposed to hang around a skate park looking for some psycho kid I don't even know?"

My cheeks burned with frustration and tears filled my eyes. "I don't know what else to do," I croaked. "I can't take much more of this."

"Fine," he grumbled, getting up. "I'm going to bed."

Thomas spoke to Tarryn. "Go get some sleep. "I'll make sure nothing else happens."

She got up then, and in an uncharacteristic move, kissed the top of my head.

I waited until she'd gone downstairs before I burst into tears.

# Thomas

THE NEXT MORNING, I called Emma and told her to cancel all my appointments due to a family emergency.

"Is everything okay?" she asked.

"It will be." I cleared my throat. "Look, could you do me a favor?"

"Sure."

I had to handle this delicately. "Can you pull Roger Bains's sales figures for me? And details of his recent listings?"

"Ummm . . . I guess so. Can I ask why?"

I couldn't tell Emma that I was afraid Roger was out to get me. That I was worried I'd done something—stolen a listing, beaten his sales record—to make him sic Finn Dorsey on us. I had to spin the request so as not to incriminate myself. "I'm just . . . you know, wondering if I've been keeping pace."

"Fair enough," she said. "Happy to help."

I had a million errands to run. I had to go to the lumber store to buy a replacement beam for the one that was damaged too badly by the fire, and to the electronics store to get more cameras and motion sensor lights. In the afternoon, an installer from an alarm company would come by to put in a monitored alarm system. A friend had recommended a carpenter who might be able to fix the porch in short order, and I'd pick up paint and do the touch-ups myself.

Viv and I had stayed up most of the night talking. She was terrified, on the verge of falling apart. I'd assured her that I would make us safe again. That I'd erase the evidence of our attack as quickly as I possibly could.

"I don't know why, but I feel embarrassed. Even ashamed," my wife said.

"Don't be," I said, squeezing her knee. "This isn't our fault. We're innocent victims in all this."

"Are we, though? There has to be some reason we're being targeted."

I thought about Chanel, who was angry enough to inflict injuries upon herself to make me pay. But that was a separate issue, it had nothing to do with this. Will Nygard had said that Roger's troubled stepson had paid him to attack us. But we barely knew that kid. It didn't make any sense.

"It's random hooliganism," I assured her. "It will fade away, when they find some other trouble to get into."

The police had suggested hiring a private security company. It pissed me off that they didn't consider it their job to protect the citizens of their community, but they had bigger fish to fry, apparently. They'd promised to do more drive-bys, but their resources were already stretched too thin. I promised Viv I'd look into hiring someone, but it would be expensive. If I could deal with this stupid lawsuit, the way I'd dealt with the blackmail attempt, it would be feasible. For now, a monitored alarm system would do the trick.

As I drove home with my trunk full of surveillance equipment, I made a call to my friend Goran Kozic. He was a real estate lawyer and we'd done numerous deals together over the years. We also enjoyed hitting the links on occasion or grabbing a beer. Thankfully, he hadn't been able to make Roger's bachelor party, so I didn't need to feel foolish with him.

When Goran answered, I got straight to the point. "I need some legal advice."

"*Free* legal advice," he chided.

"Trust me, there's a bottle of expensive cab sav in your future."

"I'm all ears."

"I'm being sued."

"For what?"

I filled him in, giving him the broad strokes of the entire story. When I finished, he said, "You know I'm a real estate lawyer. I don't usually deal with this sort of thing."

"You went to law school, didn't you?"

"This isn't my area, but I think you should countersue."

"For what?"

"For the damage to your property. For emotional distress. Mental suffering."

"Viv is really losing it."

"Perfect," he said, which was a little insensitive. "You'll need a personal injury lawyer, but if you're willing to spend a couple grand, you might get yourself a decent settlement. At the very least, they'll probably drop their suit to make it all go away."

After assuring him I'd stop by with a nice bottle of wine, I hung up. Relief buoyed me up as I turned onto our street. There was still a lot to deal with—someone had tried to burn us in our beds—but I'd handled my blackmailer, and now I would handle the lawsuit. With all the increased security, Viv would be able to relax. And I knew that eventually these kids would get bored. They weren't nefarious; they were just dumb. Of course, stupid could be as dangerous as evil, as evidenced by the burning hedge that had ignited our porch and could easily have spread to our entire house. But I wasn't worried anymore. I was taking care of everything.

With an armful of lights and cameras, I let myself into the house. "Viv, I've got some good news!"

She was up in her office but came down the stairs when summoned. Her pretty face was drawn and troubled. Her eyes were bloodshot, as if she'd been crying. I felt a surge of protectiveness. My wife was cracking under the strain, but I was going to make it better. I was going to make it all go away.

When I told her Goran's advice, her response took me by surprise.

"No," she said.

"What do you mean, no?"

"I mean, I don't want to fight this, Thomas. I

don't want to go to court and have us all dragged through the mud. I just want to pay the money and make the Nygards go away."

"It's fifty grand!"

"I'll cash in my 401(k). I'll get a loan if I have to."

"But Eli and I didn't do anything to that fucking kid!"

"You didn't knock him down? Swear at him? Scare the crap out of him?"

"He deserved what he got," I muttered.

"I can't fight anymore, Thomas," Viv said. "I just can't."

She turned and walked back up the stairs.

# *Eli*

THERE HAD BEEN very little thanks after I saved our house from burning to the ground and kept my family from a fiery death. My mom had been too hysterical to articulate her gratitude. The closest she came was when she said to my dad:

"What if Eli hadn't come home when he did? What would have happened?"

"The smoke alarms would have gone off," Dad assured her. "We would have been fine."

"You're welcome," I'd muttered, but they were too busy freaking out to hear me.

At least the fire chief had given me an obligatory, "Well done, son."

But I didn't press for more thanks. Because I knew this might be my fault.

*No more secrets*, my mom had said, after the police and firefighters had left. It was the perfect opportunity to tell my parents about Noah Campbell sitting in his Mercedes in front of the Thirsty Raven. But then I'd have had to explain what had happened at college, and all hell would have broken loose. And if the police suddenly showed up at Noah's door inquiring into whether he'd set my house on fire . . . well, I could only imagine the reaction from the Worbey guys.

I still hadn't breathed a word about the night of the hazing, that sick attack on Drew Jasper, so Noah Campbell had no reason to do something so extreme. His presence at the gastropub was just a warning. He hadn't come to Portland to hurt me. So, I would keep my secrets, and do what my mom had asked. I would find out what I could from Finn Dorsey.

Since I was on family business, she let me use her car. "Don't antagonize him," Mom instructed, as she handed me the keys. "He could be dangerous."

But I wasn't scared of a seventeen-year-old kid. I was three years older than he was. I'd been away at college, had significantly more life experience than he had—not to mention about thirty pounds of muscle. I would confront this boy and make him stop. I'd tell him that it wasn't funny anymore, that he was scaring the shit out of my mom, my whole family. If I had to rough him up a bit, I would, but I could be intimidating without getting physical.

I drove to Southwest Portland and parked on a suburban side street. It was Saturday, late morning. People were mowing their lawns, power-washing their siding, trimming their hedges; the endless buzz of suburbia. It might be too early for Finn to be skateboarding, but I had to work at four. I'd picked up a coffee and I had my phone. If I had to wait a couple of hours for him to appear, I could occupy myself.

As I walked toward the skate park, I recalled the blond kid from my dad's company picnic. I'm not sure why he'd stuck in my memory. I would have been about eleven, so that would have made Finn eight. He'd been hanging out with my sister, and I remembered thinking he seemed too wild for her, too rambunctious. I'd worried he might hurt her. Not on purpose—he had seemed innocent then—but he might accidentally knock her down, kick her in the face, lead her into traffic. We would have gone to high school together, too. Centennial High was grades nine through twelve, so Finn Dorsey would have been a freshman when I was a senior. But I'd been too wrapped up in school, my friends, and Arianna to notice him.

There were a couple of picnic tables scattered around the park. One was only a few yards from the skate bowl, affording me a prime view. A few kids were already skating lazily, attempting a few weak tricks. They were younger, thirteen or fourteen. Finn Dorsey wouldn't be hanging out with them. Perching on the bench, I sipped my coffee and waited.

After about half an hour, I turned my attention toward my phone. Arianna had posted a photo of herself in a tiny black bikini, lying on her patio in the sunshine. She was surrounded by the flowerpots her mom tended, bright-red blooms highlighting her dark hair, her tanned skin. I felt a surge of lust, and of loss. And when I swiped to the next photo and saw her eating a strawberry ice cream cone with Derek, my stomach churned with jealousy.

That's when I heard them approach. A cluster of five boys, skateboards under their arms, were walking across the grass. They looked about seventeen or eighteen, all of them slim in their oversize jeans and T-shirts. I spotted Finn right away, his pale-blond hair visible in the group of darker heads. One of the boys was sucking on a glass pipe as he walked. He handed it to Finn and the group paused while the fair-haired boy sucked in the smoke. It would be weed wax—a potent marijuana concentrate smoked in a pipe. It was not for the novice drug user. These kids were hard-core smokers.

When the boys hit the bowl, the younger skaters dispersed. They knew these bigger kids were a hazard. They skated fast and aggressively, barely in control of their movements. Finn and his crew were reckless, laughing when they fell off their boards, even when they hit the concrete. They didn't seem stoned; they seemed wired.

"Hey, Chad!"

I didn't realize the kid was addressing me at first, even though I was familiar with the derogatory term. *Chad* was a white, muscular douchebag, arrogant and empty-headed. I knew I looked the part; especially in contrast to the shaggy boy who was now facing me, his skateboard propped against his leg.

"Why are you watching us?"

The other boys soon joined him, the whole group giving off a manic, hostile energy.

*Fuck.*

"Are you perving at us, Chad?" another kid asked.

Finn Dorsey stared at me with empty blue eyes. "I know this guy."

I stood up, ignoring my racing pulse. "I want to talk to you, Finn. Alone."

"Why do you want to be alone with him, Chad?" the first boy demanded. He was practically vibrating with aggression. I noticed the others fidgeting and twitching, their eyes wild and soulless. Maybe they hadn't been smoking pot? Maybe they'd been smoking something chemical, something that made them violent and dangerous?

"What do you want?" Finn asked.

"He wants a blow job," one of them said, and they all chuckled maliciously.

"I just want to talk to you."

"About what?"

"About your sweet ass!" the first kid said, and they all doubled over with laughter.

I could feel my face burning. "Can we just . . . go somewhere? Alone?"

"You sick fuck!" a boy cried. "You're a predator."

"Get lost, pervert," the first kid jeered.

Finn's mouth curled into a sneer. "You heard

them, Chad. You'd better get the fuck out of here."

I was no match for five aggressive kids, high on shatter or worse, wielding heavy wooden skateboards. Feeling sheepish, I turned and loped back toward my car.

"See you later!" Finn called after me.

I took it as a threat.

WHEN I GOT home, my mom was sitting in the kitchen staring at her phone. When I entered, she turned off the screen and moved toward me. "Did you find Finn Dorsey? What did he say?"

I looked at her wan complexion, her wrinkled forehead, the thin hard line of her lips. She was usually so put-together, but today she looked like she'd forgotten to put on makeup, and her hair was lank and unwashed. If I told her that the kid behind our attacks and his friends had scared the shit out of me, she'd fall apart. She would collapse.

"He wasn't there," I said. "Sorry."

I headed up to my room.

# *Viv*

WHEN THE E-MAIL first came in, I thought it was spam. Chanel69 did not sound like a legitimate name, was certainly not anyone I knew. But the subject line made my stomach drop.

### Thomas and me

My suspicions were about to be confirmed. I was about to learn the truth about what my husband had been doing and with whom. Was it Emma, after all, or someone new? Was I ready to see them holding hands, kissing, maybe even being intimate? My world was already in shambles. If I lost my husband on top of it all . . . But Thomas's lover was determined to reveal their relationship. Denial was no longer an option.

So, with my heart in my throat, I opened it.

There, embedded in the e-mail, were two photos of my husband and an exotic dancer. In one, he was getting a lap dance. In the next, he was lying on the bed fully clothed, with the near-naked woman astride him. It was a betrayal. It was humiliating. But it was also a relief. I'd envisioned romantic photos of my husband holding hands with the woman he loved. What I saw was a drunken mistake.

Later that night, when Eli was at work and Tarryn was ensconced in the basement with her friends Luke and Georgia, I handed Thomas my phone. I watched his face blanch, but his words came quickly.

"I can explain."

"I'm listening."

"I got drunk. Way too drunk. I don't know how it happened, Viv. It was so stupid. I passed out in the middle of the party and my so-called friends turned me into a joke. They took pictures of me dressed up like a fool. They put me in compromising positions and photographed those, too."

I took back the phone. The pictures backed up his story. During the lap dance, he looked terrified, and I saw how his eyes were unfocused, his face slack. The photo of Thomas and Chanel on the bed was harder to make out, but Thomas appeared inert, his eyes closed.

"There are more," my husband said. "And they're worse."

My voice broke. "Did you have sex with her?"

"God no, Viv! Even if I'd wanted to, I couldn't have . . . I was way too wasted. But I didn't want to. I never wanted to."

"What then?"

"I'm being blackmailed."

"For getting a lap dance?"

"No." And then he showed me the photos of the bruises and the bite.

I believed him instantly. He didn't even need to point out that whoever had bitten Chanel was missing a bottom tooth. We'd been married for twenty-two years; I knew that he wasn't capable of this kind of violence. He would never have choked a woman, never have bitten her. Despite the recent distance between us, I knew my husband.

"I paid her ten grand from our line of credit," Thomas said. "But I told her I'm not going to pay anymore. That's why she sent the photos to you."

"Has she sent them to anyone else?"

"I don't know."

"Oh god, the kids."

"I-I'll talk to the kids. They'll understand that I made a terrible error in judgment, but I would never hurt a woman."

My stomach clenched with apprehension. I prayed that they would. "And your clients?" I added. "Your boss?"

"I'll deal with it," he said. "I'm not paying for something I didn't do. And if you want me to pay the Nygards, I can't afford to give this woman any more money."

"How much does she want?"

"She asked for fifty grand initially. I got her down to thirty-five." He sounded rather impressed with his own negotiating skills, but I wasn't about to compliment him.

"Christ, Thomas," I said. "What are we going to do?"

"We're going to get through it," he said, wrapping me in his arms. "We're going to deal with this, and we're going to be okay."

I wanted to melt into him, grateful for his comfort and loyalty. I wanted to believe that we were a team again, capable of getting through anything. But we were being sued. We were being blackmailed. And on Friday, just one night after our home had nearly been burned to the ground, the boys had returned. This time, they had spray-painted ugly words across the front of the house: FUCK YOU. COCK. And DIE. Eli had scrubbed them off, the red paint running down the driveway like blood. But the neighbors had all seen it. They would all be talking about us, whispering, speculating.

I wasn't sure I would be okay. I wasn't sure at all.

# *Tarryn*

IT WAS OFFICIALLY the last week of school. We all had final exams, so Georgia, Luke, and I studied together on a patch of grass on the hill beside the school. The warm June sunshine, the scent of lilacs in the breeze, and the buzz of kids high on the prospect of release made it hard to concentrate. We'd chosen our secluded spot intentionally. The playing field was littered with groups of kids, their books open but ignored as they talked about end-of-year parties. Bryce Ralston was hosting a big bash at his place. Obviously, I wasn't invited, so neither were Luke and Georgia. We didn't want to be subjected to all the excited chatter, so we had chosen to isolate ourselves. Still . . . I couldn't focus on history.

"Do you guys remember Finn Dorsey?" I asked, chewing the end of my pen.

"Eww," Georgia erupted. "He's such a dick."

"Why?"

"He beat the shit out of Tyler Wendell. He pulled a knife on him!"

"Oh, right." I'd forgotten about the violence.

"He was so cute and then he turned into such a messed-up druggie," Luke added. "Such a waste."

Georgia asked me, "Did you see him or something?"

"He came up in conversation. My dad works with his ex-stepdad. We played together at a company barbecue when we were little. I'd forgotten about it."

"He's a psychopath," Georgia offered.

"Oh my god," Luke said, "do you think he's the one attacking your house?"

"Why would he? I barely remember him."

"Maybe he loved you from afar," Georgia teased. "Maybe he's been pining for you all this time, and he just snapped."

Luke continued, "Do you think he's the one messag—" He caught himself, but it was too late.

"Someone's been messaging you?" Georgia asked.

"I got a couple of stupid messages," I covered. "Just random shit." I got to my feet. "I left my precalc book in my locker. Be right back."

THE SCHOOL HALLWAYS were cool and quiet, just a few kids wandering to the bathrooms or their lockers. I walked to mine in a haze, still thinking about Finn Dorsey. How could I have forgotten about his fight with Tyler Wendell? I hadn't witnessed it, but the carnage was legendary around Centennial High. Finn had nearly put the kid in the hospital. And then he'd pulled out a knife. The size of the blade varied depending on who was telling the story, but still . . . a knife. Would Finn have stabbed Tyler if teachers hadn't intervened? Was he really that messed up?

My dad seemed to think Finn Dorsey was behind the attacks on our house. But why? He had no reason to hate us. Unless . . . my parents had secrets that I didn't know about. Maybe my dad was sleeping with Finn's mom. That could be why my mom was so mad at him. Or my mom was having an affair with Finn's dad. Or his stepdad or whatever. Or maybe Eli had done something to Finn Dorsey. If this kid was behind the mischief, it had nothing to do with me. Of that, I was certain.

I'd been too scared to cam since our hedge had been set on fire. If Luke's suspicions were correct, one of my viewers could have done it. Someone online knew who I was in real life. I hadn't gone live, but I'd checked my DMs on the camming site. My regulars were concerned:

**Pardyguy:** Are you okay?
**Bender50:** Where did you go?

**Zon5:** I miss you, Natalia!

They wouldn't wait long for me. There were hundreds of girls out there, ready and willing to fill the void. If I didn't get back online soon, I'd have to start all over, build a new community. But one message kept me from resuming my role as sexy Natalia. One message, from yet another unknown name, had made me feel sick with fear and dread.

**WAL62:** Don't play with fire, little girl.

This guy knew that our house had nearly burned down. But did that mean he had done it? Or had he just watched it happen? I thought about the neighbors. . . . Maybe creepy Mr. Jens watched me on the camming site. But his wife,

Camille, would have murdered him if she ever caught him. There were other possibilities— plenty of neighborhood men or boys could have secret lives online, could be watching what happened to our home. The thought sent a frisson through me.

As if on cue, Mr. McLaughlin came out of his classroom, walking toward me. His face lit up when he saw me.

"Hi, Tarryn."

"Hey."

"How's the studying going?" He paused, like he wanted to chat. But I didn't.

"Good," I muttered, quickening my pace.

"Let me know if you need any help. I'm available if you need any tutoring."

I stopped a few feet away from him. *Tutoring?* He was offering to help me just like he'd offered to help Jordan Henry. To spend time alone with me, in his classroom, talking about literature, talking about life. Then he'd suggest we move our tutoring sessions to his little house, where he'd give me liquor or weed, to lower my defenses. That's what he'd done with Jordan, everyone knew about it. And then, he'd make his move.

"I'll be fine," I said.

"You've got great potential, Tarryn." His tone was pleasant, but his eyes were dark, hard to read. "With the right support and guidance, you could get an academic scholarship."

It was a carrot he was dangling, trying to lure me in. Could Mr. McLaughlin sense that my life was a mess, that my family was being harassed, my parents were fighting, that I was being stalked? Predators sought out the vulnerable, used affirmations and attention on their victims. But I would not be groomed.

"I'll be fine," I snapped.

"Okay," he said, to my departing back. "But you know I'm here if you need me."

I opened my locker and dug for my precalculus book. It had been an excuse to get away from Georgia's questions, but some review wouldn't hurt. I took my time, dropping a couple of pens and a lip balm into my pocket. In a few days, we would have to vacate our lockers, and I'd have to pack up all my belongings. But for now, I just grabbed a few things, busying myself until I was sure Mr. McLaughlin had moved on. When I closed my locker door, he had. But Bryce Ralston was standing right there.

"Uh . . . hi," I said, taking a step back from him.

"Hey, Tarryn." He seemed awkward. "You probably heard I'm having a party on Friday."

"Yeah."

"If you and your friends want to come, you can."

It was a pity invite. "No, thanks."

"Maybe Luke and Georgia want to come."

"They can go if they want to. I'm not stopping them."

"The whole class is coming. You'll be the only one not there."

"Don't worry about me," I snapped. "I'm fine."

His demeanor shifted then. "That's not what I hear. . . ."

I looked at the smirk on his face, and my cheeks burned. "Oh really? What do you hear?"

Amusement danced in his eyes. "It sounds like someone's out to get you."

Word had gotten around, as I'd known it would. The minute my mom walked into the principal's office, she had sealed my fate.

"Maybe you should think about how you treat people," Bryce gloated. "Maybe you should stop being a total bitch to everyone in this school."

His words should have made me angry, furious even. I should have told him to fuck off, to go to hell. But instead I found myself perilously close to tears. Because he was right. No one liked me. And someone wanted to hurt me. But I would not cry in front of Bryce fucking Ralston. I wouldn't give him the satisfaction.

Without a word, I turned away and hurried toward the girls' bathroom. Bryce's mocking words trailed after me.

"So, I'll see you at the party then?"

# *Thomas*

Dear friends, family, colleagues, and clients;

This is a difficult message for me to write. In the next few days, you might receive an e-mail containing some unsettling photos of me. Please know that I am deeply ashamed of myself for drinking too much alcohol and allowing myself to be put in a compromising position. But the woman in these photos is attempting to blackmail me for a brutal act that I did not commit. That I would *never* commit.

I abhor any sort of violence against women and I have irrefutable proof of my innocence. If you would like to discuss this further, please reach out to me. Thank

you in advance for your support and
understanding during this excruciating time
for my family and me.

Sincerely,
Thomas Adler

The mass e-mail was Viv's idea. She thought
we should "get out in front of it," but I didn't
have the guts to send it. Not yet, anyway. I was
still hopeful that Chanel might realize there was
no point distributing the photos of me. She'd
sent them to my wife, the person who would
care the most, and they'd had no effect. In fact,
Viv had responded to Chanel's e-mail:

Thomas explained these photos to me.
He was extremely drunk, and you took
advantage of that. He also showed me the
photos of your injuries and I know that he
didn't hurt you. I stand by my husband one
hundred percent. You won't get any money
from us. Please stop trying to destroy an
innocent man and his family.

There had been no response so far. Hopefully,
that meant Chanel was backing down. Hopefully,
it meant she would give up.

But tonight, Viv had insisted I talk to the kids. I'd never felt more terrified in my life. In fact, I'd tried to wriggle out of it, arguing that Chanel wouldn't send those horrible photos to my children. Even blackmailers had hearts. But if there was even a slim chance that those images could be sent to Eli and Tarryn, Viv said, I had to address it. They couldn't think, for even a minute, that I would hurt a woman.

We were finishing up the last of our dinner, though I had barely touched the spaghetti and faux meatballs. I hated the soy product, but that wasn't the reason I couldn't eat. My stomach was in knots of anxiety over the impending conversation with my children. They had to know that I was a good person, incapable of the vile acts of which I was being accused. Didn't they?

When they were little, the kids had adored me, clambering all over me for piggybacks and wrestle-time. Viv was always the strict parent, enforcing clean plates, brushed teeth, and bedtimes. I was the fun dad, the pushover. But then they grew up, grew independent and sometimes obstreperous. Somewhere along the way, I'd turned into the gruff father who worked too much and barked orders at them when he was home. In some ways, I felt like I barely knew them.

Things were still okay between Tarryn and me . . . at least she seemed to prefer me to her mother. Poor Viv was always trying to mend their relationship, but my wife seemed to represent everything Tarryn despised. Viv was pretty, stylish, traditionally feminine. She'd been a graphic designer until she started helping me stage my listed homes and then segued her flair for design into a part-time career. Tarryn didn't seem to respect her mom's talents or choices. She wasn't going to look too kindly on my drunken lap dance either.

But my relationship with Eli was another story. I knew he resented me. He didn't understand that I only wanted what was best for him. If I was hard on him, it was because I could see that he was messing up his life. I wanted him to have more opportunities, better experiences, an easier path than I'd had. If I could go back in time, I wouldn't change anything, but it had been a struggle. Eli could have it so much easier, if only he'd listen to me. I was his father, and it was my job to make sure he didn't fuck up his entire life. And yet, he hated me for it.

"I'll clean up," Viv said, interrupting my reverie. "Why don't you three go into the living room?"

"Why?" My daughter was instantly wary.

"Dad has something to talk to you about."

"Oh my god!" Tarryn whirled toward me. "What's wrong? Are you sick? Do you have cancer?"

"I don't have cancer."

"Then what?" Eli asked. "Why do we have to talk to you in the living room?"

"We don't. It's just more . . . comfortable."

"Just tell us," Tarryn demanded.

I looked pleadingly at Viv, but she picked up the plates and hustled into the kitchen.

"There's nothing wrong with my health," I assured them. "But . . . I made a stupid mistake."

Tarryn's face crumpled. "You and Mom are getting a divorce. I knew it."

Eli muttered, "Figures."

"You had an affair," my daughter accused. "Who with? Do we know her?"

"I didn't have an affair," I said. "And we're not getting a divorce. Stop jumping to conclusions."

"Then what?" my son demanded.

I cleared my throat. "A couple of months ago, I went to Roger Bains's bachelor party on the coast. There was a lot of drinking. And there were some strippers there."

"Dancers," Tarryn corrected me. "*Strippers* is outdated and demeaning."

"I drank too much," I continued. "Way too much. In fact, I was basically comatose. And now one of the *dancers* is trying to blackmail me."

"For what?" Tarryn's narrowed eyes bored into mine.

My face burned as I explained about the photos of Chanel giving me a lap dance, astride me on the bed, the bruises on her neck, and the bite mark. "But I didn't do it, of course."

"*Of course*?" Tarryn snapped. "Why do you say 'of course'?"

"Because you know I'm not a violent man, Tarryn."

"Not with us. That doesn't mean you wouldn't harm a sex worker because you don't have any respect for her."

"I-I did respect her. I mean . . . I don't care what she does for a living. I'd never hurt her. Or anyone."

"You wanted to hurt Will Nygard," Eli said.

"For Christ's sake!" I barked. "That's totally different."

"Is it? He's fifteen."

"I can't believe my own children think I

would try to choke an exotic dancer! That I'd be capable of biting her!"

"I can't believe you expect us to blindly believe you," Tarryn retorted.

Viv must have overheard their verbal assault because she returned from the kitchen. Her face was wan, and she looked concerned, shaken. But she looked that way a lot lately.

"Your dad would never hurt a woman. Ever." She moved to me and put a supportive hand on my shoulder. "I've been with him almost twenty-five years. I know him."

"Show me the photos," Tarryn demanded.

"No, Tarryn."

"Why not?"

Viv said, "You don't need to see them, honey."

"If you didn't do it, why can't I see them?"

"I didn't hurt Chanel," I said quickly. "But someone did, and her injuries are disturbing. Plus"—I could feel my face turning red—"I was very drunk. I'm embarrassed. And ashamed."

"How much money does this woman want?" Eli asked. "Are you going to pay her?"

"No," Viv said firmly. "Because your dad did nothing wrong."

"But . . . you're going to pay the Nygards. We didn't do anything wrong that night either."

"I know, but—"

My daughter cut me off. "This poor woman was injured and humiliated. But you're just going to walk away from her and give your money to some rich assholes who don't want to take any responsibility for what their spoiled brat did to us."

"The poor woman wasn't injured and humiliated by *me*," I said. "And the rich assholes have a lawyer. A very good one."

"Wow." Tarryn got up. "Just . . . *wow*."

"Wow what?" I called after her, as she strode to the top of the basement stairs.

She paused there. "This family is so fucked up!"

"We're not fucked up!" But she was already gone, stomping angrily down the stairs. I turned to face my son, and I suddenly felt overwhelmed, like I might even cry. "We're not fucked up," I said, my voice husky with repressed emotion.

Eli said nothing. He stood and left the table.

# *Eli*

MY DAD'S BEHAVIOR was disturbing. And gross. But I wasn't as upset about it as my sister was. Maybe because Tarryn was a feminist and had a lot of opinions about sex work and misogyny. Or maybe it was because my expectations of my dad were already lower. For me, he'd fallen off his pedestal years ago. But I knew he wasn't abusive. And he didn't hate women. He had a lot of faults—he was irritable, controlling, shallow, vain, overly concerned with appearances—but he wouldn't choke a woman. He wouldn't bite a stripper.

Besides, I had other things to worry about.

I scrubbed at some beer rings on a sticky table. They were permanent, but the task let me be alone with my thoughts for a few minutes. That night, after my dad's confession, I'd gone to

my room to play computer games. When I
checked my phone, I saw that Drew Jasper had
sent me another message.

Eli. Please.

With a sick feeling in my stomach, I'd tossed
my phone on the bed without responding. I
launched into my game, but even League of Legends couldn't distract me. I felt badly for Drew, I
did, but there was no way I could go to Worbey
College administration and rat out my teammates. It would be two against six, eight, even
twelve. The whole team would rally against us. It
would be a huge scandal. It would be all over the
news. I'd be interrogated about my role that
night and harassed by the media. Noah and the
guys would come after me then, for sure. They
might be arrested. They might go to court, even
to jail. But they'd make sure they got to me first.

And I couldn't do it to my family. We were already being harassed, sued, blackmailed. . . . My
mom didn't look well. She was pale and jittery. Her
eyes were often red, like she'd just stopped crying
moments before. She couldn't take much more.

Lucius interrupted my reverie. "Table four has
been waiting for their bill for twelve minutes."

"Thanks for timing me," I snapped. God,

what an asshole. I strode toward the kitchen to grab the bill.

It was the end of the night, the last few patrons trickling out. I went through the closing procedures on autopilot, still thinking about Drew, about my dad, about the kid who had set fire to our front porch. . . . Everything was such a fucking mess. As I was depositing the cash from my apron into the till, the front door opened.

"We're closing," Lucius barked.

"I'm waiting for Eli," a female voice replied.

I looked up to see Arianna Tilbury.

SHE WAS ON the sidewalk, standing next to a solid but battered 1997 Volvo that I recognized as her mom's car. Arianna wore a tiny white tank top and high-waisted jeans. She looked sexy, perfect, but it was too cold for the outfit, and she was rubbing her bare arms in the late-night chill. I'd rushed through my duties, eager and anxious to hear what she had to say. Maybe she had broken up with Derek. Maybe she wanted to try again. If we got back together, I could tell her everything. She had always listened, always supported me. The thought made me feel a bit emotional.

"Hey," I said. "Good to see you."

"I wanted to talk to you."

"Do you want my jacket?"

She shook her head. "This won't take long."

My stomach dropped. "Okay. . . ."

"I wanted to explain. About Derek and me."

"You don't owe me an explanation, Arianna. I'm the one who ended it."

"I know, but he's your friend. He *was* your friend."

"I deserve this," I said in a husky voice. "I fucked up. And I hurt you."

Arianna toed the sidewalk. "Derek is a good guy. And I like him." She looked up then. "But . . . it's not like it was with us."

A glimmer of hope stirred in my belly. Or maybe it was just validation, that we had had something special, something real.

"I miss you," I said. "I miss us. What we had."

"I'm not interested in getting back together, Eli. Your parents made it pretty clear they don't think I'm good enough for you."

"They're assholes," I said. "If anything, you're *too* good for me."

She allowed a hint of a smile. "You'll be back at college soon. You'll find a girl more suited to you. A girl who's going to go to law school or business school. Someone that your parents will like."

"I'm not going back to college," I blurted. "I can't. It's fucking . . . awful."

Emotion stopped the words in my throat, and, to my horror, tears began to stream down my face. I was mortified to break down like this in front of my ex-girlfriend, but it all felt so fucking sad and overwhelming.

"Eli, what happened?"

But I couldn't answer. I just shook my head while the tears poured from my eyes. Arianna stepped forward and took me in her arms. She was so small, but she held me as I cried. I stooped over to bury my face in her neck, wetting her skin and her hair with my tears.

And then, her familiar warmth, the scent of her shampoo, the softness of her skin . . . I'd missed her so much. I kissed away the salt of my own tears on her neck. My hands roamed over her back and her hips, pulling her close to me, pressing her into me. My body was responding to her closeness, I couldn't help it. And then she pulled away.

"No, Eli."

That's all she said. Then she walked over to the Volvo and got in.

I stood alone on the sidewalk, my heart still thudding in my chest, watching her taillights disappear.

# *Viv*

ON FRIDAY MORNING, I stared at my reflection in the magnifying mirror. The circles under my eyes were visible through the expensive concealer, and foundation couldn't hide the sallowness of my complexion. With a fluffy brush, I applied a bright-pink blush, then dusted on some highlighter. I'd hoped it would make me appear healthy, perky, well-rested, but the woman staring back at me looked haggard and worn down. She looked like a woman whose life was falling apart. And that couldn't be covered up with even the best cosmetics.

There was no more time to fuss with my appearance. I was meeting Dolly Barber, a former client—a friend, I guess—at her new home for a consult. Dolly and I didn't see each other often anymore—our boys had grown up, gone in different directions—but we shared a history. During those long hours on the edge of the soccer field, in all sorts of weather, Dolly had been so open, so intimate. She'd told me about her bouts with depression and anxiety, about her son's learning disability, and her daughter's issues with food. A few months ago, when I'd decorated her kids' bedrooms, she'd told me, in unflinching detail, about her perimenopausal symptoms (night sweats! vaginal dryness!). I'd wondered if she shared so openly with all her friends, or did she consider me a special confidante?

But, clearly, she didn't. Unbeknownst to me, Dolly had moved into a new home in the Willamette Valley, Oregon's wine country. It was about a fifty-minute drive from my house in Arlington Heights. The move surprised me. It was a beautiful area, but the Barbers had been entrenched in our community. They'd had a lovely home at the south end of our neighborhood. Their kids had attended a well-respected private school nearby. Her son was Eli's age, so he'd graduated, but their daughter was still in high school. It wasn't that long ago that I'd redecorated their bedrooms. Why would Dolly go to the time and expense if they were just going to leave?

When I pulled into her curved driveway, I

suddenly understood the appeal of country living. The home was new and sprawling, situated on several acres of bucolic splendor. When I got out of the car, I breathed deeply of the cool, fresh air, and felt a flicker of longing. It was serene, idyllic. And there would be no packs of bored troublemakers roaming the streets armed with eggs and tomatoes. But I knew my family would revolt if I suggested a similar relocation. The thought made me feel strangely lonely.

Dolly was dressed in designer jeans and a silky blouse, jewelry dripping from her neck, ears, and wrists. Despite her obvious wealth, there was always something slightly unkempt about her—her hair a little wild, her eyeliner slightly uneven—that made her approachable. She met me with her usual warm hug. "It's *so* good to see you."

"It's good to see you, too. And what a beautiful area."

"It is." She looked around at her surroundings. "It's taken a little while to get used to the quiet. And the critters. But we really love it."

I moved into the open entryway, took in the massive staircase leading to the second floor. "It's stunning."

"Well, it needs some updating. That's why you're here."

"I'm happy to help."

"Let's sit in the living room. I made tea."

The living room was a vast space, filled with dark wood built-ins that gave it a distinctly masculine feel. We perched on Dolly's teal, midcentury-modern sofa: gorgeous, but entirely out of place in its new home. Before getting down to business, we caught up on old friends and neighborhood gossip.

"When did you move?" I asked. "I had no idea you were planning to leave the neighborhood."

"It was a sudden decision." Dolly set her teacup down. "We had to get our son out of the city."

"Oh." I didn't want to pry. And I didn't need to.

"He was dealing drugs," Dolly stated. "Mark and I had no idea."

I thought about the freckle-faced boy I'd watched on the soccer field. He'd been a dreamer, more engaged by the clouds or a beetle on a blade of grass than the game at hand. "I'm so sorry."

"We might never have known, but he crossed his supplier. The guy beat Nate up so badly that he ended up in the hospital."

"God. That's terrible."

"It was." Her eyes were shiny with emotion. "They broke his jaw. And cracked two ribs."

"Oh, Dolly." I reached for her hand and held it as she continued.

"Nate's always felt . . . alone. He struggled in school. He chose the wrong friends." She dabbed at her eyes with a tissue in her free hand. "We thought he needed a fresh start. A new environment and a new beginning. He's taking college classes online, and he says he's cleaned up his act. But . . ." She blew her nose into the tissue. "He's so angry. And so unkind."

I thought about my own children. "That's normal for his age."

"We saved his life! Mark had to pay the supplier for the missing drugs. Almost ten grand! He had to take a backpack full of money into a dark alley. It was terrifying."

"That sounds awful."

"We left our home, and our friends. . . . Is Nate grateful? No, he's not. It's almost like he blames us for everything that's gone wrong."

"He's not mature enough to see all that you've done for him. But he will. One day."

She gave me a misty smile and squeezed my hand before letting it go. "I've always felt like I can open up to you. You always know the right thing to say." Then she stood up. "Let me freshen up, and then we can get down to business."

I sipped my tea, my heart tight with pity for my friend. Setting the cup down, I admired the delicate china. Vintage, clearly. There was a silver teaspoon next to it, an ornate design with inlaid enamel. I picked it up and examined it. Weeks ago, I might have dropped it into my purse in some sort of self-destructive trance. But I wouldn't now. Dolly was hurting. I was here to support her, to be her friend, and to help her redecorate her living space. I would paint everything white, bring in a soothing, neutral palette to create a calm and healthy environment. I would do what I could to ease her stress and suffering.

Suddenly, I felt a warmth welling up in my chest and my throat. It was gratitude, I realized. Because my children were not selling drugs. They had not been beaten up. Thomas had never had to venture into a dark alley with sack full of cash to get Eli or Tarryn out of trouble. For the first time in a long time I realized . . . my life could be worse.

Dolly returned then, her makeup refreshed but still a little messy. I set the teaspoon down next to the veiny cup and smiled at her.

"I've got some great ideas for this room," I said. "Let's get started."

# Tarryn

ON FRIDAY NIGHT, I sat alone in my bedroom with a pickle jar half full of smuggled vodka and a Mountain Dew. It was a celebration. School was over. I'd written my last exam—English—at two that afternoon. When it was over, I'd met my two best friends at my locker.

"What should we do tonight?" I'd asked. "Should we go to a movie or something? Or bowling?"

They didn't answer right away, but their guilt was obvious in the way they fidgeted, how their eyes darted to meet each other's but avoided mine. Georgia cleared her throat.

"Bryce invited us to his party."

"He said you can come, too," Luke added quickly.

"No, thanks," I snapped.

"Why not?" Georgia said. "Literally every-one's going."

"I hate Bryce Ralston," I said. "You know how he treated me. You know the shit he said to me."

"Isn't it time to let that all go?" Luke suggested.

"No," I retorted. "I'm not going to forgive him for slut-shaming me, just so I can hang out with the popular crowd."

"Don't be mad at us," Georgia whined. "We just want to have some fun. *For once*."

Her words stung. "Go right ahead." I slammed my locker door and stormed off.

As I'd pushed my way through the crowded halls, I'd felt the weight of eyes on me. I'd turned, expecting Bryce or some other popular douche-bag to be watching me, laughing at me, but my gaze locked with Mr. McLaughlin's. I'd scowled at him, and he'd quickly turned away, caught.

I took a drink from the pickle jar and chased it down with the sickly sweet soda. The noxious combination made me shudder, but I needed its numbing effects. My friends were traitors. My family was a disaster. And my dad was, quite possibly, a misogynist.

He'd never seemed violent or aggressive, but I

knew, better than most, that men could have a secret life they kept from their families. I knew all about the private online personas they adopted, where they lived out their dirty sexual fantasies. Maybe under his slightly grumpy family-man surface, my dad had issues with women. Maybe he'd gotten fucked up enough to let them out on this Chanel person. The thought made me sick. And sad. And angry.

The alcohol was beginning to work its magic, loosening my tension, releasing my inhibitions. Since our porch had been set on fire, I'd been too nervous to go online, scared that the creep who'd been watching me would be there. But tonight, I was ready for him. I was full of rage, resentment, and smuggled liquor. If he showed up, I would take him on.

Crawling onto the floor, I reached under my bed to retrieve the hatbox and the shoe box. My hand was a little shaky when I applied my makeup, but I didn't care. I didn't have to look good; I just had to look *different*. With the dark rings around my eyes and the slightly smudged pink lipstick, I looked older. And a little crazy. When I plopped the wig onto my head, the needle moved to full-blown lunatic.

Removing my clothes, I flicked on the directional lamps and turned on the webcam. I was wearing a sports bra and cotton underpants; I couldn't be bothered to dig out the lacy lingerie. It had been too long since my last live. Would my regulars come back to me? Would my stalker be there?

"Hey, guys," I slurred. "Did you miss me?"

I read the messages as they came in. Most of them expressed concern about my disheveled appearance.

**DeeDee2:** Natalia . . . are you okay?

**Bender50:** You look different.

**Pardyguy:** Did something terrible happen?

I ignored them, leaning close to the camera. "So . . . it seems that someone in this chat room knows who I am in real life." More messages scrolled by—outrage and worry—but I ignored them and kept going. "And that person is trying to scare me away. But I'm not afraid of you, you gutless piece of shit. Stop hiding and tell me who you are."

I waited, watching the message box, but nothing came. Even my regulars were silent, watching me unravel.

"Come at me, you fucking pussy!" I hissed, my spit flecking the screen. "You can't hide forever." I took a drink from the pickle jar, straightened the wig that was dipping into my eyes. "Is it you, McLaughlin? I will get you fired, you sick perv."

No response. Clearly, he wasn't about to confess online.

Maybe Bryce was behind this after all. Maybe the entire end-of-year party was watching me right now, laughing at me. "Bryce," I said, trying to keep my voice steady, "If it's you, I will kill you. I will come into your house at night and I will murder you in your sleep."

They were just words, just drunken threats, but, apparently, they were super unsexy. One by one, the viewers began to drop away. DeeDee1 and 2 were the first to vanish, followed by Bender50 and Pardyguy. Soon, my entire community was gone, turned off by my drunken outburst, my messy appearance. They were fickle, just like my friends. They were creeps, just like my father. They didn't care about me at all.

Suddenly, I knew what I had to do. I slammed my laptop closed and yanked the wig from my head. The vodka might be messing with my judgment, but it was also giving me courage. I had to find out, once and for all, who was stalking me online.

Slipping out of the house was not as easy as it

had once been. I had to tiptoe upstairs to turn off the alarm system, then make my way back downstairs to sneak out. All the doors had cameras on sentry, but there was a window in the laundry room that I was able to squeeze through. I left it ajar so I could sneak back in. The motion sensor lights flicked on as I skittered across the back lawn, but my parents slept at the front of the house. They didn't notice. Luckily, my bike was locked up behind the garage near the trash and recycling cans. I walked it out the back gate, and I was free. Undetected.

My headlight created a pool of light as I rode toward the school. I was drunk, and it was dark, but the streets were quiet, and I managed to get there with only a few wobbles. Centennial High was quiet and still; it seemed almost lonely without its usual buzz of energy and activity. But I rode past it with barely a glance. I had to stay focused on the path ahead. My destination was not far away.

The small house where Mr. McLaughlin lived was dark. It was Friday night, I realized, and it was late. He might be out at a club, drinking, dancing, luring young women back to his place. More likely, he was inside with the lights off, on his computer. He'd be on a camming site or on OnlyFans, chatting anonymously to pretty girls.

He'd offer them tips to do perverted things for his viewing pleasure. He would look and he would lurk, hoping to find a current or former student. I dropped my bike on the lawn and made my way to the door. As I reached for the bell, my fingers trembled. But I had to do this.

My teacher opened the door wearing plaid pajama pants and a concert T-shirt, his hair a little messy. "Tarryn?" He looked befuddled. "What are you doing here?"

My heart was hammering in my chest and sweat dripped down my back—from exertion and anxiety—but my voice came out strong. "I need to know if it's you."

He glanced over his shoulder, then stepped outside, closing the door partway behind him. "If what's me?"

Did Mr. McLaughlin already have a girl inside? Did he live with someone? Maybe his mother? It was clear that he was hiding me from someone. But I focused on my mission.

"I'm being harassed online," I said. "I want to know if you've been—" I stopped short. Because I heard a baby cry.

A *baby*? Mr. McLaughlin didn't have a family. He was a creepy predator who lived alone. He was obsessed with teenage students—like me, like Jordan Henry. But suddenly, a woman in a robe appeared in the gap behind him. "Ian? Is everything all right?"

"It's fine, hon. I think. . . . ." He scratched his head. "This is Tarryn. One of my students."

The woman's brow furrowed. She looked exhausted and concerned, but still very pretty. "Are you okay, Tarryn? Do you need to come in?"

"Yes. I mean, no. . . . I just—"

The baby squawked again, and Mr. McLaughlin turned to his partner. "Go check on Theo. I've got this."

"Okay." She gave me a sympathetic smile as she padded away.

My teacher turned back to me. "Have you been drinking, Tarryn?"

"A little."

"Why don't you come in?" He stepped back, holding the door open. "I'll make you a cup of tea. You can tell me what's bothering you. And then I'll call your parents to come get you."

"No!" I said, backing away in a panic. "I-I have my bike. I live really close. I'll be fine."

"Tarryn, I don't think it's safe—"

But I was already on the lawn, hopping on my bicycle, and speeding away.

# *Thomas*

VIV LAY BESIDE me, completely still and silent. She'd taken a pill to help her sleep. For the past few weeks she'd tossed and turned, whimpering in her dreams. The exhaustion was wearing her down, making her tearful one moment, irritable the next. Viv didn't like to take medication, but she needed the rest. Now she was so peaceful that I couldn't even hear her breathe. She seemed dead. I leaned over and put my ear close to her mouth. Alive. Thank god.

Maybe I should have taken one of her tablets, but someone had to be alert, on guard. The house was a veritable fortress now, with cameras and lights, a professionally installed and monitored alarm system. But I couldn't shake the feeling of impending disaster. Yesterday had been the deadline to pay Chanel, and I had officially missed it.

At Viv's urging, I'd sent the preemptive e-mail to my entire contacts list. Of course, my inbox had been instantly flooded with responses.

> If you would like to discuss this further,
> please reach out to me.

It was my own stupid fault.

Some people were concerned: my sister demanded that I call her immediately; my best friend from high school asked if I needed to borrow money. Others were judgmental. A client told me she'd been flirting with changing realtors and this was the final straw. But most of the responses expressed curiosity thinly veiled as concern—*I'm here if you need to talk. . . . If you want to open up to someone. . . .* Others didn't try to mask their delight.

> Whoa, buddy, Roger had said. Is this
> about the stripper? What did you DO?

Surprisingly, Leo Grass had not replied to my message. It was possible that he hadn't read the e-mail yet, but his silence was suspicious. Did Leo know more about that night than he'd let on? Did he know Chanel? Were they in cahoots? But that was stupid. Leo had no need to extort money from me. My paranoia was getting the better of me.

"She can't hurt you now," Viv had assured me.

But she was wrong. Chanel had already hurt me. My honor was in question, my reputation suspect. Where there's smoke, there's fire—that's what people would think. And the kids . . . Eli had been aloof since the conversation I'd had with both of them, but Tarryn seemed downright disgusted.

I glanced at the digital clock on the bedside table: 3:42 A.M. Eli would be home from work by now. I hadn't heard him come in, evidence that I must have dozed off for at least a few minutes. He'd been instructed to set the alarm once he was inside, but had he remembered? It was a new system, and he wasn't in the habit. And Eli always seemed so far away, so in his head. Throwing off the blankets, I got up.

As predicted, he had forgotten to set the alarm. "It can't protect us if you don't turn it on," I grumbled to myself. I'd give Eli a stern lecture on responsibility in the morning. I punched in the code—our birth months in order from oldest to youngest—arming the system. My family could sleep secure in the knowledge that I was here, on guard, protecting them. I paused in the living room. Moonlight slipped through the front blinds, giving the darkened space a faint glow. Everything was so silent, so peaceful. Viv talked about mindfulness, about the present moment, but I wasn't into that stuff. Still, I drank in the calmness, the knowledge that, in this moment at least, there was nothing to fear. And then, my stomach growled.

I went to the kitchen and turned on the lights inset under the cupboards. They provided a gentle illumination; the overhead pot lights would have been too bright and jarring. I would make a sandwich, I decided. There was leftover chicken in the fridge. And a ripe avocado in the blue porcelain bowl Viv kept on the island. I would pile on the mayo. Viv scolded me, said it was bad for my cholesterol, but nothing was going to disturb her slumber tonight. I pulled open the door of our Thermador fridge.

The shriek that came out of me sounded feral, almost catlike. I had never made a sound like that before, but I had never seen anything like this before. Not in my home. Not in my fucking fridge! I slammed the door closed, pressing myself against the center island, letting my heart rate return to normal.

"Fuck," I muttered to the empty room. "Fuck, fuck, fuck."

After a few moments, I opened the fridge door again and looked at the offending object.

It was a dead rat, its entrails spilling out of its body and onto the white porcelain plate.

# *Eli*

THE NOISE WOKE me up. I wasn't sure what it was—a raccoon being hit by a car? A cat being attacked by a dog? The scream didn't sound human. But the string of curse words that followed it did. It was my dad.

I sat up in bed, my heart hammering in my chest. I was about to go downstairs, to find out what had made him cry out like a small animal. But then I heard him slamming around, banging cupboard doors and the lid of the garbage can. His fear had morphed into annoyance. Clearly, there was nothing to worry about.

Lying back down, I tried to fall asleep, but the thumps, the muttered swearing continued. It was almost like Dad wanted to wake us all up. At the very least, he didn't care if he did. I kept waiting for my mom's voice. She was a light sleeper and would surely be woken up by the clatter downstairs. But I didn't hear her. Somehow, she was sleeping through the whole thing. She'd been really exhausted from everything going on. I guess she was wiped out.

As it often did, my mind drifted back to Arianna. When I'd returned home from work, I'd gone straight to the shower, my mind stuck on that moment between us. Her body pressed against mine, the scent of her . . . it had been too much for me to take. And I hadn't been with a girl in months. There had been a couple of hookups at college—okay, five hookups at college—but no one since the night of the hazing. And no one, ever, who compared to Arianna.

My chest constricted with a longing that was not just physical. I wanted to sleep with her, but I wanted more than that. I wanted to be with her again, like a couple. I wanted to open up to her, to tell her how alone I felt, how sick and afraid. And she wanted to be with me, too. In her heart, I knew she did. But she wouldn't give me another chance because of my parents. They'd made her feel like she wasn't good enough. They'd made her feel second-class.

But my parents didn't know that their son

was a piece of shit. That he'd stood by and watched a kid get raped with a wooden paddle. And now he was too much of a coward to do anything about it. Arianna would have tried to stop it. She would have gone to the college administration. She was a thousand times better a person than I was.

Folding my pillow over my head, I tried to block out the sound of my dad's tantrum. It was only then that I realized my pillow was damp. With tears.

I was crying like a little kid.

# *Viv*

THOMAS AND I sat at the table with our coffee cups, waiting for the police to arrive. It was seven thirty on a Saturday morning. The kids would be asleep for hours yet, but we kept our voices low.

"Who would do this?" I asked. "Who would break into our house?"

"It's those fucking kids! They're fearless. They know nothing's going to happen to them. They know that Mommy and Daddy will protect them."

I took a sip of coffee and shuddered. Thomas had been awake all night, so he'd made it far too strong. "Can you play the footage again?" I asked.

My husband had his iPad propped up on the table. He hit the security camera app and we leaned in, peering at the screen. At 1:28 A.M., three hooded figures appeared on the road in front of our home. They stood talking for a few moments before one of them darted to the right, disappearing off camera. The other two moved on and were soon out of view.

Our harassers knew the cameras' blind spots by now, knew where to stand to avoid detection. And as usual, the three individuals were completely impossible to identify. The perpetrators could be any age, any gender, any height, any race. The cameras were useless, serving only to unnerve me with their creepy recordings.

"We need more cameras in the back," Thomas said. "And I thought that window was secure. I'm sorry."

The intruder had entered our home through the laundry room window. We'd found it slightly ajar; the locking mechanism that Thomas had installed to stop it from sliding wide open had fallen off the sill and down behind the washing machine.

"It's not your fault," I said. "But maybe we should move Tarryn back upstairs?"

"Good idea."

"Will you tell her?"

"She already hates me," Thomas said. "I may as well."

"Eli has to remember to set the alarm when he comes home late. It would have gone off and scared them away. The security company would have called the police."

"He's going to get an earful when he wakes up."

"Don't be too hard on him." I pushed my cup away. "You know he's sensitive."

Thomas rolled his eyes slightly, but didn't comment.

"What if . . ." I swallowed the thickness in my throat. "What if it wasn't kids, this time?"

"It *was*, Viv. Who else would it be?"

"But this is next level. Breaking and entering? A mutilated rat?"

"They're getting braver."

I took a deep breath through my nose. "You missed the deadline to pay Chanel. And then a dead rat ended up in our fridge."

"It's a coincidence. She's not going to go from sending e-mails to breaking into our house."

My heart rate was escalating with dread, but I had to ask. . . . "You didn't hurt her, did you? I need to know the truth."

My husband's face reddened. "Oh my god! You know I would *never* do that."

"But you were so drunk. And she's so angry.

She's trying to ruin you. If you didn't hurt her, then why?"

"I don't know why!" Thomas's chair screeched across the floor as he stood up. "I've been up all night protecting this family. If you think I'm really capable of something like that . . ." He ran his hands roughly over his stubble. "I don't fucking know, Viv. I just . . ."

He was on the verge of tears. Thomas never cried. He never broke down. Like many men his age, feelings of hurt, fear, or desolation manifested in anger.

"I'm sorry." I stood and tried to go to him, but he was already moving away.

"I'm going to take a shower," he said. "Let me know when the cops get here."

# *Tarryn*

MY MOUTH WAS furry and coated, my head pounding. I opened one sandy eye and saw the Mountain Dew bottle on the dresser, and the empty pickle jar on the floor. Oh god . . .

Last night's events were hazy and unfocused, but I felt distinctly apprehensive, subtly ashamed: drinker's remorse. What had I done? I didn't want to think about it, not right now. I needed to go back to sleep for at least an hour, maybe two. Then I would feel human again. But the people whose voices I heard outside my window seemed to have different plans.

Rolling over, I opened my eyes and listened. Their words weren't decipherable, but I recognized the authoritative hum of male voices, my mom's shrill interjections. The police were here—again. This was becoming a regular occurrence. When the cops got dispatched to my house, they probably rolled their eyes. *Not the Adlers again.* Like people weren't being robbed and raped and murdered all over the city. But my mom and dad insisted we needed law enforcement to deal with some stupid mischief.

What had happened now? It had to be worse than eggs or graffiti if the police were here. That meant it had something to do with my dad. If he really was a violent misogynist, if he really had hurt that woman, then he deserved all he got. The rest of us were just collateral damage.

But I was hungover, exhausted, and totally over it. I was done wondering who was behind it, done worrying what they'd do next. They could burn the house down with all of us in it, for all I cared. Because I was totally alone now. My friends had abandoned me to reach for the brass popularity ring; and my camming community, the place where I had felt adored, accepted, even worshipped, had evaporated. One by one, my viewers had disappeared.

Fuck them. Fuck everyone.

I snuggled deeper into my covers, reaching for sleep, when the events of last night snaked their way into my memory. "Oh no, no, no," I groaned out loud, as I thought about what I had done. Mr. McLaughlin . . . I'd gone to his house. I'd met his wife. I'd heard his baby cry. What had I said to him? What had I accused him of? I'd gotten it all so wrong, and I was mortified.

Clearly, I was going to have to change schools. But that could wait until classes resumed in September. Right now, I only cared about one thing: finding out who had been watching me in real life, who had been sending me the messages online. It wasn't my English teacher—I knew that now for certain—so there was only one other possibility: Bryce Ralston. And I was going to make him pay.

I pulled the covers over my head to drown out the voices and closed my eyes.

# *Thomas*

I WAS JITTERY from lack of sleep, hopped up on caffeine and adrenaline as I maneuvered the BMW through traffic. It was a bit reckless, but I had an open house at eleven, and I wasn't going to make it on time. The cops had arrived around nine thirty, had gone through the motions, inspecting the laundry room window, looking for footprints, dusting for fingerprints. . . .

I'd shown them the rat in the trash can.

"Looks like the work of a cat," one of the officers said.

"Well, a cat didn't put it in my fridge," I'd retorted.

"Obviously not," he'd replied calmly. "But there's a significant difference between someone finding a dead rat that was killed by a cat and putting it in your fridge, and someone killing and mutilating that rat in order to put it in your fridge."

"Right," I said sheepishly. I supposed that was marginally less psychotic. The officers exchanged a look, then continued their superficial inspection.

They didn't care, not really, and I couldn't blame them. In the grand scheme of things, this was not a major crime. But to me, it was the ultimate violation. Someone had invaded my home, stalked through my sleeping house to leave a gory message for me. What if Viv had gone into the fridge before I had? She would have had a heart attack . . . literally. My wife was already struggling with anxiety and sleeplessness brought on by the lawsuit, the blackmail, the never-ending harassment.

*What if it wasn't kids this time?*

I'd assured my wife that it had to be. I'd become angry and defensive when she'd questioned me about Chanel. But I'd been trying to protect her. Viv was on edge, wasn't sleeping without sedatives. I couldn't admit that I agreed with her. An adult, someone who meant business, was out to get us now. I hadn't heard a word from Chanel since I'd refused to pay. I'd been naïve to think she'd just go away. She was showing me that she could get to me. And to my family. I hadn't choked or bitten her—I knew that for sure—but had I hurt her in some other way?

The night was still a blank, but I simply wasn't capable. I'd been blackout drunk in college a couple of times, and no one had ever accused me of violence. I'd been stupid, a buffoon, but totally benign. If Chanel wanted to hurt me, she had. She'd humiliated me. My daughter hated me. I'd already lost one client. But . . . what if that wasn't enough for her?

"Hey, Siri," I said. "Call Emma."

The phone rang several times. It was Saturday—Emma didn't officially work Saturdays, but she'd usually help us out in a pinch. She'd been a bit cool toward me lately, ever since I sold the Hancock place. Maybe I should have given her a bonus out of my commission. Her staging had been instrumental, after all. But that money was now earmarked for the lawsuit. Like everyone in my universe, Emma had received the e-mail about the blackmail. She might be too disgusted to work for me anymore.

"Hey, Thomas." Her greeting was cold, but at least she'd answered.

"Hi, Emma, sorry to disturb you on the weekend, but I need your help."

"What?"

"I'm not going to make it to the open house on Webber Street by eleven. Could you open up for me? I'll be there by noon at the latest."

"I have plans with my fiancé."

"I know it's a lot to ask. I just . . ." My voice cracked. "It's urgent, Emma. There's some serious shit going on in my personal life."

There was a long pause while she debated bailing me out of yet another mess. "Fine," she said. "But I'm leaving at noon."

"Thank you. I'll be there by then. I promise." But she had already hung up.

The store was in a retail park, surrounded by other big-box stores. I parked my car in the massive lot and practically jogged inside. My mouth was dry while my palms felt clammy, but I knew what I had to do. This was necessary. This was right. I walked directly to the back of the store where a large sign read: GUNS AND AMMUNITION. A heavyset man stood behind the counter, fiddling with the till. I approached him.

"I need to buy a handgun," I said.

# *Eli*

ON SUNDAYS, MY dad barbecued if the weather was decent. Our family usually ate really healthy food, but when my dad was manning the grill, we had burgers, sausages, or steaks. Tarryn wouldn't eat any of it, of course, so my mom always made a big salad to go along with it. I wasn't sure my sister would even join us for dinner. She still seemed pretty angry with my dad. And disgusted by him. Although Tarryn's default personality was angry and disgusted, so maybe she was already over it.

My parents were trying to act like everything was normal, going about their usual routines, but things were far from normal. Someone was seriously out to get us. It could be the Worbey guys, but I bet it had something to do with my dad. His confession and my run-in with Arianna had reinforced what I already knew in my heart. My father wasn't a good person. He was shady and shallow and maybe even abusive. He had provoked someone into breaking into our house, leaving a gory message for him. I felt sorry for my mom. She was determined to stand by him even though it was tearing her apart.

I found her in the kitchen making tabbouleh, one of my favorites. It required a lot of chopping, which seemed to be a release for her. She was slamming the blade onto the wooden cutting board with excessive force. It was just parsley, not rocks. Her eyes looked far away, and her forehead was crinkled with the exertion. If her finger got in the way, it would be a goner.

Muting my earbuds, I asked, "Do you need any help?"

She paused, looking up at me. For a moment, it seemed she didn't know where she was. Then she gave me a weak smile. "Can you take the meat out to your father?"

"Sure."

"Thanks, honey." She resumed her attack on the parsley.

I carried the plate of steaks to the backyard. My dad was scraping the grill, a beer in his other hand. Unlike Mom, he seemed to be handling the stress quite well. If anyone should be buckling under the strain, it was him. But he didn't seem to care that his family was falling apart.

"Thanks, pal." His words were too loud, too upbeat. He felt the hostility of my presence, the weight of my gaze. "Go help your mom with the salad."

"She doesn't need help."

"Okay." He took a swig of beer, then peeled the bloodied plastic wrap off the meat. "Can you put this in the outdoor trash? I don't want it stinking up the kitchen."

Clearly, he didn't want me around. The effort of being jovial was too much. I didn't want to be around him either. I took the wet plastic, felt the blood on my fingers.

Our trash can and recycling bins were behind the garage. It was a pain when I had to roll them out to the street for collection, but my parents wanted to keep them out of view. Hide the garbage, any signs of ugliness. With my music blasting in my ears, I strolled to the back of our substantial yard. My stomach was already growling, and I was looking forward to a good steak and some pulverized tabbouleh.

Maybe I would have heard something if I

hadn't been wearing my earbuds. There must have been some sort of noise emanating from the green plastic bin. But I had no warning, no sense of dread as I opened the lid to toss the soggy wrapping inside. And then, they were on me, a hot black swarm, a hundred needles stabbing into me all at once. I screamed, my voice barely audible over the loud music in my ears. My arms flailed to protect myself, but it just made the attack fiercer.

Dizzy with pain, I turned and staggered blindly toward the house.

# *Viv*

MY SON HAD thirteen angry red wasp stings on his arms, neck, and face. He looked swollen, almost monstrous, and I'd wanted to take him to the ER, but Eli insisted he was fine. I had bathed the stings with soapy water and then applied ice to reduce the swelling—though it had done little good. He wasn't in pain anymore, but he'd been stung close to his left eye. It was already closing, giving him the look of a boxer after a bad match.

Thomas had received three stings while dealing with the wasps' nest that had been planted in our garbage bin. He'd found a can of insecticide in the garage, then opened the lid of the plastic container and sprayed the poison into it. Most of the angry insects had already escaped when Eli attempted to deposit the bloody plastic wrap, but a few still trapped inside had taken the opportunity to attack Thomas. The rest had been killed by the insecticide.

When the wasps were gone, Thomas removed their papery hive. It had not been built in the can by the insects; it was not attached to the sides or the lid. Someone had planted it; there was no doubt. But when? And how? Wouldn't one need significant protective clothing to transport a live wasps' nest? How had we missed someone in beekeeper's garb walking down our driveway? Of course, if a kid was brave enough, he could capture the hive in a garbage bag. The cameras showed nothing. Our attackers were wise to them now, skirting past them or avoiding them altogether. Perhaps they'd come through the backyard? We had motion-sensor lights and a camera over the French doors at the back porch and the basement entrance, but they could have gained access to the bins without detection. Christ . . . now we needed surveillance of our garbage.

The morning after the wasp attack, I had an appointment at Dolly's house. I'd considered canceling, but Eli said I was being ridiculous. I checked on him before I left. He was covered in red welts and, as predicted, his eye was swollen shut. He looked horrifying, but he insisted he was just a bit itchy now. "I'll text work," he said, "tell them I can't go in."

"Good idea." I squeezed his hand. "I'm sorry about this."

"It's not your fault."

"I know, but . . ." My throat closed and my cheeks got hot. "We're your parents. We should protect you."

"Mom, don't." He rolled over, embarrassed by my show of emotion.

AS I DROVE down the I-5, I felt rattled and weary, but I had to drop off fabric swatches for Dolly's new sofa, and paint chips for her to mull over. The Fourth of July holiday was approaching, and Dolly was taking her family to California. Thomas and I had considered a brief family getaway, but we were afraid to leave our home unprotected. The hooligans would be out in full force, fueled by beer, hot dogs, and fireworks. These youths clearly delighted in their vandalism, thrilled by the devastation. *Boys will be boys*, people said, as if being a cruel, destructive monster was a rite of passage. Society was meant to be shifting away from its acceptance of toxic masculinity, yet these kids harassed us with impunity, enabled by indulgent parents, a harried police force, and a school quick to pass the buck. And now my son lay in bed covered in horrible welts. What if he'd been allergic? He would have been killed. Our attackers didn't know, and they didn't care.

I didn't even realize I was crying until I reached the highway exit and could barely read the sign. There was a tissue in my purse, and I fished for it with a hand still on the wheel. I dabbed at my eyes and blew my nose, pulling myself together. It was highly unprofessional to show up to a meeting in tears. And Dolly was going through worse. So much worse. They'd been run out of their neighborhood by a drug lord, an actual gangster who had nearly beaten their son to death. A few wasp stings were minor in comparison.

In Dolly's driveway, I checked my reflection in the rearview mirror. My mascara had miraculously stayed put, but tears had left pale streaks down my cheeks. I smudged at my blush with my fingers, but it didn't help. At least this would be a quick meeting. Maybe Dolly wouldn't notice my disheveled state.

With the fabric and paint samples in a manila envelope, I approached the door and rang the bell. I would take Dolly through my top choices, the costing for each option, but the decision was ultimately hers. I would suggest she mull it over during her vacation. I'd be in and out in under half an hour—before Dolly noticed my fragile demeanor. And I was eager to get back to Eli.

The door opened, answered by a teenage boy. He was a big kid, almost Eli's height, but with a less athletic build. His hair could only be described as beige, his complexion was sallow, and his eyes were a washed-out shade of gray. The only color on his entire face came from the angry red pimples on his forehead and chin. It came to me then: this was Nate, Dolly's troubled son. He'd been such a cute little boy, with a smattering of freckles across his nose, a twinkle in his lively eyes. Was this what the drugs had done to him? Or was it the stress and the fear of crossing his supplier?

"Hi, Nate," I said brightly. "I'm Viv Adler, Eli's mom."

"Yeah," he snarled. "I know who you are."

I was taken aback by the hatred in his voice. I hadn't seen Nate in nearly ten years. And even when he was a child, I hadn't known him well.

Had he ever come to our house for a playdate with Eli? If he had, I couldn't recall. True, I had redecorated his bedroom in his old house, but he had always been at school, and his mother had made all the decisions. His anger couldn't be about that.

"Y-your mom has hired me to do some redecorating," I stammered. "Is she home?"

"You shouldn't fucking be here."

Dolly suddenly appeared next to her son. The look of horror on her face made it clear she'd overheard his hostile greeting.

"Viv, hi . . . come in." She turned to the boy, still glowering at me. "Apologize to Mrs. Adler right now."

"No. Why should I?"

It felt like a slap. Even a punch. I was already so brittle, so vulnerable.

Dolly's face crumpled "Just . . . go to your room, Nate. Please."

The boy obliged, storming off. "Don't let her near me. Or my room." He stabbed a finger toward me. "Or any of my fucking stuff."

Dolly closed her eyes for a moment, as if she was willing him to disappear. "I'm so sorry," she said, opening them again. "Please. Come in."

But I couldn't. Nate Barber scared me. "I just

wanted to drop these off," I said, thrusting the envelope into her hands. "For the sofa and the feature wall."

"Thank you." She ushered me onto the front steps and closed the door behind her. "Nate should never have spoken to you that way. I apologize for him."

"I don't understand. Does he have some issue with Eli?"

"No . . . I mean, just the usual stuff."

"The usual stuff?"

"Eli was so popular. Nate never was. I suppose there was a little resentment there, but it was nothing, really."

"So then, what is it?

"He's not himself," she said, her voice thick with sadness. "We're afraid he might be using again. Although I don't know how. We've basically got him on house arrest. We don't let him use our cars. And he's been passing his home drug tests. But . . . addicts will find a way."

It was intrusive to ask, but I needed to know. "What kind of drugs was he taking? And selling?"

"Fake oxy," she said, her voice low. "I didn't even know such a thing existed before all this. The pills almost look like the real thing, but they're dull and rough, made in some underground lab. They're toxic and dangerous."

*Jesus Christ.*

"I really have to go," I croaked.

"Of course." Dolly held up the envelope. "Thanks for bringing these by."

But I was already hurrying away, already approaching my car. "Have a nice holiday," I called as I jumped into the front seat. Slamming the door on her reply, I tore out of the driveway.

# *Tarryn*

AFTER OUR HOUSE was broken into, my parents insisted I sleep upstairs in my mom's office. At least I was allowed to keep my clothes, books, and devices in the basement. There wasn't space for them upstairs anyway. My mom had a computer desk and a worktable cluttered with design books, paint chips, and bits of fabric. My childhood bed was pressed against one wall. When I climbed into the twin, I felt like a little kid again, all of us sleeping upstairs with no space and no privacy. It had made me feel safe then. But not now.

This relocation had put an end to my camming career. There was no way I could go online in the middle of the night with my parents and brother just down the hall. And when I checked my online messages, I realized that Natalia was done. Over. She'd been too much work, too un-stable and unpredictable. Camming was all about the fantasy, not dealing with messy reality. I'd been angry at first, and then sad. But now I had a new strategy. And I was excited about it.

When these kids stopped attacking us and I could move back downstairs, I would start over. I'd create a new camming persona, under a new name, on a new platform like OnlyFans. I'd wear a different wig—maybe blond this time, or jet black. I'd buy some new lingerie, not lacy and pretty but sleek and sexy, a little dangerous. It would take time to build up my community. But it would take even longer for Bryce Ralston to find me online.

The school had promised that our exam marks would be e-mailed to us within a week. I wasn't eager to get them. I already knew I'd done poorly. It was a bit difficult to study when you were being stalked and you'd just discov-ered your dad might be a violent pervert. But with luck, I'd passed. I didn't care if I couldn't get into a good college, but I sure as hell didn't want to spend any more time in high school.

On Tuesday, I checked my e-mail. There were no exam results, but there was an e-mail from Mr. McLaughlin.

Hi Tarryn,

I'd like to talk to you. Could you come to
my classroom this afternoon? I'll be there
between 1 and 3.

Thank you.

Mr. McLaughlin

Oh shit.

Clearly, this was not about my English exam.
I was pretty sure I'd passed that one, at least. I'd
probably pulled off a C, would have gotten an A
under normal circumstances. But nothing had
been normal lately. In addition to the mess at
home, Luke and Georgia hadn't spoken to me
since Bryce's party. Not even a Snapchat. Not
even a text. Had they watched my camming
meltdown with all the popular kids? Now that I
was sure Bryce was behind the creepy messages,
I figured the whole school was probably laughing at me. The thought made me feel ill.

The hallways of Centennial High were quiet,
a few other low-achievers wandering morosely
to meet with teachers. In my English classroom, I
found Mr. McLaughlin at his desk, his head bent
over a ream of papers. As I entered, he looked
up, his expression tense.

"Thanks for coming in, Tarryn," he said, pushing the stack of papers to the side. "Have a seat."

I grabbed a chair and pulled it up to the opposite side of his desk. My face felt like it was on fire.

"Ms. Harris will be joining us momentarily."

"I don't need to talk to the counselor," I said quickly. "I'm fine."

"You're clearly not." He leaned forward. "What was that all about the other night?"

"Look, I'm sorry I went to your house," I said, my voice hoarse with shame. "I was drunk. It was stupid."

"It's obvious that something's going on with you," he said, his face troubled. "Ms. Harris and I just want to help."

"But this has nothing to do with school," I cried. "You guys can't meddle in my private life!"

Mr. McLaughlin steepled his fingers together. "You mentioned that you were being harassed online. . . . The school has resources. There are support systems that can help you."

I wasn't going to stick around for pamphlets and pep talks. I stood. "Honestly, everything's fine. Really. I just have to go."

I hurried out of the classroom. At the other

end of the hall, I saw Ms. Harris headed my way, a clutch of reading materials in her hand. Without looking back, I jogged to the exit and burst out of the school. My teacher and counselor could not fix the mess I was in. Only I could do that.

# *Thomas*

WITHIN A COUPLE of days my background check had cleared, and I was able to pick up my gun. It was a secondhand revolver, a .38 Smith & Wesson in perfect condition. The store clerk had given me brief instructions on how to use it, and then he'd tried to sell me a gun vault.

"It's the best way to keep the weapon safe but accessible in case of an emergency."

"I'll be fine," I said. Because I could hide a gun from Viv, but I couldn't hide a vault.

My wife was anti-firearms. I suppose I had been too until someone had come into my home and left a gory message next to the poached chicken. Until my house was set on fire and my son was attacked by wasps. I'd never thought I'd be capable of shooting someone, until now. The police would not protect my family, so I would do it myself.

This wasn't the work of kids anymore. The eggs, the rocks, the graffiti . . . that was kid stuff, but the attacks had turned sinister. They had moved beyond paint-filled balloons, fruit attacks, and smoke bombs. Children did not break into homes with mutilated rodents. They didn't have the capacity to plant a wasp nest in a trash can. And they wouldn't try to burn us in our beds. The assaults had taken a deadly turn. And I finally knew who was behind them.

Unbeknownst to Viv, I had messaged my blackmailer.

> Harassing my family is not going to make me pay for something I didn't do. I advise you to stop before you get hurt. I will do what is necessary to protect my family.

And I would. I considered myself a nonviolent person, but if I had to, I would shoot. And I would kill. If Chanel—or more likely, her henchman—tried to hurt Viv, or Tarryn, or Eli, I would do what was necessary.

Chanel's response came quickly and briefly.

> Pay. Or your family will pay.

It was an outright threat. Jesus Christ. How had things taken such a dark turn?

I looked at the revolver, felt the weight of it. I double-checked that it was loaded, that the safety was on. And then I put it in the drawer of my bedside table.

"What are you doing?"

I whirled around to see my wife in the doorway. Her face was white, her posture beaten down. What had she seen? "Nothing." I jumped to my feet and moved toward her.

"Did you just put a gun in that drawer?"

I was caught. There was no use lying. "Look, Viv . . . I know how you feel about guns, but we're under attack here. You said yourself that this has gone beyond child's play. There's been a man out there, with a knife. With gasoline and matches. I hope I never have to use it, but I'm not going to stand by and let someone hurt you or the kids."

Tears welled in her eyes. "I can't believe it's come to this. A weapon. In our home."

"Eli could have been killed by those wasps. The house could have burned down with us in it. And someone came in here while we were asleep." My voice cracked. "The police won't help us. I don't know what else to do."

"I-I'm sorry," she said.

I took her in my arms. "Why are *you* sorry? This is all my fault." I stroked her hair as she cried softly on my chest for a few moments. And then she pulled away.

"This isn't your fault," she said. "There's something I need to tell you."

# *Eli*

I WAS IN the kitchen, applying a paste of baking soda and water to my welts to relieve the itching, when the doorbell rang.

"Door!" I yelled. My parents were upstairs. My sister was in the basement. Someone in this family who wasn't covered in crusty white bumps could answer it. But no one responded. "Don't worry! I'll get it," I called, heavy on the sarcasm. It wouldn't be for me. No one came to see me anymore.

But when I opened the door, I saw my friend Sam on the doorstep. He was in his usual shorts, and a T-shirt that read: GOD MADE US SISTERS, AL-COHOL MADE US FRIENDS. "Dude," he said. "What happened to you?"

"Bee stings," I said, feeling foolish. And ex-

hausted. I didn't want to explain that the wasps'
nest had been planted in our garbage can. That
someone was out to get my family.

"Do they hurt?"

"Nah."

"I've got the day off," Sam said. "I was hoping we could chat. Catch up."

"Sure." I stepped back and ushered him inside.

We sat in the living room. My parents and sister hadn't emerged to see who was at the door,
so we had the main floor to ourselves.

"How's work?" Sam asked.

"Good. Except I'll have to take a few days off
now. These stings are pretty ugly."

"Sucks, man. How did it happen?"

"Doesn't matter." I waved my hand dismissively. "How's the bank?"

"Fine. Yeah, good." He shifted in his seat, his
eyes darting around the familiar house. "There's
something I thought you should know. . . . It's
about Arianna."

My pulse quickened at the mention of her
name. "What about her?"

"Well, I guess it's more about Derek." Sam
leaned toward me, lowered his voice even though
we were alone. "He's been seeing someone else.
A girl he met online. Arianna doesn't know."

I felt a swell of anger and protectiveness, but it was misplaced. Arianna wasn't mine anymore. "Why are you telling me?"

"I thought you cared about her," Sam said. "She's a sweet girl. She doesn't deserve this."

She didn't. But I couldn't save her. Arianna had made it clear that she didn't want me anymore. "Why don't you tell her?"

"Dude." He didn't need to explain. He couldn't betray Derek.

I heard the door from the basement open, and my sister emerged. Sam looked up. "Tarryn. Hey."

She glowered at him as if she'd never seen him before, even though he'd been my best friend for about seven years, even though he was her friend Georgia's cousin. "Hey," she finally muttered.

"How's it going?" Sam asked. "You good?"

"Sure."

She strode toward the door with Sam's eyes on her. He seemed oddly interested in my gloomy sister. Even when she slammed the door behind her, he kept watching in her wake.

"Yeah," I said, bringing him back to the issue at hand. "I can't tell Arianna. She'll think I'm jealous and trying to ruin things with Derek. She won't believe me."

"You're probably right." Sam rested his elbows on his knees. "I just hate that she's getting played. She was really broken up after you dumped her."

"I know," I said, a catch in my voice. But thanks to my parents, Arianna didn't want anything more to do with me. She was over me now. "I don't want her to get hurt, but . . . what happens between her and Derek—it's none of my business."

"Maybe she'll figure it out on her own," Sam said.

"Hopefully."

He stood up. "Okay, then." I followed him to the door. "Take care of those bee stings."

"Yeah. Thanks for coming by."

He got on his bike and rode away.

# Viv

MY HUSBAND AND I were sequestered in my walk-in closet, staring at the bag of tiny blue pills, Dolly's words looping through my mind.

*Fake oxy. I didn't even know such a thing existed before all this. The pills almost look like the real thing, but they're dull and rough, made in some underground lab. They're toxic and dangerous.*

"So, you stole these from Dolly Barber's son?" Somehow Thomas was keeping his voice level, controlled. But when I answered him, mine trembled.

"Yes."

The memory had come rushing back to me, there on Dolly's doorstep. I'd remembered finding the pills in a linen closet, hidden behind a stack of towels. I hadn't recalled whose home I'd been in until that moment. It had been in Dolly's old house. The illicit pills had belonged to Nate Barber.

"What are they?" Thomas poked the bag with a tentative finger.

"Fake oxy."

"Jesus Christ, Viv."

"I know." Tears welled in my eyes.

"How long have you been stealing things?"

"I've stopped," I fibbed. "It was a stupid little thrill."

"What else have you taken?"

"Just small things, like nail polish, an earring, a corkscrew. . . ."

His brow was wrinkled with concern, confusion, distaste. "But why?"

"I-I don't know, Thomas. It felt like I was losing you. And the kids were so unhappy, but they wouldn't talk to me. Taking things gave me a sense of power, I guess. It was something I could control. But I always ended up hating myself."

He was looking at me like he'd never seen me before, like some strange kleptomaniac had just appeared in his wife's renovated walk-in closet.

"I never took anything big," I continued. "I never took anything meaningful or important."

"Except these." Thomas's gaze was affixed to the plastic bag containing the pills. "How much are these worth?"

"Ten thousand dollars." I swallowed. "Mark Barber had to pay off the drug supplier. Dolly said he had to take a backpack filled with cash into an alley. They were terrified, but they had to pay the money back, to protect Nate."

"Christ."

"When I stole the drugs, Nate's supplier beat him up. He broke his jaw." My voice was barely a whisper. "It's all my fault. And Nate knows it."

"So, he figured out that you took them." Thomas looked up at me, and his eyes were cold. "He must really hate you."

"He does. And he has every right to."

"Do you think Nate Barber is behind the attacks on our house?"

"He can't be. Dolly said he's practically locked up at home. And they're out in the valley now. Nate doesn't even have access to a car."

"So, who else knows you have these pills?" Thomas pressed. "Who did Nate tell?"

The question took me aback. "I-I don't know."

"Did he tell his supplier? Some of his dealer friends? Some of his junkie clients?"

The possibility had not even occurred to me. *Oh god.* My knees weakened.

"You brought ten thousand dollars' worth of illicit drugs into our home, Viv," my husband snapped. "You didn't think you were placing us in danger?"

"I didn't think anyone would know," I cried. "I didn't expect Nate to realize it was me."

"When this drug lord was beating the crap out of him, you don't think Nate might have mentioned that he knew where the drugs were?"

"You think a *gangster* is behind our harassment?"

"You've seen the footage," Thomas said. "It's not always little boys scurrying around in the night. There's been a man out there."

"Is that really how drug lords operate?" I said. "With rats and wasps?"

"I don't know, do I?" Thomas was angry now. "But Nate Barber had his jaw broken. Who knows what could happen to us?"

God, he was right. And it was all on me.

"I'll take the drugs to the police," I said, tears spilling from my eyes. "I don't care if I get charged. Or if Dolly ruins my business and my good name. I'll tell them what I did. They'll protect us."

If I'd expected some sort of thanks for falling on my sword, none was forthcoming. "What about the rest of us, Viv?" My husband's face was dark and twisted with rage. "If you admit to stealing from a client's home, my reputation as a realtor will be ruined. And what about the kids? They'll be mortified! Eli played soccer with Nate Barber, for Christ's sake!"

"Oh god . . . you're right."

"And there's no guarantee that the cops will protect us, just because you walk in with a bag of pills you stole."

"I-I don't know what else to do!" I cried.

"Neither do I." My husband said nothing for a long moment, his eyes on the fake pharmaceuticals. Finally, he looked up at me. "This is serious, Viv. We're in danger."

He was right. And the thought that I'd put my family's lives in jeopardy threatened to overwhelm me. I gripped the top of the island, my legs sagging with fear, regret, self-loathing. "I'm so sorry," I said, the tears slipping from my eyes.

But Thomas didn't comfort me, didn't hold me and tell me it would be okay. He just turned and strode out of the closet. My stomach twisted sharply, and I doubled over with pain.

What had I done?

# *Tarryn*

I HAD EXPECTED Mr. McLaughlin or Ms. Harris to call my parents, but when a couple of days passed without contact, I allowed myself to relax. My English teacher must have believed me when I told him that I had my problems under control. Or maybe he and the counselor had bigger issues to worry about. Maybe they just wanted to enjoy the Fourth of July holiday. Whatever the reason, it seemed like I was off the hook. And now I could focus on getting revenge on Bryce Ralston.

Humiliation was the ticket. Bryce had slept with me, fallen for me, and I'd rejected him. Now he pretended he barely knew me, that I was too far beneath him to warrant even the most basic civility. All the while, he was watching me online, messaging me, obsessing over me. It was time the kids at Centennial High knew the truth.

A Snapchat story would be the most efficient way to get the word out. I had quite a few followers, but I could count on the story being shared throughout the school community. I would go on camera and tell everyone exactly what had happened between Bryce Ralston and me. He could try to deny it, but I would mention the cute little birthmark on his lower left hip. The boys in the locker room would have noticed it. And anyone else who had seen him naked.

I held my phone out, about to record, when Luke texted me. *Finally*.

> Hey stranger. Want to hang? Or are you still mad at me?

I *was* still mad. Luke had gone to Bryce's end-of-year party while I'd sat home alone drinking vodka out of a pickle jar. I'd seen the Instagram photos of Luke and Georgia spending Independence Day by her parents' pool, while I'd been forced to endure an overcooked veggie burger and the forced cheerfulness of my family. But Luke had a way of disarming me, of making me feel petty for being angry. And he was the only person who knew I had been camming, who knew about the creepy messages I'd received. I was desperate to tell him that I finally knew the identity of my stalker. So, I replied:

Smoothie?

I MET LUKE on Northwest Twenty-Third, at our usual smoothie place. The drinks cost upwards of ten bucks, but they were delicious and healthy, and I still had plenty of money saved in my bank account. Soon, I would start camming again . . . as Collette. Or maybe Anjelica. And the money, along with the attention, the adoration, would roll in again.

"I've missed you," Luke said, as we sat at a small round table, our pricey smoothies before us. "Bryce's party sucked, by the way."

I'd planned to play it cool, but my friend knew how to diffuse my anger. And I had missed him, too. Luke was my only confidante, and I had so much to tell him.

"You were right about Mr. McLaughlin," I said, sucking thick green liquid up a compostable straw. "He wasn't sending me those messages."

"How do you know?"

I leaned forward. "I went to his house."

"Oh my god, Tarryn!"

I told him everything then, about the vodka, the bike ride, Mr. McLaughlin's pretty wife and crying baby. I told him how I'd been called into the English classroom, how I'd wriggled out of the counseling session. "At least now I know who's been harassing me."

Luke leaned closer. "Who?"

"Bryce." I stirred my smoothie, the straw squeaking in the plastic lid. "It has to be him."

Luke sat back with a shrug. "Maybe not."

"It definitely was. And I'm going to make him pay."

"How?"

"I'm going to do a Snap story. I'm going tell everyone what happened between us. How he was a virgin, how he fell for me, how he couldn't handle it when I turned him down."

"No, Tarryn." Luke's face looked hot and red. "You can't do that."

"He deserves it," I retorted. "His messages scared the shit out of me."

"He didn't do it, Tarryn. It wasn't Bryce Ralston."

"I know you don't want to believe it because he invited you to his party, but he's a dick!" I consciously lowered my volume before continuing, "He's the only person who hates me enough to send those messages."

"Maybe he is a dick and maybe he does hate you, but he wasn't sending you those messages." Luke sounded rueful. "I know who it was."

My stomach dropped. "Who?"

"It was Georgia."

"What the actual fuck?" The betrayal made me feel sick, the banana, coconut milk, and kale churning in my stomach.

"She was worried about you," Luke tried to explain. "The camming site is not a safe space for someone our age. And you're so smart. You have college to look forward to. This could haunt you. It could ruin your chances of getting into a good school."

Since when were Luke and Georgia so concerned about my future prospects? They sounded like my fucking parents. "So, you knew about this?" I spat.

"Not at first. . . ."

"Then how did Georgia know I was camming?"

"Her cousin came across your page and he recognized you. If Sam could tell it was you, then anyone could."

Oh god. Eli's friend Sam had been watching me cam. He'd seen me in my sexy lingerie, talking about TV shows and vitamins and my favorite type of pressed juice. And he'd been over at our house only a couple of days ago. Had he come to tell Eli that he'd seen me? Would my brother tell my parents? The knowledge would kill my mom right now. She was already so close to falling apart, this would definitely tip her over the edge.

"Is Sam going to tell my brother?" I said, my voice hoarse with fear.

"No. He told Georgia to deal with it. He told her to make you stop . . . and she did."

"By scaring the shit out of me!" I snapped. "I've been fucking terrified, Luke. I've been driving myself crazy trying to figure out who was sending me those messages. I went to McLaughlin's house! Why didn't you tell me it was her?"

"I promised I wouldn't. And . . . I wanted you to stop. I was worried about you, too."

"Then why not tell me that? Why not just *ask* me to stop?"

My friend looked at me, his eyebrows raised. "We've known you since first grade, Tarryn. If we'd asked you to stop, you'd have said we were shaming you for doing sex work. You'd have accused us of judging you."

He was right, I would have. But I wasn't about to admit it, not now. I was still simmering with anger, reeling from the betrayal.

"We thought this was the best way to protect you," Luke said.

To my horror, I felt tears well in my eyes. I didn't want to fall apart in this smoothie bar, in front of Luke. I stood up. "I don't know if I can forgive you and Georgia this time."

"Maybe we were wrong, but we did it because we love you."

The thickness in my throat kept me from answering. But even if it hadn't, I didn't know what to say. I wasn't sure if I'd ever felt more betrayed. Or more alone.

I turned and I left, the ten-dollar smoothie on the table, melting in its plastic cup.

# *Thomas*

THE OPEN HOUSE would not be well-attended, that I knew. It was a run-down bungalow with a bad layout. Plus, no one was searching for a house on the Saturday evening after the Fourth of July. It was a time for family vacations and out-of-town visitors, for parties and barbecues. Not for us, though. Thanks to our faceless attackers—be they neighborhood kids or drug lords—we couldn't leave town. Who knew what would happen to our property in our absence? And we weren't about to invite guests over. They'd be terrified, if not actually injured. And we'd be mortified.

Still, I welcomed the chance to get out of the house for a few hours. Viv's confession was weighing on me. My wife was a thief, a klepto-maniac even. She'd downplayed it, said she'd talk to a therapist, but was it that simple? Maybe Viv's mental-health issues had impacted the kids, too? Eli was dropping out of college and refused to see any of his friends. And Tarryn was so angry . . . at everyone and everything. Maybe their problems were genetic?

At seven o'clock, the summer sun was still high, but the sky was overcast, a scrim of pale clouds blotting the light, making the already un-inviting bungalow downright dismal. I opened the windows and turned on all the lights, my mind still on my wife's admission. Would I have found out about her habit if she hadn't stolen a bag of pills? If she hadn't realized that her theft might have brought on the escalating episodes of harassment? I had been blaming myself, wondering if Chanel was behind this, but it was just as likely Viv's fault. She had taken drugs away from a dealer. And for that, we all had to pay.

Emma had printed the feature sheets and I removed them from the manila envelope. I'd requested twenty pamphlets, though I'd be lucky if I gave away two tonight. I'd do another open midweek; surely I'd use them then. As I spread them out on the dining table, something caught my eye. Buried within the promotional materials was another image. It was a photograph of a young couple, the words *Save the Date* across the top. It was for Emma's wedding.

She had obviously been using the work photocopier for personal business, but I didn't begrudge her. I knew she was underpaid, and her elaborate dream wedding was going to be expensive. I hoped her computer guy made a lot of money or they'd be in debt for years. His name was Paul, according to the *Save the Date* card. Had I known that? Surely, Emma must have mentioned him. Maybe I'd even met him, though I couldn't recall.

I looked at the attractive couple, standing in each other's arms. They were posed but laughing, a candid outtake from a professional shoot. They looked really happy, really in love. Viv and I had looked that way when we were engaged, before we knew what the years ahead had in store for us. Emma was young and naïve, optimistic by nature. She'd never expect the things life was going to throw at her.

Her fiancé, Paul, was a good-looking guy with a shaved head and artful stubble. There was something a little off about his smile, though, an asymmetrical quality. Looking closer, I saw what gave his grin the lopsided effect.

Paul was missing a tooth.

It was barely noticeable, a small space where

a bottom incisor should have been, but it sent a prickle down the back of my neck. The bite marks on Chanel's breast . . . the culprit was missing a tooth, a *bottom* tooth. But it didn't make sense. How could Emma's fiancé have bitten the stripper? Unless . . .

*Oh shit.*

I had to talk to Emma. I dialed her number, but she didn't answer. She couldn't have gone away for the weekend, not with the wedding looming. Was she screening me? She probably thought I was calling to ask her to do me a favor, to cover the open house for me. But she had to answer, because I had to know—what was Paul's connection to Chanel?

A couple entered then, their disappointment already evident as they looked around the bungalow. "Welcome!" I said, too loud, too bright. "Please—take a feature sheet. I'm here if you have any questions."

When I closed up, I would go to Emma's condo. I knew where she lived. I'd helped her find the place when she and her boyfriend first moved in together. A disturbing picture was taking shape in my mind, but I shouldn't speculate. I would talk to Emma. And she would tell me what the hell was going on.

# *Viv*

THOMAS'S OPEN HOUSE ran from seven till nine. He'd promised he'd be home by ten at the latest, so at nine fifty-five, I took an Ambien. There was no way I'd be able to sleep without medication. I would lie awake all night, stressing, worrying, and hating myself for what I had done to my family. I was already exhausted: eyes sandy, thoughts muddled, nerves on edge. A drug-induced sleep was not as restorative as a regular one, but it would keep me functional, and keep me sane.

In the morning, I would go to Dolly Barber and admit that I had stolen the bag of pills. She would be furious with me. She might decide to destroy my reputation and career; to negatively impact Thomas's. My children would be embarrassed and upset. But I could see no other way. The Barbers had dealt with Nate's supplier. They knew the people he had hung out with when he was dealing. They would understand the kind of danger we were in, the danger *I* had put us in. They would help us. They had to.

Just after ten, my phone pinged with a text. It was my husband.

I'm going to be late. Set the alarm.

Why? I texted back. What are you doing?

But Thomas didn't respond.

Had I known he wouldn't be home on time, I would not have taken the sleeping pill. Despite our security measures, I still felt someone needed to be alert. But I punched in the alarm code, arming our house against intruders. Did those in the drug trade take advantage of national holidays? Did they make a long weekend of it, heading to the coast with their friends and families? I hoped so. Because that meant nothing would happen tonight. The neighborhood brats might throw eggs or tomatoes or empty bottles, but nothing dangerous, nothing deadly.

"Where's Dad?" Eli had asked, as we ate our roasted chicken that evening. His welts were healing, but they were still visible and rather un-sightly. He hadn't been back to work yet. Tarryn had made herself rice and beans and taken them to her upstairs bedroom. She was clearly upset about something, but I wasn't equipped to deal with her teenage problems, not right now. Not until I figured out how to neutralize the abuse against us.

"He has an open house," I said, taking a sip of wine. My second glass—an effort to calm my frayed nerves.

"On a Saturday night? After the Fourth?" Eli scoffed.

Even a week ago, I would have been suspi-cious of my husband's absence, but not now. We were a team again. And we needed money. The end of my income stream was imminent.

My son took a bite off a drumstick. "Shouldn't Dad be home at night with all the shit going on?"

"He won't be late," I'd assured him. "And we have the alarm. No one can get to us."

I didn't need to be afraid, I told myself, as I settled into bed. The house was a veritable for-tress now of lights and sounds designed to pro-tect us. If the monitored alarm system detected any kind of danger—a fire, a break-in—a security team would be alerted, emergency responders summoned if necessary.

My children were just down the hall, which gave me comfort. My son was a full-grown man, fit and strong, and my daughter had twenty pounds on me. But if anything happened, I would protect them. The gun was in the drawer of the nightstand. Thomas had showed me how to use it. And I would, if I had to.

I tried to read, but I couldn't focus, and my eyes were getting heavy. Determined to stay awake until Thomas got home, I shuffled to the bathroom, my shoulder ricocheting off the doorframe. I leaned over the sink and splashed some cold water on my face. When I righted myself, the room tilted, and I stumbled. Shit. The Ambien and the second glass of wine with dinner were messing with my equilibrium.

Running my hand along the wall for balance, I made my way back to the bedroom. My phone was charging on the nightstand. When I picked it up, the clock read: 10:25. I texted Thomas.

When will you be home?

I waited, watching for the shimmering dots that prefaced his reply, but there was nothing.

I had just set the phone down, just pulled the

covers up to my chest when I heard it. A *THUMP*, followed by a voice, an angry hiss, coming from the backyard. The alarm was armed; no one could get in, but someone was out there. What were they doing? Setting a trap for us? Setting another fire?

With trembling fingers, I picked up my phone again and opened the camera app. Selecting the backyard camera, I watched the livestream, waiting, hoping to see a skunk or a raccoon, but nothing appeared. The camera had recorded movement just over a minute ago. I clicked the link to watch the video, my mouth dry and parched with dread.

There was nothing at first, and then a figure entered the frame. It was most definitely a man, not a boy, this time. He was too tall, too self-assured. He was wearing not a hoodie but a full face covering—a black knitted balaclava, three holes revealing eyes and a mouth. The looming figure was walking around the periphery of the yard with a confident stride, like he was looking for someone. Like he meant business.

What if Thomas came home and disturbed this intruder? Would the man attack him? He looked taller and stronger than my husband, and infinitely more menacing. Did he have a weapon? I replayed the video, looking for evidence of a gun, a knife, or a club, but it was so dark. It was impossible to tell.

On a wave of fear and adrenaline, I reached for the handgun in the top drawer of the bedside table. It was just a deterrent, I told myself as I picked my way down the darkened staircase, clutching the railing with my free hand. I certainly wasn't going to fire the weapon when I felt so wobbly and unsteady. But if Thomas needed me, I would be there. I could threaten the intruder, fire the gun into the night. I could scare the man away, at least.

The main floor was dark but for a beam of light streaming through the back window. It was from the backyard sensor lights, triggered by motion. It meant that the culprit was still out there, still creeping around in the dark. I went to the front window and peeped through the blinds, searching for my husband's car. Eli was right. Thomas should not have gone to that open house. He should have stayed here with us. But I couldn't fault my husband for doing his job. And I knew . . . this was my fault.

Besides, we were safe inside our suburban fortress. If that man tried to gain entry, an alarm would sound. The security company would call our home phone, and then, if we didn't answer or told them we needed help, the police would be summoned. To reassure myself, I stumbled to the alarm and double-checked it. To my horror, I found it unarmed.

Had I punched in the code incorrectly? Surely, it would have beeped to alert me if I had. Thomas had selected an easy-to-remember combination of numbers based on our birthdates. But in what order? And was it our birth years or our birth months? Suddenly, I couldn't recall. My fingers trembled on the keypad, afraid to enter the wrong code and require a reset. But the children and I were now vulnerable to the menacing figure creeping around outside.

As if on cue: another noise, the sound of feet on our back steps. The man—predator, drug lord, or psychopath—was just outside. He was trying to get in. Was he looking for the pills I had stolen? What would he do to me, to Tarryn and Eli, once he gained access?

I looked at the revolver in my hand and knew what I had to do. I couldn't stand here waiting, weak and pathetic. My family, and my home, had to be protected. On trembling legs, I moved to the back of the house and peered out the French doors. The figure in black was nowhere to be seen. I turned the handle and stepped out onto the porch.

"Get the fuck out of here!" I called into the silent yard. I cocked the revolver, held it out in front of me. "Get away from my family!"

I waited. Nothing. And then, from a darkened corner of the backyard, a figure emerged. He was moving toward me, so large, so menacing. His clothes were dark, his face obscured by the mask; even his eyes appeared black, the pupils dilated by the backyard lights. He wasn't stopping; he kept coming at me. "Stop!" I screamed, but he didn't.

I had no choice. I closed my eyes and I squeezed the trigger.

# *Tarryn*

I WAS IN my office/bedroom, lying on my single bed, when I heard someone on the stairs. I assumed it was my dad coming home from his open house, so I paid no attention. My mind was still reeling from Georgia's betrayal. How could my closest friend since childhood have sent me those terrifying messages? How could Luke have stood by and let her scare me like that? But then I heard the back door open, and my mom's shrill voice.

"Get the fuck out of here!" Her words trembled and sounded slightly slurred. What the hell was she doing? Why was she outside? If someone was out there, she shouldn't be confronting them alone. I sat up, grabbing for a pair of sweats on my floor.

"Get away from my family!" she cried, and I hurried for the door. I had just turned the handle when my mom screamed, "Stop!"

And then a gun went off.

My feet flew down the stairs, my stomach lodged in my throat. "Eli! Get down here!" I yelled, but I didn't pause. He had to have heard the crack of the gun—even if he was gaming, or sleeping, or wearing earbuds. But I needed my brother. Because my mom had just been shot, and I couldn't face that alone.

When I reached the main floor, I saw my mom's form through the French doors. She was standing on the back porch, her whole body visibly trembling. Relief flooded through me. She was safe. She was alive. But what the hell had happened?

Stepping out into the cool night air, I approached her. "Mom? Are you okay?" She didn't answer, didn't move. She just kept staring out into the yard, at the body lying on the grass. And then I saw the gun in her hand, and the puzzle pieces slotted into place. My mom had shot the intruder. Since when did she have a gun? Since when was she capable of shooting someone?

"What happened?" I cried. "What's going on?"

When she still didn't respond, I realized that she was in shock. And maybe I was too, because what I did next was odd, out of character for me. I stayed calm and I took control. "Go inside and call nine-one-one," I said, my voice surprisingly firm. I turned her by the shoulders and pressed her gently toward the house. And then I hurried down the steps toward the motionless lump on the back lawn.

Who had my mom shot? A neighborhood kid? Finn Dorsey? I approached tentatively, afraid of what I might see, of what he might do. The motion-sensor light illuminated the still intruder, and as I got closer, I took in his size: tall and broad and strong. He wore dark clothing, but the wound was visible on his left shoulder, and there was a pool of blood collecting underneath his head. But there was something familiar in the angles of the body, and a lock of light-brown hair peeped out beneath the knitted mask. And then, I looked at his hand, and saw the angry red welt.

"No!" I screamed, as I fell on my knees and pulled back the mask, revealing his pale, still face.

"Eli!" I cried. "Wake up!"

# Thomas

ON THE DRIVE to Emma's apartment, my thoughts were scattered, my mind flooded with questions. Was Emma's fiancé, Paul, blackmailing me? Was Emma oblivious or in on it? Did they know Chanel? When had he bitten her breast? Had the dancer let him do that to her? I'd tried to formulate some kind of spiel for Emma, but I soon gave up. When I spoke to her—*if* I spoke to her—it would be instinctive, unrehearsed. Parking my car at a meter, I practically jogged toward the block of apartments.

Emma lived in a nondescript tower in the Pearl District. I was familiar with the building, had sold a couple of apartments there over the years. I knew it had a small gym, that it was well-managed, and that it was likely at the top of

Emma and Paul's budget. I also knew that it had a secure front lobby. I would not be able to get inside unless Emma invited me. Scrolling through the digital intercom, I found their names.

EMMA HOLLY & PAUL MONTAGUE

They were in apartment 609. I punched in the code and waited, my heart hammering in my chest. It rang three times, and then four. Maybe she really wasn't home. Maybe she couldn't face me. And then, I heard her voice, cool and suspicious. "Hello?"

"Emma, it's Thomas," I called into the tiny microphone. "I'm sorry to show up here so late, but I really need to talk to you. Please."

She didn't respond, and I could hear nothing on the other end of the line. The pause went on so long, I feared she had hung up on me. "Emma?" I said again. "Are you there?"

Her response was clipped. "I'll come down."

A few minutes later she appeared, wearing gray sweatpants, an oversize T-shirt, and flip-flops. She wore no makeup, making her look young and innocent, but there was a wary look in her eyes. She opened the glass door, but didn't invite me in. Instead, she came outside, leading us back toward the sidewalk, where she stopped and crossed her arms.

"What do you want, Thomas?"

I held out the *Save the Date* printout. "This was in with my feature sheets."

She took it from me. "What? Are you upset that I used the color printer for personal business? Is that why you're here?"

"No . . ." I felt strangely nervous, rattled. "You know I'm being blackmailed, right?"

"Yeah, I got your e-mail."

"Well, the dancer from Roger's bachelor party claims I hurt her. That I bit her and choked her. But I would never do that."

She said nothing, just shifted her weight to the other hip, a skeptical look on her face. I swallowed my anxiety and pressed on.

"I have proof that it wasn't me. The guy who bit Chanel, the dancer, is missing a tooth."

A shadow of unease flickered across her features, but it was gone so quickly that I wasn't sure if I'd imagined it. "Okay . . ."

I gestured toward the photograph in her hand. "Whoever bit Chanel is missing the same tooth as Paul."

"He plays hockey," she said quickly. "He got a stick in the mouth, like, two days ago."

"But he's missing a tooth in your photos. When was your photo shoot?"

"Yesterday," she snapped, but I could see the panic in her eyes.

"You were at work all day yesterday. You printed these feature sheets—and your invitations."

"So what?" she said. "Are you accusing him of something?"

"No," I said, trying to rein in my apprehension, "I just need to know . . . did Paul bite Chanel?"

"Of course not! We don't even know her!"

"Something's going on here, Emma." I was losing my composure. "Someone broke into my house and left a dead rat in my fridge! A wasps' nest was placed in my trash can and my son was badly stung. My family is being tortured and harassed and I need to know why!"

"We had nothing to do with that," she snapped back.

I rocked back on my heels in surprise. I had her. She'd admitted it. I kept my voice as steady as I could. "So, Paul *did* bite Chanel?"

She didn't speak, but I could see the muscles tensing in her jaw. Finally, she said, "No. He didn't." Then she wrenched down the collar of her T-shirt, revealing the top of her breast. "He bit *me*."

The injury was basically healed, but the tissue was permanently damaged. The indents would leave a nasty scar. "My god, Emma. You should call the police. Is Paul upstairs? Don't go back up there!"

She gave me a withering eye roll. "I *asked* him to bite me. And to choke me. The whole thing was my idea."

"What? Why?"

"You treat me like crap," she said, her pretty face contorted by hatred. "You're always calling me at the last minute to cover for you. I asked you to introduce me to your wife, to tell her I was interested in interior decorating, but you wouldn't. You just wanted me to keep staging your properties for peanuts."

"I've always paid you."

"You gave me a hundred bucks for staging the Hancock place. If your wife had done it, you'd have paid her a thousand."

"Viv's a professional."

"You sold that place because of *me*. You know that. What was your commission, Thomas? Tell me."

"I-I don't remember."

"It was twenty-five grand. I printed the contract."

"So, you thought you'd blackmail me for the money?"

"Paul's gaming company went under. The wedding is costing us a fortune. We just needed a little help to get us through a tough time. And then Leo sent me those photos of you acting like a disgusting frat boy," she spat. "It was gross. It was sickening. You're a married man."

"I-I know," I stammered. "I made a huge mistake."

"Yeah, well, I thought you deserved to pay. So, I made Paul bite me. And grab my neck. I wore turtlenecks or scarves to work for weeks despite the heat." She gave me a contemptuous look. "You didn't even notice."

"But Chanel had a tattoo."

"Ever heard of Photoshop?"

"God, Emma. I thought . . . I thought you liked me. That we were a team."

"Why would I *like* you?" She gave a humorless laugh. "You're shallow, and selfish, and greedy. No one in the office likes you, Thomas. You're a pompous jerk."

Her words stung, because on some level, I knew she was right. I could have been more patient, more polite and grateful. I could have been more of a team player. But I'd been so wrapped up in my own life and my own problems.

All at once, her tone changed. "What are you going to do to me?" she asked, suddenly sounding young and vulnerable. "Are you going to call the cops? Have me fired?"

I was still reeling from her revelation. I looked at her. "I . . . I don't know." And then my phone rang. I pulled it from my pocket and looked at the screen. It was my daughter.

"I have to take this," I said.

Emma snorted, as if this was *so typical* of me. But I ignored her, spoke into the device. "Tarryn? Is everything okay?"

"No, Dad. It's not okay." There was noise in the background, traffic, and voices.

"What's wrong?" I said, through the fear gripping my throat. "What happened?"

"We're on our way to St. Vincent's Hospital. You need to meet us there. Now."

"Okay, I'm on my way. What the hell happened?"

Only then did I realize my daughter was crying. "It's Eli," she said, her voice thick with tears. "He's been shot. By Mom."

# *Viv*

"WE JUST NEED to ask you a few questions," the female police officer said. She was so young, so fresh-faced and healthy-looking. Her voice was calm, steady, in an attempt to soothe me. But it wasn't working.

"Is my son okay?" I demanded, my words breathless, hysterical. This couldn't have happened. I couldn't have shot Eli.

"He's still in surgery," she said, in that same monotone. "The doctor will talk to you soon. But right now, we need to know what happened."

"I don't know what happened!" I said, because it was true. "There was an intruder. I was so scared." I thought about the dark figure moving toward me, the sheer terror that had filled me. But it couldn't have been Eli. What had he been doing out there? And how could I not recognize my own son?

"How long have you had a weapon in your home?"

"Only a few days. We've been harassed for months." I looked at this young woman, so serene and composed in the face of my nightmare. "We called you! You wouldn't help us!"

"Calm down, Mrs. Adler." I heard the hint of irritation in her tone. "Was the gun purchased legally, from a licensed firearms dealer?"

"Of course! I mean, I'm sure it was. . . . My husband would know."

"He's been contacted. He'll be here soon."

"Please," I begged, tears rolling down my cheeks. "Let me be with my daughter." Tarryn was alone, somewhere in this hospital. "I need to know my son's going to be okay."

"Did you have anything to drink tonight, Mrs. Adler?"

My chest tightened. "Just wine with dinner."

"Any drugs?"

"I was—I took a sleeping pill." The effects had long since worn off, decimated by the adrenaline coursing through my system.

"So, you were operating the firearm while under the influence of drugs and alcohol?"

Oh god, oh god, oh god. I dropped my head between my knees, anguished sobs ripping through me. Why had I picked up that gun? Why had I taken it downstairs and out into the night, when I was clearly compromised? Was I criminally responsible? Criminally negligent? But I didn't care what happened to me. Because if Eli didn't recover, I would not survive.

A warm, solid hand on my shoulder pulled me upright. Thomas. He was here. I stood and threw myself into his arms. He would hate me once he knew what I had done, but right now, I needed his strength and comfort.

"I'm here," was all he said, over and over, as I bawled into his collar. "I'm here."

After a moment, the officer cleared her throat. "Mrs. Adler, I need to—"

But Thomas cut her off. "Can't you see that she's in no state to be interrogated? Our son has been shot! He's in surgery! She'll talk to you when he's stable."

I looked up at him. *When* he's stable, not *if*. I had to believe that.

"I'll call my lawyer if I have to," Thomas grumbled; then he took my hand, and led me back toward the waiting room.

# Eli

*I'D BEEN HOME from college for two weeks when I finally got up the courage to tell my parents that I was dropping out. Their reaction was exactly what I'd expected. My mom had whimpered like I'd just told her I had a terminal disease, but my dad had lost it. "What the hell is wrong with you?" he'd said. But I couldn't tell him that I was weak, a coward. I couldn't tell him how I had stood by and let Drew Jasper be sodomized by my teammates. That I couldn't go back to Connecticut, that I had to stay home and hide. They'd make it all worse. So much worse.*

*It was late now, almost midnight. The sky was black and starless, but a bright three-quarter moon cast an eerie glow on the silent streets. I'd been walking aimlessly since I stormed out of* the house just after ten. I'd drifted far from home and my feet were starting to hurt. I knew I should turn around and head back. My parents would probably be asleep. But what if they weren't? I couldn't face them. I was still so fucking angry.

I reached a park, an expanse of cool grass with a playground at one end, a skate bowl at the other. It was so quiet, so still, except for the soothing sound of wheels on pavement as a skater rolled methodically back and forth in the darkened bowl. I found a bench and sat, tipping my head back, face to the endless sky. Everything I thought I knew, everything I thought I wanted, had been taken from me. My entire existence felt so fucking pointless.

Pulling out my phone, I typed in Arianna's name. I hesitated for a moment, thumbs hovering over the keys. . . . Would she want to hear from me? Would she even respond? I'd treated her like garbage, but I hadn't meant to. I'd been young, pressured by my family, raised to think I could do better. It wasn't my fault, not really. And now, I needed her. She was the only person who could help me through this. Arianna had always listened, had always cared.

I typed:

I'm sorry to text you so late. Can we talk?

*I waited, eyes on the screen. Arianna's response came quickly.*

R U Okay?

Not really, *I typed.* I need you.

*There was a long pause, and I knew she was processing my words. But I filled the void.*

I'm dropping out of college and moving
back home.
Something bad happened there. Something
terrible.
I fucked up Arianna. I should never have
broken up with you.
I want to try again.
Please. Give me another chance.

*And then I waited, watched the ellipsis as she typed back. Her message was short and to the point.*

Eli, I'm sorry, but it's over. It has to be.
I'm seeing someone else now.

*A sob shuddered through my chest, but I tamped it down. I wasn't going to cry; I had lost*

*Arianna, for real, over a year ago. All I had lost now was the possibility of her. I felt jealous, frustrated, angry. My whole life had gone to shit, and it was my parents' fault. They had convinced me to go to Worbey College, to leave Arianna behind, to become the man they wanted me to be. They didn't care what I wanted; they never had.*

*And then I heard the clatter of the skateboard against the pavement, the clunky sound of a trick gone wrong. "Fuck." It was a boy's voice. I couldn't see the kid—it was too dark, too far away. And then another sound came. Breaking glass.*

*I stood up and peered toward the skate bowl. I could just make out the figure in the distance. There was another shattering sound as he threw something at a small, squat building. It was a storage shed where the park workers kept their gardening equipment. At first, I thought he was breaking the windows, but the structure didn't have windows. The kid was throwing glass bottles at it.*

*Something drew me over there—curiosity, I guess. He didn't see me or sense my approach, so he was shocked when I spoke.*

*"What are you doing?"*

*He startled but recovered quickly. "What's it*

to you?" he snapped. I saw the beer bottle in his hand, though he quickly hid it behind his back.

"Nothing," I said, stepping closer. I saw the blondness of his hair in the moonlight, his fair skin. He looked a bit younger than I was, Tarryn's age maybe. There was something familiar about him. Was he my sister's friend? No . . . Tarryn only had two friends, and this guy wasn't one of them. But I knew him from somewhere.

"Why are you doing that?"

"Why not?" He turned and hurled the beer bottle at the shed.

There was something satisfying in the senseless destruction, in watching the glass shatter. I saw the box of beer at the edge of the skate bowl. "Can I throw one?"

He stopped and looked at me for a second. "You're Eli Adler."

So, I did know this kid. But from where? "Who are you?"

"Finn Dorsey," he said. "You wouldn't remember me."

"Where did we meet?"

But he didn't answer. He reached into the box and handed me an empty bottle. "Go for it."

I threw the bottle as hard as I could, watched it explode against the wood siding. I imagined it *was my parents' house, that they were asleep inside, startled and terrified by the sound. The thought made me laugh out, like a total psycho. But then I remembered that we were in a public park, that some kid could cut himself on the broken glass, that a park worker would have to clean up our mess.*

*I turned back to Finn. "My dad's company barbecue, years ago. You were playing with my sister, Tarryn."*

*"You have a good memory." He handed me another a bottle, a full one this time. I cracked it open and took a drink.*

*"Want to do something for me?" I said. "I'll buy you more beer. Or weed. Whatever you want."*

*Finn took a drink of his beer and smiled. "Like what?"*

*"Something like this," I said, indicating the broken glass next to the shed. "Except at a house. In Arlington Heights."*

*"Whose house is it?"*

*"Mine."*

*The boy laughed. "Wow. That's—"*

"Eli . . . ? Can you hear me?"

A man's voice was pulling me out of the memory, back to the present. But it sounded tinny and far away, and I didn't recognize it.

"Eli, my name is Dr. Connelly. You're in the hospital. You've just had surgery, but you're going to be okay."

*What happened?* But I couldn't form the words. I was too tired, my mouth was dry, and a weight was pulling me back down, back under.

"Eli . . . you have a gunshot wound to your shoulder, but we were able to remove the bullet fairly cleanly," the voice continued. "And you hit your head when you fell. You're going to feel rough for a while, but you'll get through this."

Again I tried to speak, to ask what had happened, but the doctor was leaving, moving on to the next patient, the next injury. "Your family is here for you," he said. "You just rest."

And with his permission, I slipped back into darkness.

# Tarryn

WE SAT BESIDE my brother's bed, waiting for
him to wake up. He was going to be fine, the
doctor told us, though there could be some last-
ing damage to his shoulder. "Luckily, the bullet
missed the brachial artery, or this could have
been fatal," he'd said.

My mom had broken down then and hadn't
stopped sniveling since. I was actually more
worried about her than I was about Eli. Why
weren't they giving her a Xanax or something?
She was so pale, and she was trembling all over.
She clutched my brother's hand, whispering,
"You're going to be okay, Eli. I'm so sorry." She
thought the whole thing was her fault. But it
wasn't.

"Mom, stop," I said, when she pressed his

hand to her forehead, her shoulders shaking with sobs. "Stop blaming yourself."

She didn't look up. And she didn't stop crying. "I did this, Tarryn. It's all my fault."

"But why was Eli out there? Why was he wearing a mask?"

I saw the look that flashed between my parents. No one wanted to ask the question, because no one wanted to know the answer.

My dad spoke then. "It doesn't matter what he was doing. I should never have bought the gun." He squeezed my mom's shoulder. "It's my fault, too."

"When did you buy it?" I asked.

His expression was pained. "I picked it up a few days ago. I thought it would keep us safe."

My throat felt like glue as I swallowed. "Was it because you found the rat in the fridge?"

"Yes." His face was so pale, it looked like wax. "That's when I knew that all the lights and alarms couldn't protect us. Someone got inside. Someone crept through our home while we slept. So . . . I got the revolver."

"Then this is my fault, too."

Mom looked up then, her confusion mirrored on my father's face. I had to tell them. I had to explain.

"I turned off the alarm that night. And I left the window open."

My mom gasped. "Tarryn, why?"

"I sneaked out. I was upset. At Dad, because of those photos. At my friends, for abandoning me. At my teacher . . ." I didn't articulate my former suspicions about Mr. McLaughlin, and I wasn't about to tell them I'd gone to his house. ". . . for giving me a crappy grade. I just went for a bike ride. But I couldn't go out the door or the cameras would have seen me. So, I went out the back window. Someone must have been out there, watching and waiting. They got into the house because of *me*."

"No," my mom said. "You are not to blame for this."

Dad's voice was firm. "Finding fault is not going to change anything. All that matters now is that we're honest with each other. And we're there for each other."

But I wasn't finished. My voice was small when I said, "There's something else—"

A weak, groggy voice interrupted. "Way to make this all about you."

It was Eli. He was awake! We all swarmed around him, gently touching him, patting him, or kissing him, in my mom's case.

"You're going to be okay, Son." My dad's voice was choked up. My mom sobbed, "I'm sorry, Eli. I didn't know it was you."

"It's not your fault, Mom," Eli said. "You have to let me explain."

"Not now. You just rest."

But he wouldn't.

"A couple months ago, I asked Finn Dorsey to throw eggs at our house," he said, his voice slow, slightly slurred. "I was so mad . . . about college. And Arianna. And everything . . . But then Finn got his friends involved and they wouldn't stop. They took it too far. I knew you guys were falling apart."

My parents' eyes met over top of their son's hospital bed, and I knew what they were thinking. So many secrets. So many lies. And so much anger. How had our family gotten so messed up?

Eli kept going. Maybe the anesthetic was acting like a truth serum. Or maybe he just couldn't keep it all inside anymore.

"I went out there to talk to them. To tell them to stop. I didn't want you to recognize me on camera, so I wore the mask. . . . I scared you, Mom." He squeezed her hand weakly. "You were just trying to protect us. Anyone would have done it."

My mom started sobbing again, her anguish filling the small room, likely carrying down the hallways. My dad and Eli tried to comfort her, but I stood back. Watching. We were all unburdening ourselves, all confessing our sins. But I realized I couldn't tell them about my secret life, my alter ego. Not with my brother lying in a hospital bed, not with my mom overcome with guilt and self-hatred. It would be too much. It would tip them over the edge.

One day, when the time was right, I would unburden myself. Because secrets had almost destroyed my family. Secrets had almost gotten my brother killed.

I moved into the family scrum and hugged them.

# Thomas

LATER, WHEN ELI was stabilized, the police interviewed my wife and cleared her of any negligence. They had our continual harassment on record; the gun had been legally obtained; and Oregon was a "stand your ground" state. Viv had reasonably perceived the threat of serious physical injury or death before she used deadly force. And, perhaps, pity had played a small role in the cops' decision. Only a monster could inflict further trauma on a woman who had accidentally shot her own child. Her devastation was so clearly evident. She had suffered enough.

The police would visit Finn Dorsey and any other boys he was willing to identify. They wouldn't be charged—they were minors, there was no evidence against them—but the cops would make them see that they'd been playing a dangerous game. It could easily have been one of them that Viv shot, instead of Eli. They wouldn't be bothering us again.

Eli was released from the hospital after three days. He was going to be fine, but his shoulder had sustained permanent damage. It would always be weaker, would have limited mobility. His soccer goalie career was likely over—at least at the college level. But none of that mattered now, not to any of us.

As it turned out, our son had one more confession to make. He called us into his room, where Viv had him propped up on pillows, his bedside table laden with tea, toast, and a cut-up apple, and he told us the real reason he had dropped out of Worbey College. His face was red, his voice shaky, but he opened up to us, and told us what those boys had done to Drew Jasper. He told us how he had stood by, afraid to intervene as the horrific crime played out before his eyes.

"Oh my god," Viv said, taking his hand. "That's so awful."

"It was." Eli sighed. "I just stood there and watched. I-I should have done something. I'm ashamed of myself."

"Don't be," I said. "It was group contagion. They would have turned on you. Beat you up or worse."

Eli sat farther up in bed, wincing from the use of his injured shoulder. "After everything that's happened . . . after everything I've done . . . I need to back Drew Jasper up. I'm going to call the dean at Worbey and I'm going to tell him what happened."

"We support you, one hundred percent," I said.

"We're proud of you," Viv added. "You're strong and you're brave."

"It could get ugly," Eli said. "The guys could come after me. Maybe they already have. . . ."

"What do you mean?"

"The fire . . ." His face was troubled. "I don't think that was Finn Dorsey and his friends."

"Of course it was," I said quickly. "They were bored little delinquents. They got off on it. It gave them a high."

"But they were attacking us for kicks. For fun. We could have been killed!"

"They didn't think it through," I said, something desperate in my tone. "Kids have poor impulse control."

Viv added, "And they don't understand repercussions."

"Maybe," Eli said softly. "But we all saw that figure walking down the driveway with a knife. That was a man. It wasn't a kid."

My wife looked over at me, and I saw my fear reflected back at me. We needed it to be those kids. Because we needed it to be over.

"Noah Campbell lives in Vancouver," Eli said. "He could have done it."

Viv took our son's hand. "Whatever happens, we'll deal with it."

I squeezed his foot under the blankets. "We've got you, buddy."

Viv kissed his cheek, and we left the room.

WHEN THE TWO of us were alone in the kitchen, I poured two glasses of water. "Do you think Eli's right? Do you think the more serious attacks were done by someone else? Like this Noah kid?"

"I don't know." Viv took a drink. "It's possible."

"It could have been Emma. Or her fiancé. But they're gone now," I said with more confidence than I felt. "For good."

I had given my former assistant an ultimatum: I wouldn't press charges if she agreed to quit the firm, immediately. She had acquiesced, leaving the whole office talking and speculating as to why she would resign so suddenly. Only I knew the truth. Although . . . Leo Grass had been giving me the cold shoulder ever since. I wondered if Emma had confided in him.

"You win," Emma had said, when I saw her in the parking garage. I'd returned from a showing as she was loading a box of her belongings into the trunk of her car. "Men like you always do."

"Men like *me*?"

"Arrogant. Privileged. Entitled." She closed the lid with a slam. "You make me sick, Thomas. One day, you'll get what you deserve."

"I'm not a bad person, Emma."

But as she drove away, I'd felt a swell of guilt. Of shame. And of dread. Her words weren't an outright threat, but they sent a chill through me. Would she and Paul be back? Were they determined to make me pay?

"There's one more possibility," Viv said, bringing me back to the moment.

"The drug supplier?"

"I need to talk to Dolly," she said. "I know it will be humiliating. I know it could impact my reputation. And yours. . . ."

"Do it," I said. Because all that mattered now was keeping our family safe.

She set the glass down on the counter. "Okay."

"Do you want me to come with you?"

"No." She sounded strong and resolute. "I need to do this on my own."

# *Viv*

THE LAST TIME I'd driven to Dolly Barber's Willamette Valley estate, I'd been vibrating with anxiety and blinded by tears. This time, I felt strangely calm. Perhaps I could thank the therapy sessions I'd had since that horrific night when I had shot my son. I was still awakened by devastating nightmares of Eli lying bloodied and lifeless on the lawn, but the doctor was making me understand that I had been trying to protect my family, that the lengths I had gone to were proof of intense maternal love. And my therapist was also helping me understand my compulsion to steal.

She thought, as did I, that it was about control . . . or my lack of it. My need to orchestrate every aspect of my life, and those of my husband and children, had set me up for failure. The children were growing up and pulling away, naturally. And Thomas and I had had the usual ups and downs of any long marriage. Taking things that weren't mine had made me feel powerful, in command, if only for a moment before the darkness descended. It was a coping mechanism, she said, a response to stressful triggers in my life. Perhaps it stemmed from my relationship with my own parents? She wanted to delve into my past and examine my childhood. But even if I could understand *why* I'd stolen things, it didn't absolve me.

I knew this confession could destroy my career and even my husband's. It would humiliate me and likely damage us socially. And yet, I was firm in my resolve. Because the only way I could ensure my family's safety was to talk to Nate Barber. He was the only one who could tell me who knew I had the pills.

When I parked in the long curving driveway, I sat for a moment, steeling myself for the confrontation. Dolly was expecting me, probably excited to hear the gory details of the worst night of my life. She had texted me when she heard (through the grapevine of mothers) about Eli's "terrible accident." She'd assured me that her home makeover could wait, that I should focus on my son and his healing. A box of gourmet cookies had been sent to Eli's hospital room from the Barbers. It was sweet and thoughtful. And now, I was going to confess that I was the source of so much of her misery.

Walking to her stately front door, I rang the bell. It opened almost instantly, as if she'd been standing behind it, waiting for me.

"How *are* you?" she asked, sweeping me into a hug.

"I'm okay," I said. "Getting better day by day."

"How's Eli?"

"He's young and strong. He's recovering well."

"I'm so glad. That night must have been absolutely horrifying. Come in . . . tell me what happened."

Her curiosity was normal. Even the barely concealed excitement in her tone was understandable. I stepped into the open foyer. "Can we talk . . . privately? I'll try to explain."

"Of course. Mark's at work. And Nate's still asleep."

Dolly led me into her sunny kitchen, with its dark, chunky cabinets. I would have installed white cupboards and more glass to open up the space, but my design ideas didn't matter now. Once I told Dolly everything, I wouldn't be working on her home anymore.

When we were seated in the cozy breakfast nook, and I'd declined her offer of tea, I cleared my throat. Might as well start at the beginning. . . .

"When I was decorating your old house," I began, "I found a bag of pills. And I took them."

"I'm sorry . . . what?" She shook her head, as if she was seeing spots.

"I think they were the fake oxy pills. The ones that Nate was dealing."

Dolly's face was pale under her heavy makeup. "For god's sake, Viv. Why didn't you tell me?"

"I didn't know what they were then. In fact"—my face burned with shame—"I took them on a whim. Without thinking at all."

She was looking at me with thinly veiled disgust. "My son was beaten to a pulp by some drug kingpin. You could have prevented that."

"I'm so sorry, Dolly. Had I known—"

"I don't understand this." She stood up, putting distance between us. "Why would you do that?"

"I-I don't know," I stammered. "I wish I hadn't."

She pressed her thumb and forefinger to her eyebrows. "I'm trying to process this. I think you should go, Viv."

But I couldn't. Not yet. "I understand that you're angry, Dolly. And I know that Nate is, too. But . . . I need to speak to him."

She whirled on me. "About what?"

"I need to know who he told about the drugs. That I took them. That . . . I *have* them."

"Are you kidding me?" she snapped. "Those drugs nearly destroyed my son's life. He's healing and he's moving forward. You can't come over here and expect him to revisit the most horrible thing that's ever happened to him. To all of us."

"Someone's after us," I said. "They set our front porch on fire. They broke into our house with a dead rat and put a wasps' nest in our garbage can."

She gave a mirthless laugh. "And you think that's related to the illegal drug trade?"

"I-I don't know. Just . . . can you get Nate, please?"

"No, Viv. I won't get Nate."

"The police won't help us, Dolly. I'm trying protect my family."

"So am I," Dolly snapped. "I'd like you to leave now." She pressed the heel of her palm to her forehead. "Before I lose my temper."

I slid off the leather seat. "I'm really sorry. It was such a—"

"GET OUT!" she screamed.

I ran for the door.

# *Eli*

I SAT AT my computer desk, sifting through economics courses at the University of Oregon. There were several local colleges that would accept the credits I'd earned at Worbey. I could return to school in Portland and finish my degree on schedule. But I'd decided to take it slow, working part-time at the Thirsty Raven while taking a lighter course load. My healing was more important—both physically and mentally.

When I came forward to corroborate Drew Jasper's story, Worbey College informed me that a full investigation into the hazing incident was under way. Some of the other guys had confessed, pointing fingers at Oscar and Manny as the ringleaders, the abusers. I didn't ask the dean what would happen to them, but Drew and I messaged now and again. He told me that Oscar and Manny had been expelled, that the other guys were currently on academic suspension. Noah Campbell had broken down, apparently. He had written a letter of apology to Drew and his family. He said he'd been overcome by peer pressure and horde mentality, had been trying too hard to fit in. He was really sorry, he said. Drew seemed to think he meant it. I wasn't so sure.

I hadn't heard from any of them. There was no social media harassment, no angry messages calling me a traitor or a coward. And no one had attacked our house since that night. Whoever had been behind it wouldn't be coming back. Everyone in Portland knew that a crazy lady with a gun lived there. They'd be nuts to bother us again.

A rap at my bedroom door interrupted my musings. My dad poked his head inside, a smile on his face, a twinkle in his eye. "Someone's here to see you," he said. And then he ushered Arianna into the room, closing the door behind him.

"Hey," I said, spinning to face her in my chair.

"I made you some cookies." She held out a plastic container. I reached for it, and then grimaced with pain. "How's your shoulder?"

"It's okay. It only hurts when I use it."

She smirked. "I'm sorry. For . . . everything you've gone through."

"You mean my mom shooting me? It's all good." Why was I being so jokey and flippant? I was nervous. And excited that she was here. She set the cookies in my lap, then sat on my bed.

"You seem like you're doing pretty well. All things considered."

"I am." I indicated the computer screen behind me. "I'm going to take some courses this fall. At the University of Oregon."

"No way. Me too!" Her face was bright. "I got accepted into the nursing program."

"You'll make a great nurse. You're really caring, and good with people."

She blushed a little. "Thanks, Eli."

"Maybe we'll see each other around campus."

"I should probably go." She stood. "I just wanted to see how you were doing."

"Thanks for the cookies."

"Peanut butter chocolate chip."

"My favorite."

"I know."

Arianna took a step toward the door. "Are you still seeing Derek?" I blurted, halting her exit.

She turned to face me. "I ended it. He'd been cheating on me with some girl he met online."

"Shit." I played dumb. "You don't deserve that."

"No. I don't."

"I hope you're okay."

Arianna shrugged. "It was no great love affair. I told you that."

She was going to leave, and I didn't want her to. Not yet. "Do you think . . . maybe you and I could be friends? Since we're going to the same college next term?"

"That might be okay. . . ." She smiled. "Your parents actually seemed really happy to see me. Maybe I imagined all their condescension?"

"Or maybe they've changed. We've been through some pretty heavy stuff."

"That's an understatement." She reached for the door handle. "Take care, Eli."

"You too."

I turned back to my computer screen, but I couldn't stop smiling.

# *Tarryn*

IT DIDN'T TAKE long for every person at Centennial High to hear that my mom had shot my brother. Even though school was out for the summer, the Adlers were the talk of the entire student body . . . not to mention the faculty. I'd had a call from Ms. Harris, the school counselor. Even though she was on vacation, she wanted to make sure I was okay, that I was getting the support I needed. I assured her that I was fine, that I had access to my mom's therapist if I wanted to talk, that our family was healing. If Ms. Harris knew what had happened that night, that meant *everyone* knew.

I decided to delete my social media accounts, at least for a while. Instagram, Snapchat, even TikTok would be burning up with gossip about my fucked-up family. Clearly, my mother was a lunatic, my brother a psychotic lurker, and my dad and I were guilty by association. I had never cared that my schoolmates had a low opinion of me—or no opinion of me at all—but the thought of them gossiping and laughing about our tragedy made me feel sick. And angry.

Obviously, someone from the school, or maybe another parent, had contacted my mom and dad. They came into my room one morning, steaming coffee mugs in their hands, to address the rumor mill swirling around me. Mom perched on my twin bed, while Dad stood at the end. "I know this has been hard on you, honey," she said. "And I'm sorry for that."

My throat felt thick with emotion. Recent events had been a lot harder on Eli and my mom, obviously, but it was me who had discovered my brother's inert body; me who'd instructed my mom to call 911 while she stood frozen with shock, a gun in her hand. Sometimes, I felt like an afterthought in my own family, but here they were, making sure I was okay.

"Kids gossip," my dad said. "But they'll soon get bored. By the time you go back to school, this will be old news."

I doubted that, but I just shrugged.

"And it doesn't matter what people think about us," my mom said. "We know the truth."

I couldn't help but snort. My mom and dad cared more about appearances than anyone I knew. They had to have the perfect home, the perfect yard, had to drive status-symbol cars. They dressed the part of the attractive, wealthy, stylish couple, had kept it up even when their world was falling apart. A glance passed between them. They knew I was onto them.

"This has been a real wake-up call for me," Mom said, her voice husky. "The only thing I really care about is this family. The only thing that really matters is that you and your brother are safe. And happy. And thriving."

"Same," Dad said, and his eyes looked misty. Oh god! If my dad started crying, it would be beyond awkward.

To my relief, my mom stood up then, signaling that the heartfelt confessional was mercifully over. "You know we're here if you want to talk." She stroked my hair. "And Dr. Chang will see you anytime. Or we could get you your own therapist. Someone who specializes in treating teenagers."

"Yeah, I'll let you know," I said. I wanted

them to leave. I hated to admit it, but I felt like having a little cry myself.

A COUPLE OF days later, Georgia reached out to me via text.

> I know you hate me, and I don't blame you
> But I hope Eli's ok
> And your mom
> And you
> Luke and I are here if you need us

I wanted to hold on to my hatred and anger. My best friends had betrayed me in spectacular fashion. They had been sneaky and cowardly and downright stupid. Their anonymous messages had terrified me, had exacerbated all the scary shit that had been going on in my family. But the fact was, I missed them. And I needed them.

So, when Luke texted to check on me shortly after Georgia had, I responded:

> Doughnuts?

Yes please, he wrote back.

We met at our usual spot, a cheaper, less trendy

place than the famous Voodoo or Blue Star. I got there first, and found a table, nervously picking at a whiskey-apple fritter and sipping a chai latte. When my friends entered, they looked as uneasy as I felt. They gave me a tentative wave, and then headed to the counter to get their doughnuts and coffees, before joining me at the table.

"How's your family doing?" Georgia asked, as she sat.

"They're good," I said, sipping my latte. "All things considered."

"That must have been a nightmare." Luke pressed his hands to his chest. "Are you okay?"

"Yeah." I tore off a piece of my fritter. "I mean, I hate that everyone's talking about us, that my mom and my brother are the *scandal of the year*, but I'm hanging in there."

"Fuck everyone," Luke said. "Who cares what they think?"

"Their lives are so boring, they *wish* one of their parents would shoot their brother," Georgia quipped.

We all laughed then, and it felt comfortable and right. It felt like old times. I had thought I was outgrowing my two oldest friends, but now, after everything I'd gone through, it felt so good to be back with them.

"I'm really glad you wanted to see us," Luke said, clearly feeling the same sentiment. "You have every right to be mad at us."

"I know I do."

"I really fucked up." Georgia's Earl Grey and rose petal doughnut sat ignored on the plate before her. "You were being attacked and it was stressful and horrible, and I made it worse."

I gave a half nod, half shrug. She *had* made it worse. But I didn't want to be angry anymore.

"We screwed up," Luke said. "But we were concerned about you. And scared for you."

"I never judged you," Georgia added quickly. "I just felt like you were too young and too vulnerable to be involved in sex work. I mean, Sam found you on the site. That meant *anyone* could have found you."

"Any creep," Luke volunteered. "Any psychopath."

"Or a teacher," Georgia added. "Or someone from college admissions."

"But what you do with your life is up to you," Luke said, breaking off a piece of his salted chocolate doughnut. "We'll support you. And we'll keep your secret."

"Thanks," I said, licking the icing from my

fingers. "But I'm not going to cam anymore. Not right now, anyway. Not while I'm underage and living in my parents' house."

"Good," Georgia said, then quickly covered: "I mean, whatever you think is best."

I sipped my tea. "Your messages really did creep me out. Especially when you called me *baby doll*. Ick."

Georgia's brow furrowed. "I never called you baby doll."

"You did. I remember it."

"I didn't, Tarryn. That's so pervy."

The conversation shifted then, back to familiar topics like hot guys and annoying celebrities, but my mind was stuck on that message. Ur playing a dangerous game, baby doll. I hadn't imagined it. If Georgia hadn't sent it, who had? But it didn't matter now, I told myself. I was closing the door on that chapter. I hadn't changed my moral stance on sex work. I still believed it was a viable way to earn an income, that it should be safe and respected, not judged and shamed. But I didn't really need the money. And I didn't really need the attention. So, whoever had been watching me, whoever had called me baby doll, was irrelevant.

"Harry Styles is *sexually ambiguous*," Luke

was saying, as I tuned back into my friends' chat, "which just means he hasn't met the right guy yet."

I laughed and took the last sip of my latte, pushing the niggling concern to the back of my mind.

# Thomas

THE HOME PHONE rang, a rare occurrence. I almost didn't answer it, but then I remembered that Tarryn and Eli were still asleep, and the constant ring would wake them. It was Sunday morning, my time to do yard work, to mow the lawn and power-wash the house. Viv was puttering in the garden, but I was drinking my coffee, scrolling through my phone, taking my time. The noise of the electric mower would wake up the kids, and they needed their rest. And since that terrible night we were all moving a little slower, looking after ourselves.

I picked up the handset in the kitchen. "Hello?" My greeting was guarded; I suspected it was a telemarketer.

"Thomas?"

The voice was familiar, but I couldn't place it. "Speaking."

"This is Mark Barber calling."

My stomach dropped. Mark was a jovial, good-natured guy. He'd worked in marketing for Nike for years, had just moved to a smaller outdoor clothing company. We weren't buddies or pals, but we'd occasionally bumped into each other at school events or neighborhood functions. I liked him. But I knew all about Viv's ugly confrontation with Dolly last week. And I knew this was not a social call.

"Hey, Mark." My casualness was overt, forced.

"Dolly's upset. She doesn't want to talk to Viv but . . . there's something we wanted you to know."

I set my coffee cup on the counter. "I'm listening."

On the other end of the line, Mark inhaled and exhaled heavily. "My son, Nate, has admitted to attacking your house. He said he slashed your tires. And . . . he lit your hedge on fire."

"What?" Anger made my pulse pound and my face burn. "We could have been killed," I snapped. "If Eli hadn't come home when he did, our whole house could have burned down."

"Nate didn't intend for the fire to spread. He's just a troubled kid."

*Oh, that's okay then!* I wanted to bark, but sarcasm wasn't going to make this conversation go more smoothly. "I thought you kept him at home? I thought he didn't have access to a car?"

"He's not a prisoner," Mark retorted. "I guess he found a way."

"What about the wasps' nest in our trash can?" I moved into the living room. "Did he break in and put the dead rat in our fridge?"

"I don't know, Thomas." Mark suddenly sounded small, exhausted. "He shut down after he told me about the fire. He's been through a lot. He's . . . got some serious problems."

"I'll say," I snorted.

"What about your wife's problems?" Mark's ire was up. "She stole Nate's stash of pills. She admitted it!"

Through the window, I saw Viv on her knees, digging in the flower bed. She looked small, gentle, vulnerable. Protectiveness swelled inside me. "It was a stupid impulse," I said. "She wasn't thinking straight."

"My son was beaten to a pulp. Because of *her*."

"Well, if he hadn't been dealing drugs in the first place . . ."

"Thanks for your compassion," Mark spat.

Our argument was escalating, becoming heated. I thought about Viv's phone call with the Nygards, and how much it had cost me. "Look, Mark . . . this whole thing is a huge fucking mess," I said, an attempt to defuse the tension and anger. "Pointing fingers isn't going to solve anything."

"I agree," Mark said, similarly resigned. "But we need to know . . . do you plan to press charges against Nate?"

"I don't know. I'll have to talk to Viv about it."

"Well, if you do, we'll have to tell the police about Viv stealing the pills. They'll need the whole story."

It was an ultimatum. A threat. And it worked. Viv was dealing with her issues, privately. She was getting therapy and she was healing. If her secrets were made public, it would destroy her. And the kids. All of us.

"Your son needs help," I said. "We just want him to get that."

"He will." Mark's response was tinged with relief. "He's going away for a while. A treatment facility in Idaho. They've got an excellent track record with substance abuse issues and anger management."

"Glad to hear it."

"Yeah. It's for the best."

Outside, Viv was standing up, removing her gardening gloves finger by finger. "Thanks for the call, Mark," I said, hanging up the phone. My wife entered moments later, her gaze falling on the phone still in my hand.

"Is everything all right?" she asked.

"Of course." I put the phone down and moved toward her. I took her in my arms and kissed her cheek. "Everything's absolutely fine."

# TWO MONTHS
# LATER

# *Viv*

IT WAS MID-SEPTEMBER, the first nip of autumn in the air, the sun setting earlier with each passing day. I welcomed the new season with its changing leaves, cooler temperatures, and pumpkin spice everything. It felt like the end of a long hard trial, the beginning of something new. We had just endured the worst summer of our lives. Things could only get better.

I slipped deeper into the bath, the warm water soothing the ache in my lower back. At the end of the tub, my chipped burgundy toenails peeped through the bubbles. I'd been on my feet all day, staging a home in Eliot for Thomas. My design work had been slow—perhaps Dolly had something to do with that—but my staging business was as busy as ever. And that was fine with me.

My ambition had been thwarted by recent events. Maybe it would come back, with time, but for now, I was satisfied working within my comfort zone. Tomorrow morning, I was looking at one of Leo Grass's listings.

Somehow, we were moving on. Eli's injury had healed, mostly, but the muscles in his shoulder had been permanently damaged by the bullet. He didn't suffer great pain, but his mobility would be forever limited. I thought he might blame me, hate me, but my son actually seemed relieved. The pressure of competitive sports, college, and the social scene had been too much for my sensitive boy. Thomas and I had pressed him too hard, and he had lashed out at us. We had convinced ourselves that we only wanted the best for our kids, but we hadn't taken the time to understand what that really meant for each of our children. We were all learning to redefine the meaning of success.

The water was cooling off, so I pulled the plug and got out of the tub. I was toweling myself off when I heard the front door open. Either Thomas was back from his open house, or Tarryn had returned from the movie she'd gone to see with a new friend. The girl's name was Ambreen. I wasn't sure if their relationship was romantic or platonic, but it didn't matter. Tarryn seemed happy. The footsteps on the stairs indicated my daughter's lighter step. As I slipped into my robe, I opened the bathroom door and poked my head out.

"How was the movie?"

"Lame. Cliché." But she was smiling, and there was a softness in her expression. Since that terrible night, Tarryn hadn't changed in any outward way. She still refused to conform to high school norms and would not play the popularity game. As usual, she was dressed in her uniform of sweatpants and an oversize T-shirt, a huge flannel shirt over the top to combat the night's chill. But there had been a subtle shift in her energy. Underneath her veneer of apathy, she seemed lighter, warmer. Recently, she'd even started talking about her future. Tarryn was in her senior year now, and she was considering the University of Washington, majoring in either sociology or women's studies. Thomas and I would support her, financially and emotionally, but we would not pressure her. We had learned our lesson.

"Are you off to bed?" Tarryn's room was upstairs now. She said the basement was too cold, too remote. Eli had gladly taken it back. It af-

forded him quiet for his homework, and privacy
when his pal Sam came over. Or his friend Arianna.

"I'm going to read for a bit. Good night,
Mom."

"Good night, honey."

I padded to my bedroom and into the walk-in
closet. It was still my sanctuary, my little slice of
heaven, but the drawer with the false bottom
was empty now. I'd trashed all of my ill-gotten
gains and would not be replacing them. The illicit pills had presented a problem. They were
too toxic and dangerous to toss in the trash or
flush down the toilet. If I took them to the police, there would be questions, questions that
would incriminate me and Nate Barber. We'd
reached an unspoken agreement with his family.
We didn't need to get law enforcement involved.

In the end, I'd taken the deadly pills to a
pharmacy for proper disposal. "I found these on
the street," I'd told the pharmacist, a woman
about my age with an air of extreme compe-
tence. "I have no idea what they are." And then
I'd hurried away, relieved that they wouldn't destroy any more lives.

Opening a top drawer, I selected a nightgown
and put it on. Thomas would be home soon, and

I would wait up for him. Not because I felt nervous without him in the house. We still armed our security system every night, even though we'd suffered no harassment for months. And I no longer worried that Thomas was *up to something*. I trusted him completely. We were talking to a therapist and to each other. There were no more secrets between us, there was no more suspicion. The horrible events we had endured had brought us closer, in a strange way. So, I wanted to wait up, to ask about his evening, and to kiss him good night.

As I moved toward the bed, gratitude, that sentiment I had struggled so hard to find, filled my chest and lifted the corners of my lips. It came so effortlessly these days, and often. Moved by the feeling, I settled myself down on the plush carpet, pressed my hands together at heart-center, and closed my eyes. I gave thanks for all that we had, and for all that we had survived. My family was safe and healthy now. My marriage was strong again. And the endless stress and torment had ceased. We had all learned so much: about ourselves, about one another, and about what it truly means to be happy.

I was just about to get up when I heard the egg hit the front window.

# *Acknowledgments*

I'M VERY GRATEFUL to the team at Gallery Books: Jackie Cantor, Molly Gregory, Jennifer Bergstrom, Andrew Nguyên, Michelle Podberezniak, Jessica Roth, Anabel Jimenez, Aimée Bell, Sara Quaranta, Jennifer Long, Liz Psaltis, Abby Zidle, Diana Velasquez, John Paul Jones, Davina Mock-Maniscalco, and everyone else behind the scenes. Thanks to my eagle-eyed copyeditor Joal Hetherington, and to designer Spencer Fuller/FACEOUT STUDIO for this wonderful cover.

Thanks to my kind, calm, always supportive agent from day one, Joe Veltre, the faultless Tori Eskue, and the entire team at Gersh.

To my friend and legal adviser, Jon Lazar. Thanks for talking me through the legalities of this fictional situation and being such a good friend and support in real life.

Thanks to the team at Simon and Schuster Canada: Nita Pronovost, Karen Silva, Felicia Quon, Kevin Hanson, Adria Iwasutiak, Rita Silva, Rebecca Snodden, Sarah St. Pierre, Mackenzie Croft, and co. You are the best! Thanks to the wonderful Fiona Henderson, Anthea Bariamis, Kirstin Corcoran, Rachael Versace and everyone at Simon and Schuster Australia.

I'm so grateful to all the booksellers and librarians, the bloggers, bookstagrammers and Facebook groups who do so much to spread the word about books. And thank you to the wonderful community of writers. I miss you all and can't wait until we can go to conferences again!

As always, thank you to my mom, my family, and my friends. And all my love to John, Ethan, Tegan —and the naughty chihuahuas Victor and Wendy.